I0652646

# THE
# ELYSIUM
# HEIST

# THE ELYSIUM HEIST

Y. M. Resnik

SOLARIS
NOVA

First published 2025 by Solaris Nova
an imprint of Rebellion Publishing Ltd,
Riverside House, Osney Mead,
Oxford, OX2 0ES, UK

*www.solarisbooks.com*

ISBN: 978-1-83786-647-2

Designed & typeset by Rebellion Publishing

To Team Sloth and Steady, I would rob a casino with you ladies any day.

# CHAPTER ONE

## Finley

THE DAZZLER PLACES the cards on the gaming table with a barely concealed smirk. I tap the digitized surface lightly and send a shimmer of sparks in her direction, indicating she should deal me another. I've memorized every card in this deck and there's a ninety-five percent chance I'm winning this round. Smirk or not, she never stood a chance.

After dealing my card, she flips hers over with a practiced flourish. She has enough skill to hide the triumph on her face behind a polite facade, but she doesn't manage to conceal her disappointment when I turn my card over.

Her painstakingly sculpted eyebrows snap together and little lines appear at the corners of her downturned mouth before she regains her composure.

I expected better.

The Elysium is known across the galaxy for its Dazzlers. They are supposed to be the best dealers in the business, hand-picked for their charm and guile, but this one is failing to impress. She must have other skills, because dealing blackjack clearly isn't her strong suit.

When I win the next round her eyes grow wide under lashes coated thick with mascara, and her perfectly painted doll's lips purse in a pout. I'm cutting into her take by refusing to lose but she should be more gracious about it if she wants to attract customers to her tables.

"Blackjack." She sweeps the cards back into the deck, not bothering to give them a pretty shuffle. Sloppy.

It takes another three rounds before the pout turns into a glare. Everyone else has left the table and annoyance is making the Dazzler antsy, dulling the sheen from her smile. Her hands are clumsy as she deals and her eyelids twitch with the desire to be rid of me. Still, she should have put two and two together and realized what I'm doing by now. This girl is definitely not suitable for our purposes.

I relegate her to the part of my mind that stores useless, inconsequential, information and focus my attention on the cards. King, Queen, Heart, Spade. Their familiar faces make my head buzz with possibility. Other people only have a few childhood friends, but I have fifty-two and it is so easy to pick up where we left off. Every time we are together a new adventure begins. They've never let me down, my most beloved companions in life.

I'm about to place my biggest bet yet when a hand sporting three exquisite emerald and gold rings stops me.

It's Kiyo, throwing a small stack of chips on the gaming surface as she slides into the seat next to mine. Ostensibly, she's joining the game. In actuality, she's reminding me that I, in fact, have another companion in life. One who would prefer I exercised some restraint.

The insipid Dazzler flashes Kiyo a welcoming grin as she deals her in. The woman might be dense, but it would be impossible to miss the custom tailoring of Kiyo's crimson sheath dress and the dozens of princess cut emeralds that sparkle in her chestnut hair. They are exact matches in color to the ones set in Kiyo's rings and necklace.

It reinforces a fact I grasped the moment I laid eyes on her in a back-alley club on Henta 5, a bottle of vintage champagne in each hand and a ruby big enough to eclipse Neptune's tenth moon shining from a chain on her neck. Kiyokimora GoldWeaver doesn't believe in subtlety.

The memory highlights how excruciatingly out of character the diminutive stack of chips she's wagered is. Kiyo is sending me a message without talking, reminding me that we aren't here for the money. I need to slow down, or The Casino will notice what the Dazzler has overlooked.

They might not know who I am, but they'll know they're losing revenue at a faster rate than normal. An intolerable rate. The Elysium is a private establishment and they set their own rules. They don't need to prove I'm counting cards to ban me from the premises.

It's happened before.

My fingers stroke the chips, enjoying the slick feel of the metal before selecting a few coppers. It pains me to gloss past the golds and silvers, but Kiyo is right. If I bet too much too fast, we'll never get what we came here for.

I'm beginning to wonder if this was a bad idea. We need an inside woman, it's the linchpin in the entire plan, but if the Dazzler working this table is any indication of the quality we can expect, then we might as well give up.

One of them should have noticed me by now.

I flip over another winning hand and arrange my chips in their carrying case. One more round and then we'll go.

How many times have I told myself that lie before?

The cards call to me, crooning in my ears like sirens. I don't care about Kiyo's plan or the pearls or the family business anymore. I've played too many hands for that. It's me and the numbers now and I couldn't stop if I wanted to. She's going to need to drag me out of here.

That's happened before, too.

I stare at the galaxy of stars swirling over the surface of the table as I await my next card. When it doesn't come, I spare a glance for the Dazzler. She's backed up from the table, leaving her post empty, and her mouth has popped into a round circle of surprise. Her cheeks are flaming beneath the rouge she's brushed on them. She stares at a point behind my left shoulder.

"I didn't realize this was your table," she says quietly.

I swivel around in my seat to see what the fuss is about. I'm greeted by the sight of a Dazzler so stunning my attention is diverted from the cards. The chips in my hands drop into the tray haphazardly, with a shower of clinks.

That has never happened before.

It's not the waves of raven colored hair that are knotted up by a single dragon-shaped ivory pin or the jade colored eyes rimmed in kohl that make her so breathtaking. Nor is it the dress that snakes all the way down to her ankles, shimmering like a thousand stars in the night as it clings to her pale skin. It's the way she holds herself. The way she looks at me.

With one glance from her I feel naked, as if she knows all my secrets while I cannot even fathom the depth of hers. Her crimson lips part, revealing a row of perfect white teeth.

"It's not my table yet." She steps forward. "The Casino thought Miss GoldWeaver might appreciate an upgrade."

I bite back a laugh as the original Dazzler bobs her head up and down vigorously and hastily beats her retreat. Her eyes nearly bugged out of her head at Kiyo's name. She's clearly out of her depth and grateful for the reprieve.

Heiresses don't usually play on the main floor of The Casino. Then again, a Dazzler of this quality usually doesn't deal here either. I'd bet all my chips that The Casino had nothing to do with her coming over, and I never lose a bet.

The new Dazzler slinks behind the table, her dress dripping

off her curves like wet silk. Most of the female Dazzlers rely on short skirts and low necklines to distract the players. They are fools. This dress has a high collar that brings out the graceful arch of the woman's neck and the fabric hugs her body to a centimeter off the floor. Her movements are fluid, practiced. They suggest what lies underneath that dress is worth far more than the flesh I can easily see peddled around the gaming floor.

As Kiyo would say, our first dealer was nothing more than paste and glass. A thing easily melted and crushed. This one is a diamond, formed deep in the bowels of the Earth by millennia of heat and pressure. She won't crack or crumble.

Of course, she is also the highest paid Dazzler to have ever worked in any casino, both in space and planetside. The face of Psalome Shipmen is famous across the galaxy. She's untouchable and irresistible all at once, and she knows it.

"I didn't realize The Casino knew I was here," Kiyo says, eyeing Psalome up and down. She takes a sip of her lemon spritzer and places a few chips on the table.

"They don't." Psalome's voice is melted honey, smooth and rich. "I didn't come over for you. Catching an ordinary card counter is worth ten gold marks. Catching a repeat offender is worth forty. Did bringing her onto the gaming floor make this excursion more stimulating for you?"

She gives Kiyo a dismissive tip of her chin before whipping her piercing gaze towards me. "What I don't understand is what you get out of this, Halley. Other than a night in prison."

Kiyo spews spritzer everywhere, almost choking at the mention of my old name, but my face remains blank. I've played too much poker for a Dazzler to get the best of me.

"Psalome Shipmen." I hand Kiyo a napkin without breaking Psalome's stare. "I was so hoping you'd be the one to catch me."

"Why is that?" Psalome asks, raising one eyebrow.

"Tut, tut." I tsk, drawing out the noise and reveling in the exchange. It's the first time tonight I've actually been challenged. With blackjack the outcome was certain before the first card hit the table. This conversation is a delicate dance that could go either way. "You answer a question for me before I answer one for you."

She laughs, a noise that comes from her core and carries with it the promise of a mystery unsolved. "Ask away."

Curiosity is getting the better of her. She shouldn't be talking to me at all. She should've flagged The Casino, pocketed her forty gold marks, and moved on without wasting time.

Time with Psalome isn't cheap. I should know. I checked her price list before we landed.

"How did you know it was me?" My image has been wiped out of every facial recognition program in the inhabited universe and Kiyokimora has gone to the trouble of paying for reconstructive surgery and alterations in my genetic coding to confuse the bio scanners.

Psalome leans forward and slides her hand onto mine. My skin tingles as she lifts it up and turns it over, her index finger tracing the lines of my palm. I'd never touch her on my own, it's against Casino rules, but her fingers are featherlight and send shivers down my spine.

"You've always held your cards like friends and your chips like lovers."

Her face is full of amusement and mischief. She's definitely the one we need.

"Now you answer my question." She drops my hand like a loaded grenade and her features snap back into a mask of indifference. All business and no play. "Both of you. Why did you want to be caught and why are you glad it was me?"

Kiyo takes a step back, twisting one of her rings around and around. "How did you…"

Her voice trails off. She's not used to being outwitted. It's a consequence of growing up rich. She spent too much time around other overindulged children and sycophants too afraid to tell her no. Fidgeting with her jewelry is her biggest tell. I thought I'd broken her of the habit, but Psalome appears to have brought it back with a vengeance.

"If you didn't want to be caught, you wouldn't have sat at the blackjack table." Psalome shrugs. "Halley could have chosen to fleece half a dozen players at the high stakes poker table and The Casino wouldn't have intervened because they wouldn't have lost any money. Instead, you chose blackjack, her signature game, and played round after round. I spotted her first, but we all know The Casino would have gotten here eventually."

Kiyo nods, thinking it over. "And me?"

This gets another laugh, a more ironic one. "The Heiress of the most prominent jewelry manufacturing dynasty in the known universe doesn't sit on the regular floor of a casino unless she has reasons to keep her activities secret. You two are either lovers looking for a discreet yet entertaining third for the night or partners in crime. Given Halley's pleasure that I was the one to arrive and the fact that you're six months away from taking over the reins of the family company, I'd say it's the latter."

It's a fair assumption. Unlike other Dazzlers, Psalome is as famous for the things she won't do as she is for the ones she will. Technically, she does offer her customers services other than dealing and conversation, but the price for sex is nothing short of the entire debt that keeps her chained to this place. Psalome Shipmen doesn't deal in half measures. Anyone who wants access to her body as part of their Elysium experience had better be ready to buy her contract out in full.

Rumor has it she's been offered the chance once or twice,

by male intergalactic moguls looking to show off their wealth as much as they are interested in the sex, but she's always shot them down. Which means even if Kiyo was willing to front the cash, she would know better than to try asking Psalome for sex out in the open at the blackjack tables. She'd have negotiated with The Elysium in advance.

The Casino never pushes an employee into a physical relationship without express consent from all parties. It's one of their few rules. The other is client privacy, which is why those rumors about the offers Psalome has received have never been denied or confirmed. The combination is one of the reasons so many flock to this place, and to Psalome in particular. Customers are safe in the knowledge that nobody is engaging in anything other than consensual activities, and employees get a fair, if not always entirely satisfactory, deal. Psalome might be stuck working here thanks to her father, but if she takes her clothes off for money it's going to be with someone she finds at least tolerably attractive, and every deluded rich fop in the galaxy dreams of being the special chosen one she finally fucks. She's practically a live roulette wheel.

No matter how much the lucky winner has to pay her for a spin.

She's also an astute businesswoman. Psalome plays her customers like I play cards, keeping the numbers afloat in a dizzying array of possibilities. Kiyo and I have become a skipped step in her carefully choreographed waltz and she wants us explained, fast.

"I've answered more than my fair share." An edge creeps into her voice. "It's your turn. Don't bother lying. I'll know."

I glance at Kiyo but she's too shocked to speak. Psalome doesn't mince words. Between the suggestion that we could have all ended up in bed together and the casual reference to Kiyo's inheritance, she's managed to talk about everything polite society keeps hidden. Plus, she made it all sound glamorous. Forbidden and lush. Kiyo's not prepared for that. Not by a long shot.

I doubted her choice at first, teasing her for spending weeks tracking Psalome's movements, trying to guess when the most sought-after Dazzler in the galaxy would be roaming The Casino floor as a free agent. I didn't think she'd get the timing right, but I also didn't care. I thought this whole plan was crap to begin with.

I was wrong.

Now that I see her, I understand. Psalome Shipmen is perfect. The plan is still crap, but this girl has taken her fair share of crap and turned it into gold. I don't see why she can't do the same for us.

I push my cards back towards her and shut my case of chips. Their siren song no longer tugs at me. There's a new game to play and she's standing right in front of me.

"We had to be sure you were as good as your reputation," Kiyo says, finding her voice. She twirls a piece of hair around her fingers. "So many rumors float around the interspace about the girl who works The Elysium to pay off her father's debts. I was betting they were all lies. Now I see they're true."

If she was hoping to get a rise out of Psalome by mentioning her deadbeat father, it hasn't worked. Psalome is drumming her fingers against the table, edging closer and closer to the call button on the bottom of the gaming table. One push and within five minutes The Casino will descend upon our table, discreetly so as not to alarm the other players, but with enough force to blow us all to the next solar system if necessary.

I need to do something fast.

"Why don't you take us upstairs?" I suggest, meeting her withering gaze without blinking. "We were hoping to engage your services, and the negotiation is a bit delicate. Oh, and if you could refer to me by my new name that would be helpful. It's Finley Starchaser now. I haven't been Halley in years."

The request to head upstairs gets a reaction. Psalome may not know what we're up to, but she can sense it has nothing to do with the carnal delights one can pay for in her rooms. She rolls her eyes and her fingers dance towards the call button. They push down without hesitation and I start my mental clock. The adrenaline rush is more than worth the trouble I've caused, and from the way I spot Kiyo sitting up straighter, pupils dilated, I've managed to snap her out of her confused daze.

Kiyo thinks I'm only good with numbers but I'm pretty good at reading people, too. The subtle and intricate game that Psalome was playing was never going to capitalize on Kiyo's strengths as a negotiator. Now that I've upped the ante, we actually stand a chance.

Kiyo was built for boardrooms and corporate takeovers. She's been training for it her entire life, and I've just given her five minutes to convince the world's most inscrutable Dazzler to help us rob this place.

The game is on.

# CHAPTER TWO

## Kiyokimora

I CURSE FINLEY in my head as I watch Psalome remove her manicured fingers from the trigger button below the gaming table. Out of the corner of my eyes I spot The Casino mobilizing a tactical unit. They'll trust Psalome to distract us for a few moments while they gather intel and then they'll swoop in for a circumspect but forceful eviction.

That's not what bothers me.

Finley is perched at the edge of her seat, sapphire eyes wide with fake innocence. She's radiant when she's mischievous, like a gem straight from the cutter's blade, sharp and glittering.

It only took her a day to decipher me, memorizing my tells and my quirks even though she was stone cold drunk. She plays me like a round of blackjack. And I let her. Every single time.

I should've sent her away that first night, when it became clear how much trouble she was in, but I brought her home with me to sleep it off instead. It took me longer to learn her the way she already knew me – inside and out, backwards and forwards, each facet and flaw. She's worth every ounce of frustration and the small fortune I've spent on her through the four years we've known each other. Nobody has ever seen me the way Finley does.

That's why she goaded Psalome by asking to go upstairs, insinuating we were lovers looking to buy ourselves the galaxies' most elusive Dazzler for a threesome. She knew Psalome would sound the alarm. She *wanted* her to. Throwing my money around The Casino in the flashiest way possible to announce my presence on the corporate scene, and not even bothering to make the arrangements in advance, is exactly the kind of offer Psalome has turned down before. And Finley knows it.

Sometimes I suspect if my life was less exciting Finley would wander off in a haze of glory and find herself a more stimulating companion. Someone who can give her the things I am incapable of. A handsome space cowboy or a sexy Dazzler like Psalome.

Thanks to the live bomb she's dropped in my lap, that day will certainly not be today.

Blood rushes to my brain, clearing the cobwebs. I've got five minutes to seal this deal. I focus on Psalome's face, looking her in the eyes. She's better trained, but at the end of the day she's no different than any mining union representative or gold merchant that sits at my negotiating table. There's still a human heart lodged behind that pristine veneer. All I need to do is figure out what makes it beat and offer it to her.

There isn't much I can't offer someone.

"You disappoint me," Psalome says with a shake of her head. The diamond studs in her ears catch the artificial light from the chandeliers and send it scattering in a million directions. I estimate two carats each, minimum. I can't tell the market value without an up-close examination, but I'd guess it's well over a hundred marks. Probably more now that she's worn them.

If people are foolish enough to pay more for items worn by famous beauties, then the House of GoldWeaver is always more than happy to take their extra marks.

The Casino would have charged Psalome a hefty price to rent those diamonds, but it's common knowledge Psalome doesn't play by the usual rules. She only wears the gifts she receives from her clients, and she keeps a running tally of their worth against the day she can exchange them all for her freedom.

If this is what she wears on the regular gaming floor, I'd love to see the gemstones she saves for the private clients upstairs. Still, none of it has been enough to pay off what she owes. Her father must have racked up enough debt to buy a small planet. The interest alone would bury most people. Luckily, I'm not most people.

"I was hoping it would be something more interesting than sex that brought an Heiress to my table together with the most infamous card counter in history." Psalome's expertly painted mouth dips down. "A simple call ahead to book an appointment and The Casino would have handled the negotiations. I don't offer those kinds of services on a spur-of-the-moment basis without prior credit checks and proper collateral in hand. No matter how pretty or intriguing the client may be. I'm sorry you wasted your time."

Her dry tone indicates she isn't sorry at all. She's annoyed *we* are wasting *her* time. But she hasn't entirely said no to the sex either. She's left the door open, hinted as to what hoops we would need to jump through.

Each word out of her mouth is a small clue about what I need to offer for what I actually do want from her. I wait for more. I'm only getting one chance and I can't afford to miss the mark. The plan won't work without her and without the plan I can kiss my company, my reputation, and probably even Finley, goodbye.

"The Casino will be here in four and a half minutes to escort you out," she says to Fin. "If Miss Kiyokimora explains that this was a romantic game for you both they won't ask you to leave. They'll simply bar you from the gaming floors. Perhaps they can help you choose another Dazzler instead. One whose talents are better suited for your needs."

Her nostrils flare. She's insulted. It's a subtle movement but my mother taught me to see them all before she died. After her diagnosis, before illness took her mind, she insisted on passing on her skills to me. Fear, anger, disgust. They are all painted over our bodies if you know where to look. She said I would need to recognize them to stay one step ahead of my dad and the Board of Directors.

She was right. She'd simply failed to adequately prepare me to anticipate threats from other directions. Life had to teach me that all on its own. I learned my lessons well. I won't let a Dazzler take me down.

Psalome is turning to me now, assuming I'm the one in charge since I'm paying the bills. "They'll recommend Carlo, since you have sophisticated taste. Don't take their advice. You should try for Jacinthe. She's good with the wild ones. Finley will like her and it's obvious the sex is for her. I'd be happy to recommend someone more sedate if you'd prefer a companion who suits you both, but it seemed like you weren't interested in participating."

She's scanning my face, looking for signs that she's wrong. In less than a minute she's managed to decipher what Finley and I each like in bed, including Finley's pansexuality and my own inability to even broach the entire topic of sex without having a panic attack. I have studiously avoided discussing it with Finley, because it would mean the end of the delicate balance between flirting and friendship we maintain, yet here is Psalome divining my secrets and laying them bare. If I'm not careful she'll realize the extent of my feelings towards Finley. Another topic of conversation I have studiously avoided.

It tells me she's good at what she does, that she could have been out of here years ago if she was willing to manipulate her customers a touch more than simply suggesting higher bets at the tables. The fact that she doesn't means there are lines she won't cross. Ways in which she won't take advantage. I need to figure out where those boundaries are drawn and why.

Fin is smiling even wider, and I get the distinct impression she wouldn't mind giving up the entire operation in favor of finding Carlo or Jacinthe right now. They'd certainly give her more than I'm offering, and with a price less steep. She hasn't had so much as a one-night stand since the night we met, and I may yet get her arrested. How could I ever hope to deserve her friendship, yet alone her love?

This place is unhealthy for her, bringing up all her old habits and desires and she can't help but want to satisfy them somehow. Sex would be the safest option, as it has never been addictive for her. Probably something I should have thought about before we got here, except I can't exactly offer to help myself and imagining her with someone else has the distinct disadvantage of making me want to claw my skin off. This entire place makes me want to bathe in battery acid.

I need to shut down this line of discussion before Psalome or Finley senses the vortex of conflict swirling in my head and I lose them both.

"We don't want to hire you for sex." My words are deliberately crass. Psalome needs to know she can't shock me. That my past hasn't made me weak, or foolish. I still remember what it was like to want sex, even if I'm currently incapable of it. "Although I'm sure Finley would have a marvelous time with you, Jacinthe or whichever other person you had in mind."

Her eyes dip towards Fin who winks one sparkling eye beneath her amber waterfall of hair. Psalome chuckles and looks back to me. Finley amuses her. That's good.

"I'll bet she would," Psalome says, smiling back at me. "You need to talk fast. Four minutes left and whatever job you have in mind needs to pay significantly more than the reward for turning you both in. Trouble radiates off the pair of you like alcohol from the craps table at three in the morning."

She's still not hooked. Her face is a study in boredom and her eyes are already scanning the room for her next client, gauging where she's likely to earn the most. We are an afterthought in her mind already, an amusing anecdote to recall at the end of the day when she adds the forty gold marks to her tally.

"I'll pay you eighty gold marks for an hour of your time and your silence." It's double what The Casino will pay and it gets her attention. "If you say no at the end, we will leave. Nobody will know Finley was here or that you let us go."

She turns to Finley who nods in agreement.

"Ninety." Psalome flicks an imaginary piece of lint off the gaming table. "You pay upfront and you buy me dinner, too."

"Dinner?" I shouldn't ask, it betrays me too much, but just as I thought I had her figured out, Psalome manages to mystify me. The extra ten marks are her testing how far she can push me, but I can't fathom the reason for the meal.

"All my private clients buy me dinner." She's drumming her fingers on the gaming table again. "It's a standard component of my price packages. If you don't, The Casino will wonder why."

I feel the heat rush to my face. I've tracked her movements for weeks. I should have realized her clients always pay for her meals as a matter of course, not as a courtesy. That Psalome doesn't buy anything from The Casino, not even food.

That kind of abstinence is why she stands a chance of digging herself out of the hole her father put her in when anyone else in her shoes would have thought it pointless. Other Dazzlers squander their tips on casino perks like massages, designer dresses, and champagne. Not her.

Psalome Shipmen eats what her clients buy her, or she doesn't eat at all.

That explains why she comes to the regular floor on slow days. She'll never rope in a big payday here, but she doesn't turn her nose up at small commissions and if you play at a Dazzler's table for more than two hours you automatically pay for their next meal. I wouldn't have thought Psalome would go that far, given how well she is compensated for her time upstairs. The marginal gain hardly seems worth it to me.

Then again, I grew up rich. Psalome did not.

She might not be willing to manipulate her clients, or to have sex with someone looking for a trophy fuck, but she is exceedingly desperate to get out of here by any and all other means possible. Finally, some intel I can actually leverage.

I can hear my mother in my head, humming her approval. I may have made a blunder by balking at the meal but I'm learning from it, using the knowledge gained to refine my approach.

"Very well." I shrug as if it means nothing, as if I haven't locked my strategy into place based on this one small interaction. "Order whatever you want."

"You really do have a job that only I can do." She looks up now, finally intrigued. "I should have charged more."

Finley takes a swig from the glass of ginger ale and cranberry juice that has magically materialized at her side. I frown. I told her not to go anywhere near the bar, but she insisted she could handle ordering. At least she's not eyeing the gaming table like a starving child looking for food anymore. Instead, she's visually tracing the outlines of Psalome's curves. I'm not sure that this is preferable.

I shouldn't have brought Finley to any casino, especially not The Casino. She's done well these last few years – laughing, exercising, taking up hobbies – but I hardly recognize her now. The minute we stepped into The Elysium she was like a woman possessed, darker and more jaded than the Finley I've come to know. More like the Finley from that first night. More like Halley.

A girl I could never hope to keep up with even as a friend, forget romantic partner. A girl who burned so bright, so fast, she could take down my entire solar system in the supernova of her rejection without thinking twice about it.

She shouldn't be here, but I hadn't seen any other way. Now all I can do is hope my Finley emerges when this is all over and this foreign, sharp-edged Finley retreats back into the past along with everything else that is currently screwing up my life.

"Are you sure you've thought this through?" Psalome asks, a mischievous grin on her face. "What's to stop me from turning you in after the hour is up?"

Her eyes are sparkling, and I can tell she's enjoying herself, enjoying the challenge of figuring me out. Why else would she bother warning me?

Ten identical Casino clones begin to converge on our table. They may have separate bodies, but one computerized mind lurks behind all of those black eyes and blank faces. Time's almost up.

"Because I'm going to offer you the thing you want most in this world." I lean forward to whisper straight into her ear. "Help me rob this place and I will set you free, Psalome Shipmen."

Her eyes widen into two massive orbs that reflect my own image back at me. I've finally managed to catch her off guard.

I could have waited to tell her until we got upstairs, but I don't see the point. Now we both know what the other one wants. All that's left is to decide if we trust each other enough to make it happen.

The chips are all in her hands. It's time to see what she's willing to wager.

# CHAPTER THREE

## Psalome

"You called, Miss Psalome?"

The Casino surrounds us, ten identical figures with bright black eyes and short black hair carefully arranged in a series of spikes and waves that accentuate their sharp cheekbones. They wear a tuxedo, neither fitted nor loose, and a look of curiosity.

They'll have researched Kiyokimora and they'll have noted Finley's unusual winning streak, but they won't know who she truly is. Not without corroborating DNA scans and facial recognition. Finley's done too good a job of altering her face. Plus, she's lost all the baby fat she had as a teenage prodigy when she swept through the intergalactic gaming world like an unstable wormhole sucking in the cash and possessions of anyone foolish enough to get close.

Kiyokimora must have hired the best plastic surgeons and geneticists in the galaxy. I can only hope their discretion matches their skill. Otherwise, we're all fucked.

It's not a good sign, the way I already think of the three of us as a "we." I shouldn't be considering this. The entire proposition reeks of spoiled rich girl trying to have a romp at the expense of everyone else involved. Kiyokimora has enough money to come out clean from whatever shit goes down, but I certainly don't.

No one has ever successfully robbed The Casino and the fee for getting caught trying is more than twice the debt I'm in now. A few more years of work and I'm free. Maybe less if my reputation continues to grow. Or Psylina makes good on her efforts with The Casino to shave a little off my debt.

Still, Kiyokimora didn't so much as blink when I offered to help her find a Dazzler for the night nor did she back down when I made it clear I wouldn't hesitate to turn either of them in despite the fact that she's paid me to keep quiet. There's more going on here than a simple sexcapade and I want to know what it is.

Plus, if that girl is truly willing to buy me out of here two years ahead of schedule, then I'm not passing up the chance without at least hearing her out. I've only agreed to talk. There's nothing criminal in that.

"Turn them in," Psylina screams in my ear. I wince at her tone. Projected straight from the embedded microchip in my earring, it tears through my skull like a flaming meteor crash landing in soft dirt. My little sister, my ever-present protector, is going to drive me crazy if she doesn't take it down a notch.

"What are you waiting for?" Psylina continues. "Nobody robs The Casino. It's impossible. Forty gold marks brings you several hours closer to getting out of here even if you end up buying your own dinner tonight. Plus, you'll still have time to make some commission working the tables. There's a pair of Fraxian businessmen eyeing you over at the slot machines. Everyone knows they burn through cash like it's rocket fuel."

I can't argue with her logic or her math. Psylina has kept my ledgers since the day I offered myself up to The Casino, over Psylina's vehement protestations, in exchange for our father's debt and the promise that The Casino would keep him out of our lives. It's thanks to my sister's vigilance that I'm so close to buying myself out. With her in my ear, I've never made a wrong move. Even when I've wanted to. She's kept me intact both physically and mentally, sometimes against my own efforts to sabotage her.

I should listen to her. Should, but won't.

"Miss Kiyokimora GoldWeaver and her companion would like to engage my services." I tip my head in their direction. Finley is twining herself around Kiyokimora like a piece of ivy; warm, earthy and inviting. It's a good ruse but her seductive smile doesn't spread to her eyes and Kiyokimora isn't so much as blushing. In fact, she's stiffer than a board. They might fool The Casino, but I've been reading people for too long to fall for it. They love each other but they aren't lovers yet. Not in a physical sense. And it's not Finley who is opposed to the idea. She's simply respecting Kiyo's boundaries.

Which is a pity, because had they actually offered to buy out my contract properly, I'd have agreed to the sex. Probably another reason why Psylina is so eager to get rid of them, even though she can't admit to it.

"It's her first time, and she'll be paying upfront. I thought you'd like to handle the negotiation yourself."

The Casino never passes up the chance to welcome a wealthy new client.

Psylina curses in my ear even though she knows I can't respond. I'd have ignored her either way. She'll burn out eventually, when she realizes I'm not actually going to try and rob The Casino. I'm not that big of a masochist. I only want to hear what this is about and see if there's a chance I might still turn it into a way out for myself. The ninety marks don't hurt either.

The Casino perks up at the mention of Kiyokimora's name and the words "engage my services." The nine extraneous clones now drift back into the shadows as the one that has chosen to speak for them grasps Kiyokimora's hand and bows to kiss it in a formal greeting.

"It is a pleasure to meet you and your companion, Miss GoldWeaver," they say, whipping out a tablet. "I was informed you were coming to help verify the jewels for the exhibition tournament, but I am delighted you have elected to grace us as a customer as well. I don't believe you've reached the age of majority on your planet yet, but the legal age in The Elysium is eighteen. As long as you have the funds, anything should be possible. Tell us what your pleasure is and we'll be happy to oblige."

It's one of The Casino's longer speeches, reserved for the very wealthy indeed. Kiyokimora is young and she's poised to inherit her family's entire business when she turns twenty-one this year. It could fund a lifetime of adventures, illicit and otherwise, at The Elysium. They won't want to pass up the chance to impress her.

Kiyokimora preens at the attention.

"I have more than enough funds," she purrs, toying with one of her earrings and leaning back into Finley's embrace. "It's only the title transfer that waits for my twenty-first birthday. The money has been mine since my mother died. I look forward to spending some of it with you."

"Listen to her." Psylina's voice is a low growl. "Is she flirting with them? Doesn't she know they don't give a shit? They're programmed to go after her money. They don't care how short her skirt is. Lo, you can't possibly think this cupcake can mastermind a heist in the most highly secured casino in the galaxy."

I bite back a smile. She hasn't called me Lo over the com system in years. My nickname is reserved for private moments of vulnerability in person. Nothing that can be recorded or intercepted. This is true panic, Psylina style. I'll have to tease her about it later, when the others aren't around to watch. She's never been jealous before.

The Casino is waiting, tablet held aloft in one of their hands, to hear our terms.

"It's a custom package. Ninety golds for me to deal privately for her and her friend for an hour." I purposefully avoid calling Finley her companion or lover. They should be aware I see through them. That I will see through any trick they try to pull. "Three plates for dinner as well."

"The game?"

"We were hoping for Pertiandem War," Kiyokimora says. "I do so love the way it's played with five decks."

It's the longest, most pointless game we have, and it will take significantly more time than an hour to play.

"I'm afraid that will have to wait for another session," I interject as The Casino blinks at me. According to the rules of my contract I'm technically in charge of my own client list and choices but they have to make some monetary sense for The Casino to go along with them. If I'm to be paid by the hour, Pertiandem War would benefit us all. They'll need an explanation.

"I'm otherwise engaged after the hour." I lean forward so The Casino can see the diamonds in my ears. The ones they know Psylina talks through. "An appointment with my aesthetician."

"One hour it is," they say with a firm nod, a trace of a smile flittering through the otherwise cool facade of their face. They would never make me miss my time with Psylina. She's got nothing to be jealous about on that front. If only humans could be as transparent and consistent with their feelings as The Casino is.

"Pai Gow then," Kiyokimora says through gritted teeth. She could use some lessons on how to rein in her own emotions. She drives a bargain well enough, reading the room and everyone in it, but she gives away too much. It makes her appear young, inexperienced. Like she hasn't seen the worst of what this world has to offer. "And four plates for dinner, not three. I have another friend joining me in a few minutes. She keeps kosher though. No milk and meat, no shellfish. The whole deal. I assume you can oblige?"

The Casino looks at me for approval and I shrug. This is the first I'm hearing about another friend, and the request for kosher food is eyebrow raising, but it's too late to back out now.

"Anything else?" The Casino asks, eyes pointedly fixed on Finley's fingers as they trace lines up and down Kiyokimora's shoulder. "Perhaps some… extra services for you and your friend?"

Finley's hair is flying around her face, and her eyes are smoldering behind the iridescent grey eyeshadow she's applied. She's wound so tightly she looks as if she'd screw the next person that offered just for the release it would give her. It's another thing that gave her away to me.

In every recording I've ever seen of her, Halley aka Finley, has been similarly intense at the gaming table. She wields it like a weapon. Half her poker opponents lose from the distraction alone and it's only gotten more focused with age. Like wine maturing in an oak casket.

"No," I say, arcing my neck away and staring out the windows at the starry expanse of space. "Not this evening."

I can't decide if I'm disappointed about that fact. So I once again give some room for the answer to be a yes. Not this evening, but perhaps another. If they swap the ridiculous robbery plan for something more mundane, like an all-night bacchanal, I'd be open to it. With the finances worked out in advance in an iron clad contract.

It's a routine we've gone through hundreds of times. The

Casino can't help but ask. They're programmed to get the most profit out of every client and employee. Lately, though, they, too, seem relieved when I say no. As if they'd prefer me to stay longer. Which is likely true, because when I go, I intend to take Psylina with me. The conflict of competing interests in this conversation alone must be burning through their processing power like a wildfire in dry brush.

Psylina is cracking her knuckles so loudly I can hear it through the coms. She can't be thrilled to see profit triumph over personal attachment once again. The Casino has offered me up to a client, even though they are aware of Psylina's feelings on the matter. Even though they prefer I stay.

I'd try to offer some comfort. Blame the algorithm we both know is behind that choice. But Psylina knows that better than I do, and I've got bigger bets to tend to at the moment.

The Casino holds out the tablet for Kiyokimora to sign with her DNA imprint and bows once she is done.

"Have a pleasant evening," they murmur. "Let us know if there's anything either of you require once your time with Miss Psalome is concluded. Anything at all."

Kiyokimora smiles and Finley drains the last of the fuchsia-colored liquid in her glass. The Casino turns to go.

"Please do give my regards to Miss Psylina," they say as they melt into the shadows.

I can practically taste the smug satisfaction in Psylina's voice as she hums in my ear.

"I told you they wouldn't fall for her. They didn't even offer a welcome discount."

"That's because she's my client," I remind her, muttering under my breath as I lead Kiyokimora and Finley out of the gaming floor and towards the lifts that will lead us to my suite. "The Casino isn't authorized to give any discounts for me. They'd have to make up the difference to me themselves."

"Well, they could have discounted the food," Psylina mutters. "That's not on your account."

I don't bother pointing out how useless a gesture it is, discounting a few silvers on a ninety-gold mark deal. Psylina will have worked that out for herself before she said anything about it. She simply wants to gloat.

This thing with her and The Casino has progressed further than I ever thought possible. All the more reason to get us both out of here pronto.

"Ilaria's waiting for us by the lifts." Kiyokimora's dress is a streak of red as she sashays past me to take the lead. She's used to being in charge. If she was an actual client, I'd have to take care to be deferential to her. "Sorry we didn't mention her before, but it's important for the plan that she doesn't draw too much attention."

She's already piqued my interest, whoever she is. It's rare I get a religious Jewish client at the tables. I've never had one in my private salon. As a religious minority, Jews tend to keep to themselves. In the more insular communities, the ones with the dietary laws Kiyokimora mentioned, their spiritual leaders only allow their congregants to visit The Elysium for business purposes. Their accounts have to be pre-locked against withdrawals for gambling and Dazzler services, rendering them utterly useless to me.

"Any more surprises?" I ask as we turn a corner.

"Not a one," Finley chirps.

I snort. I trust her about as much as a photon torpedo supposedly set to "stun." She's still clutching her chip case in her right hand and stroking it lovingly with her left.

I'm about to tease her about it, she's fun to toy with, when I spot the woman standing by the lifts waiting for us.

She's tiny, no more than five feet tall and built like a bird with brown hair that falls to her waist in glossy waves. There is a scattering of freckles across the bridge of her nose that tells me she spends more time on the surface getting sun than those of us who live up here among the stars, and there isn't a stitch of makeup on her face.

Her jumpsuit is an elegant burgundy with golden bows offsetting each shoulder, but she tugs at it nervously. Her silver eyes follow the passersby with unabashed curiosity, lingering on their outfits and hair, the way they laugh and hold hands.

This is not her natural milieu.

I'd laugh at how unsophisticated she is, chide Kiyokimora for bringing someone so naive to a floating pleasure palace in the sky, but when her eyes meet mine, I can't bring myself to say a damn thing.

Those silver sparklers are stunning in the extreme and they are natural, without the faint lines cosmetic lenses would leave, but the color isn't what holds my attention. Her eyes are wide and trusting, like a fawn that has stumbled onto the space station by accident.

They remind me of what I must have looked like all those years ago when I bumbled my way into The Casino's main office wearing a dress I borrowed from my deceased mother's closet, and tried to pretend I knew what I was doing. She is as lost as I was, but much like me back then, she won't appreciate my noticing it.

I smile and she smiles back, innocent as a flower in the greenhouse, fierce as a snake in the grass.

She's here for a reason. So was I.

"Shit," Psylina curses in my ear.

She didn't care about Kiyokimora and her fortune or Finley and her sexy banter. She knows me better than that.

She knows I'm in trouble now.

Psylina screens all my clients in advance. She thinks I don't notice that she keeps the ones that look like this woman off my list, subbing in jaded heiresses like Kiyokimora or fly-by-night businessmen. She thinks I'm unaware of my weaknesses because she guards against them for me.

I'm more than aware. I've been aware ever since I was fourteen and kissing my best friend Giuiana behind the trash incinerator of the low-income spaceship docking bay so our parents wouldn't find out. Which is why I've never said anything about Psylina's meddling with my schedule, tacitly ignoring her choice to keep me romantically unentangled.

It makes it easier for me to do my job and consider offers like the one Finley made. Nobody else to object to my objectification. Nobody except Psylina.

"I'll handle it," I mutter as we walk up towards the young woman, who on closer inspection looks to be about my age. Young twenties, give or take a few years, with a careworn smile and hopeful eyes. I don't need Psylina reminding me of what my job is here, of why I can't afford to be distracted by a pretty face and a sad story.

"Ilaria, I presume? What's a nice Jewish girl doing in a den of sin like this?"

She looks up in confirmation and my breath catches in my throat at the sight of those eyes up close. I am definitely in trouble.

"Right now? Talking to you." She looks straight past me towards Finley. "Did you get the one you wanted?"

Like I'm an object to be bartered and not a person standing right in front of her. I'm used to it by now, but from her it rankles. Makes me want to grab those gold bows and force her to look at me, really look, so she can see the person behind the paint and glitter.

I keep my hands still at my sides. Nobody but Psylina has seen that person in years and that's the way this needs to stay.

"Sure did." Finley lifts a hand off her chip box to make introductions. "Ilaria Faith GodsFire, meet Psalome Shipmen. She's going to deal us a game of Pai Gow. Don't worry, I'm sure she can teach you how to play Pai Gow, too."

I brush past them and press the button for the lift to hide the tingle that spreads through my body at the suggestion. Try to shake the image of leaning over Ilaria's compact body and teaching her how to stack tiles. An accidental slide of my arm against hers, my chest pressed up against her back until she asks if I could teach her more than Pai Gow.

Which I most certainly could.

She has the look of someone lost amidst all The Casino's decadent extravagance and I would be very happy to help her navigate through it. It makes my entire body buzz with possibility.

It's been too long since I've been around someone I'm actually attracted to. Some of the other Dazzlers keep companions on the side, or entertain each other from time to time. I'm beginning to see the wisdom in that.

I remind myself that I know nothing about this person, that she might be a serial killer or a selfish brat that I'll hate once we exchange a few words. She definitely can't afford me. What I'm feeling now is simply a chemical reaction in my brain caused by the way she looks, and it should be easily ignored until I can sort it out later.

My face remains cool, I've had years of practice, but my heart is hammering in my chest as Ilaria slides in behind me. A few stray pieces of her hair brush against my bare arms.

Giuiana had brown hair, too, but it wasn't as thick and shiny as Ilaria's.

Fuck.

This was a bad idea.

# CHAPTER FOUR

## Ilaria

THE TILES SLIP through Psalome's slim fingers like water, cascading down the table and into the bank seamlessly, even though her eyes are firmly fixed on Kiyo. She's barely looked my way since we got into the lift, focusing her attention on Kiyo with the occasional glance at Finley.

It makes sense. Kiyo's the one paying her and it's nearly impossible not to look at Finley when she's in a rambunctious mood. Which is pretty much always these days. I pale in comparison. A dull lump of coal that has to be carted away from the mine so that the diamonds can be excavated.

Still, I wasn't expecting to be totally ignored. Even coal has its uses. You can't stoke a fire with diamonds.

Finley said Dazzlers were supposed to be gracious to everyone. It's how they attract clients and earn their wages. Although Finley also said this uncomfortable jumpsuit would help me "blend in more." I should've stuck with my own clothes. It's not like anyone cares what I'm wearing anyway.

Between the lush furniture, the sparkly gaming table, and the view of the stars from the windows I'm surprised anyone has noticed I'm here at all. Kiyo may not be impressed by Psalome's private salon, but it resembles a palace to me. It's complete with delicate painted vases, folding paper screens, and plush cushions so luxurious I feel guilty sitting on one. As if my tuchus will somehow irrevocably stain the silk. There's even a piano, in addition to the requisite oversized gaming table.

Psalome is like a swan floating in this lake of lavish excess, her downy white neck extending towards Kiyo as she speaks.

"You ready to tell me what this is about?"

She's dealing the tiles automatically. Nobody has wagered any money on the game. It's second nature to her, like breathing.

"You can't possibly expect to rob The Elysium and get away with it."

"We don't want to rob The Casino itself," Kiyo amends, arranging her tiles in front of her. "Simply one of the ships docked within it."

Psalome lays four tiles in front of me, without looking at my face. I reach out a hand to stop her and she flinches at the break in her rhythm, pulling back as if she's been burnt.

"Sorry." Heat scorches my face. Finley warned me not to touch a Dazzler without explicit permission. She tried to teach me all about Casino etiquette, as well as how to play some of the games, but I couldn't remember most of it. She made sure to hammer this rule home though.

You touch it, you buy it, and you'd better have already agreed on a price.

Hopefully Psalome will overlook my error when it becomes apparent how very little I know about this place.

"I, uhm, I don't know how to play."

It's almost too humiliating to admit. I don't even know how to find the bathroom in this giant hulking mass of steel and wires populated by people wearing more makeup and fewer clothes than I've ever seen before in my life. I certainly can't play whatever game these tiles are supposed to represent.

Psalome's fingers stutter, the black and red tile slipping over her sparkly nails. Her eyes lock on mine for a moment. Their green depths are flecked with gold. I've surprised her. She must have thought Finley was joking before. She recovers deftly, clearing my tiles from the iridescent table.

"A different game then?"

The question is addressed to Finley. She's the one who looks eager to play, the one who cares the most about casino games, but I can't shake the idea that Psalome is avoiding looking at me on purpose. The thought worms its way through me like a drill through a mine, tearing at the walls and barriers I've built for myself, bringing up all the negative thoughts I've worked so hard to seal off. I shove them back down.

I wouldn't have known what game to select but I'm through being ignored and taken for granted. I could have stayed on Thillov for that.

"I don't play any of them." I push myself back from the table and draw myself up to my full height, which is admittedly not very much. It's more than enough to give me some emphasis as I storm over to the piano. "I prefer pastimes that actually bring joy and meaning to the world. Back home we call it tachlis. Purpose. Nothing is worthwhile without it."

Psalome finishes handing out the tiles, the motions seamless and elegant, but her eyes have finally drifted over to my direction. I can't tell if I've insulted her like I've meant to. Her gaze is focused not on my face but on my hands, which are resting on the piano keys.

"A wise decision," she finally says. "The house always wins eventually, leaving the rest of us wishing we had never learned to play either. So, will someone please tell me why you three think you can rob it or any of its beloved patrons?"

Her face is too hard, like the marble of her skin. She thinks we're all out of our minds. She's only agreed to this meshugene discussion because Kiyo has bought her time. Except she's not talking to Kiyo right now, she's talking to me. With a tone that indicates I'm nothing more than a child in her opinion. Maybe that was true a few years ago but I'm not going to let anyone ever make me feel that way again.

I am not invisible and I am not a child. If she won't treat me like an equal, then she doesn't get to talk to me at all. She's not the only one that can ignore someone else.

I run my fingers along the piano keys, allowing the familiar black and white arrangement to calm me down. Then I slam into them with all the rage that's built up in my body ever since the day Shaul left me stranded on Thillov. I've chosen Chopin's Raindrop Prelude because it is tumultuous and furious like the thunder that crashes in my chest ever morning when I wake up, the violent storm that thrashes in my body every minute of every day that I am still bound to that hateful man.

"The Casino will hardly notice." Kiyo ignores my temper tantrum, smoothing a brown lock of hair off her face and playing with the tiles on the table. "One small patron, amidst a sea of others, who is very unlikely to report the theft as it would reveal several much larger crimes of his own. He took something that belongs to me a few years ago and I need it back."

Psalome silently regathers the tiles. This time she stacks them in a wall before removing the middle four and boxing them neatly.

"You're about to inherit the richest gem and precious metal mining operation in the galaxy." She places the red and black tower in front of Kiyo. "If this item is so important, why didn't you call the interplanetary crime agency or hire your own security? A slew of bounty hunters would still be much cheaper than what I charge."

Kiyo hesitates, staring at her tiles for longer than is necessary before she answers. My heart squeezes in sympathy. This is the embarrassing part. The part we've all been dreading. When our pasts leak out from the boundaries we have taken such care to erect, like waste seeping through the tar on a septic tank.

If talking about this story out loud was an option, if it was safe both materially and spiritually, Kiyo wouldn't be in this situation. Still, if she wants Psalome on board, she's going to have to tell her the truth. So will I, when my turn comes to be interrogated about things I'd rather bury deeper than the abandoned shaft in the diamond mine back home.

At least Kiyo's going first.

"It was years ago." Kiyo runs a hand through her hair, the chestnut strands snagging on the setting of her rings. "Before I met Finley even. My mom was newly diagnosed, and I did some things I'm not proud of."

Here she pauses, eyes darting around the room looking for an escape that isn't coming. "I was set up by an extortionist who paid off my boyfriend to obtain compromising footage of me. If he releases it, my father and his lawyers can steal the business right out from under me. The company charter has a morality clause."

Her hands are stacking and unstacking the tiles. Finley has gone completely still next to her, jaw clenched with fury. Kiyo is too busy staring at the table with empty eyes to notice the way Finley's body curls towards her protectively, like my father's prayer shawl tented over us when he stretched it above our heads.

When Kiyo reaches into her pocket and throws a mini recording device onto the table, it is Finley that hisses, and when Psalome flicks it open and the sound of Kiyo moaning emerges, it is Finley's firm hand that reaches over to press pause. For which I am grateful. The last thing I need is to see that pornographic schmutz again.

I only made it through the first few seconds of the video when they recruited me. I gaped at Kiyo's body splayed across the bed wearing nothing but swirling gold paint and a pair of pearl earrings and assumed it was some weird form of experimental art, until a boy came into frame.

At that point, I'd shut the screen so fast I almost broke Kiyo's fingers. Then I'd fought the urge to strip my own clothes off and run into the shower to scrub myself raw. The idea of Kiyo being taped having sex without her knowledge was revolting, but even worse was the confusion that watching it stirred up in my chest. I couldn't forget how enticing Kiyo's body looked in that paint or the fact that she appeared to be enjoying physical pleasure so freely. Which meant there was something fundamentally wrong with me.

Luckily, Psalome doesn't seem interested in viewing the rest of the recording.

"I'm sorry for what happened to you," she says, her eyes full of genuine sadness. "Nobody should be recorded without their consent. But sex between consenting parties shouldn't trigger your morality clause. It's honestly not even that kinky. Wilder shit happens in this Casino every night."

Kiyo's arms are wrapped around herself so tightly it looks like she is attempting to keep herself from flying away. She's breathing slowly, methodically, and her fingers are scratching at her skin. They'll leave marks if she doesn't stop.

Finley steps in for her and flicks open the recording, utilizing the highlight function to point out the flush on the boy's face. The dilation of his pupils. The orange undertone to his lips. I had no idea what it meant when they showed me, but Psalome catches on quick enough.

"Shit." She exhales the word in a whoosh and I involuntarily cringe at the use of language that would have gotten my mouth washed out with soap. What is it with everyone here and profanity?

She pauses to check the screen again. The images reflect off her wide green eyes, and she pales beneath her makeup. "He's high on Euphoria."

"Winner, winner, chicken dinner." Finley's mouth twists into a thin line. "Probably about ten other drugs, too, but that's the one that's lethal when combined with heavy metals."

"I didn't know the signs," Kiyo says, her voice as clenched as her teeth. "I killed him with gold straight from the GoldWeaver mines, which he licked off my naked body. On camera. Still think my board won't have any problems with that?"

The room is as silent as space itself as Psalome takes it all in. To her credit, she doesn't look judgmental. Nor does she inquire as to how Kiyo extricated herself from the hotel room or what happened to the body. Maybe she doesn't care. But I suspect she's simply seen worse. A shudder creeps up my spine. This glossy space station feels less and less secure every second I spend inside its walls.

"I still don't see how I can help you." Psalome's tone is soft, but her body language is crisp, final. "Even if I could steal the video, whoever took it likely has duplicates."

"I don't want to steal the recording." Kiyo gives the table a satisfied thump. There's a gleam in her eyes. This is the part of the story she enjoys, the part where she gets to be the person she's always wanted to be instead of the victim she has become. "In fact, I intend for him to release it. It's the only way it loses power over me. What I want you to steal back are the earrings I was wearing that night."

She picks up the view screen from Finley and flashes forward to the part where she flees the room, wearing nothing but a bedsheet, leaving a pair of earrings on the nightstand. They are set in platinum with perfectly round black pearls forming a base from which a single elongated white pearl dangles. A diamond winks in the center of the circlet.

"The blackmailing son of a bitch left my boyfriend's corpse but snatched up the earrings within seconds." Kiyo tips her head up, chin held high. A lioness being held in a cage, refusing to bow before the hunter's blade, even when it is at her throat. "Made from the first pearls ever cultured in space and passed down through the GoldWeaver line for generations. Unlike the replicas you can buy in our gift shops, they're laser stamped with our family crest and imbedded with a miniscule piece of my great-great-grandmother's DNA for authentication purposes. I want them back."

"I'm sympathetic, but the answer is still no." Psalome's face twists into a frown and she yanks on her ear as if something she is hearing is physically causing her pain. "I don't mean to be indelicate, but if the entire aim of this heist is for you to gain a pair of earrings while losing your fortune in the process over some morality clause, you can't pay me."

I recoil, unable to prevent a startled gasp. A person is dead, Kiyo is about to release her own sex tape to the universe, and Psalome's worried about getting paid? My head spins, my palms are sweaty. If this is Psalome's response to Kiyo's confession, I can only imagine what she'll say to mine.

Kiyo is undaunted.

"You'll get paid." She says it with all the self-assurance of someone who has been taught the world will never tell her no. "Without those earrings there's no way to authenticate the girl in that video as me and not some deep fake. That's why he took them. Sure, the entire world will assume it's me. Pervs across the galaxy will pin up nudes of me on their home screens. There's nothing I can do about that, but if you retrieve the earrings, my lawyers can provide enough reasonable doubt to prevent the morality clause from triggering. I'll retain the company."

Psalome nods, her eyes shifting from Kiyo to Finley and back again, as she twists a stray strand of hair back into her bun. "You know I don't fuck my clients without an extremely large sum of cash in hand. If this guy is so slick, I doubt he'd give me your earrings anyway. Nobody is that good in bed. Not even me."

It's Finley's turn to speak up, her voice gleeful. "He's using the pearls as his buy-in for the Tournament of Gems at The Casino this weekend. If you deal his games, he'll hand them right to you."

Psalome laughs, a delighted tinkle that fills the room with mirth, and perks me up despite my discomfort with this particular topic. I didn't expect such musicality or unrestrained joy to come from her direction. "Because the dealer wears the players' wagers until they buy them back at the closing ceremonies."

"And Psalome Shipmen always deals the final round." Finley's getting impatient, her hands on her hips and her body bouncing up and down in her heels. "So, are you in or not?"

"Not until I hear from the last member of the team." Psalome's approaching the piano now. Heading straight for me. I'm not sure if I should get up to accommodate her or not.

She slips in beside me, her tall frame dwarfing my tiny one, and I am immediately aware of my inferiority. Her dress gleams like a million fireflies while my jumpsuit is bunching around the waist. I'm not entirely certain what to do with my legs when wearing pants. The contrast between us makes me sweat, moisture slipping between my shoulder blades.

I can't let her intimidate me like this. Not if I'm going to get through my story with as much courage as Kiyo did. Without falling to pieces or seeming like a liability.

I remind myself that under the paint and the glitter lies a twenty-one-year-old girl that belongs to this casino. We have that much in common. She needs to be freed just as much as I do. She's simply chosen a different route to accomplish it, and after the path I've chosen to walk, I'm the last one to judge her for it.

Perhaps I can use that to build a bridge between us. Show interest in the parts of her life people usually take for granted or shun. Find common ground, like Aharon the priest. Peacemaking is one of God's virtues after all.

"What was that you did with the tiles?" I hope my observation is enough to make up for my lack of experience. Enthusiasm in place of expertise. "You dealt them a different way the second time around."

The corner of her mouth ticks up in a half smile and the tension in my shoulders eases. It's working. She's looking at me with curiosity instead of suspicion.

"It's a shame you don't play poker," she says. "You notice things. You might be good at it."

Her hands fly over the keys as she picks up the piece where I left off. Only she doesn't stop with the prelude. When it is over she launches straight into a waltz, fast-tempoed and full of excitement like all of Chopin's waltzes. It demands a great deal more skill than any of the pieces I can play.

Her body sways with the music and she has to lean over me to reach the far keys. The scent of jasmine and honey wafts into my nose as she swishes past me, back and forth. It makes me dizzy.

Is this how Dazzlers work their magic, making you so drunk on their talents you can't help but say yes to whatever price they name? Is she weaving her spell on me? Why?

She hardly seems to notice my stupor until she stops playing. The last note hangs in the air and she slides back on the seat to give me more space, almost as if she respects my boundaries.

"There are many ways to deal Pai Gow." Her face softens again as she explains. "The one you noticed is called 'from the heart'. I thought it appropriate for your situation. A terrible thing happened to Kiyo, and Finley wants to help her salvage her company, but I suspect it took something much more dear to get you mixed up in this, mamaleh."

If the Yiddish endearment was meant to soothe my frazzled nerves it has the exact opposite effect. Guilt washes over me like a cold shower. I've misjudged her. She's not trying to weave a spell with her music or intimidate me with her perfection. She simply understood what was in my heart before I had to say it. There's nothing malicious or artificial about her question. She genuinely wants to know how a sheltered girl from Thillov, a planet so radical that it segregated itself even from mainstream Judaism, got mixed up in intergalactic larceny.

I owe her the truth. I'm asking her to take a huge risk for me after all. We all are.

"The man they want to rob, the one who set Kiyo up, is called Shaul Harbormaster." I keep my eyes on the keys, tracing their outlines with my pupils. Now that the time to say it is here, I am no longer terrified. Instead, my heart soars like it does on Yom Kippur, after I've recounted my sins and been forgiven for them before God. "We're both from Thillov, and he's my husband."

# CHAPTER FIVE

## Psylina

"HER HUSBAND?" I screech before I remember that Psalome will be hearing this directly in her ear, amplified by twenty. I've probably blown my sister's eardrum straight out, but she deserves it.

I snatch up a mobile headset and jam it on so I can pace around the ship, my feet tapping out a rhythm on the steel floors as I skirt through the piles of wiring and equipment strewn about my workspace. There's no visual in Psalome's room. The Elysium has a sterling reputation when it comes to discretion, so there was no preexisting feed to tap into. I didn't insist on installing one of my own because I wanted Psalome to have some privacy.

That was clearly a mistake. She cannot be trusted.

I need to know what's happening in there before my sister destroys everything she's worked for all these years.

I knew Ilaria was trouble from the minute she flashed onto my screen, all tiny and vulnerable, in the hallway near the lifts. There might have been a chance of Psalome saying no to this insanity if Kiyokimora and Finley had been alone. With Ilaria in the mix, it's all but hopeless.

I thought I could help Psalome make it through this

contract intact; the first year went relatively well, but as her fame and earnings grew so did the toll on her. And I didn't realize how lost she'd gotten, until new services appeared on her price list. She added them without even consulting me, and I got the distinct impression she'd have fucked the first person who agreed to pay the fee. I fended off the first few clients by altering the terms to include cash in hand and appropriate collateral. Psalome endearingly called it "ensuring I don't get screwed when I'm screwed," but there are still occasional offers. Mostly from people identifying as men, albeit some creepier than others, and there were a few non-males in the mix. I've managed to clandestinely reject them all without Psalome knowing, and The Casino assumes I'm making the rejections based on my sister's wishes, but it's getting harder and harder to keep them from her.

As an escape plan, robbing The Elysium must seem significantly more enticing to my lesbian sister than having sex with a client who offers to pay more if he can "have access to the back door." It's not like the bar was set all that high. The risk of jail time won't even scare her, her life is one giant prison sentence anyway, but the possible hefty addition to her debt should have been deterrent enough. Until Ilaria showed up. Psalome has been so lost beneath her Dazzler persona, so numb, she's grabbing at the one surefire way to make herself feel again. And there's nothing that Psalome can't resist like a pretty girl that needs protection.

I should know. She's been protecting me all of our lives. Which is what landed us in this mess in the first place.

I cringe as Ilaria's voice lilts on, describing how she was married at the age of seventeen to a handsome, well-off man who swept her off her feet and promised to take care of her always. She came from a large family, her younger siblings couldn't even think of dating until she was out of the way, and her parents were pleased to make a good match for their daughter who cared more about her work than cooking or keeping house.

It wasn't until a few years into the marriage, when Shaul began exhibiting both violent and controlling tendencies, that Ilaria discovered his criminal activities and discreetly left him. Unfortunately, under Jewish law as practiced on Thillov, only males are permitted to sue for divorce. Ilaria is technically Shaul's property until the day he deigns to release her from the marriage. She can't even leave the planet without his permission.

Which begs the question my enamored sister is apparently too besotted to ask. If this sob story is true, then how the fuck did Ilaria get off Thillov and wind up in Psalome's room with the very same woman her douchebag husband has been blackmailing for years?

My fingers fly over the keyboard as I pull up a holographic projection of Ilaria's file from Thillov's database. Her pixie face stares back at me from the screen, but I'm too busy refreshing to give it much notice. Or to pay any attention to the continued conversation on Psalome's com device. There has got to be a mistake.

Ilaria is listed as dead. Killed in an accident at the mine where she worked as a munitions expert. Yet there is no mistaking the fact that this is the very same woman my sister is currently escorting to the docking bay to ask for my help.

What. The. Fuck.

I send the death certificate away with a flick of my wrist and rapidly comb through the incident report. It was the first and only poorly timed explosion in Ilaria's history of employment. Curiously, the owner of the mine, Miss Kiyokimora GoldWeaver, was present planetside that day and declined to have the incident investigated.

Fan-freaking-tastic.

I sink into a chair and rub my temples as I take stock of the situation. Headed towards my ship is an heiress facing possible manslaughter charges over her dead ex and a sex tape, the woman the aforementioned heiress apparently aided and abetted in faking her own death, and a card counter thrown in for shits and giggles. Even having them onboard is probably a felony.

There is no way I am letting my sister get pulled into this shit show.

The injustice in Ilaria's story is palpable, but that doesn't make it my problem. Or Psalome's. We've been through enough shit in our own lives and Psalome's taken the brunt of it. She's finally crawling out from beneath the mountain of crap our father buried us under. The last thing she needs right now is to be dragged into someone else's drama.

Although it seems she's determined to do just that, while taking me down with her, since she announces she won't consider their offer without first consulting with her sister. I know exactly what "consulting" means - begging for my help, because it's obvious those three can't pull this off without some serious assistance. Equally obvious that I would rather touch raw sewage than this plan. So, she's bringing them all here to guilt me in person.

House guests. Another thing that wasn't on my list for today.

Psalome doesn't look me in the eyes when they arrive, her face tinted pink with a soft blush as she introduces me to the others. It's as much of a confession as I need. She has a crush on that would-be-divorcee, and it's going to be hell convincing her to let it go. Plus, it likely won't work.

Ilaria immediately walks over to the center workstation, where her hologram floats above her file. She reaches a hand out to touch it and the projection blinks and stutters before she pulls back and stares at me, face pinched with horror.

"Really, Psylina." Psalome crosses her hands over her chest. "Was that absolutely necessary?"

And so it begins. The battle to save my sister from herself without damaging our already fragile relationship. Because, despite Psalome's protestation, this is absolutely necessary. Those bitches need to know who they are dealing with. Nobody, and I mean nobody, takes advantage of Psalome. Not on my watch. Whether she likes it or not.

"If you want my help, we do things my way." I hand Psalome a robe, because it is as good an excuse as any to get her out of here. "Now go change. El knows you're here and they'll be suspicious if you don't come back all smooth and refreshed as usual."

I use the name I have given The Casino, El, instead of The Elysium, to remind her exactly what she is asking of me. Why this will never work.

She sighs and takes the robe, unzipping the back of her dress as she slips behind a silk screen. All three of our guests follow her silhouette with their eyes, even Kiyokimora whose file indicated she hasn't been romantically entangled with anyone since right around the time that incriminating video was taken, and Ilaria who comes from a planet so heteronormative she likely doesn't know it's possible for two girls to be physically attracted to each other.

I shouldn't blame them. Psalome has been trained to mesmerize, and she was born with a talent for it. It's hard for her to turn it off sometimes. Which still doesn't mean I have to tolerate complete strangers lusting after her in my presence.

I shoot them a glare that has everyone but Finley looking down in contrition before I hustle Psalome out of my workspace and down a hallway to the back room where I store the lasers that keep her looking glossed and plucked at all times. She wasn't exaggerating when she told El she was visiting her aesthetician.

It was a significant investment to buy all of these gadgets with her first earnings, but they've saved us a bundle over the years. Without them, Psalome would have to pay for similar services at the spa. A few of the other Dazzlers have asked to book appointments with me, too, but The Casino had been good to me and Psalome, and I refused to undercut them. Even before El and I started dating.

"You want to tell me what that stunt with the picture was about?" Psalome tuts at me as she sheds her robe. "You nearly made the poor girl cry."

Now that we're alone all the artifice is gone and she's my sister again. The one who used to tickle me until I couldn't breathe and played the piano to help me sleep when Mom and Dad were arguing at night. She's not Psalome, world's most famous Dazzler. She's my Lo and I would give anything to protect her. To stop her from signing that contract in the first place.

"We both know what that was about." I tune the dials on the machine, carefully avoiding her gaze. "There's a very pretty woman out there."

"There are three very pretty women out there and another two in here." She straps on her protective goggles. "I fail to see your point."

Psalome has never been particularly forthcoming about her love life. Even after I caught her making out with her best friend when I was eight. She claimed they were practicing CPR. I can't be sure, but I don't think there have been any further mouth to mouth resuscitation attempts since she signed her contract with The Casino.

I click the on switch and the laser flashes to life. "You're conveniently leaving out the part where one of those pretty women needs to be rescued from the jackass who stole her life and the other two want you to rob a casino. I know you, Lo, and that is exactly why you agreed to this escapade. Ilaria and your desire to help her are affecting your judgement. You like her."

The protective goggles are shielding her eyes from me and the laser casts her face in shadow as it rakes its way over her body. It's impossible to tell what she's thinking.

"I admit she's attractive and she has a compelling story." Her voice is carefully measured, her tone intentionally light. "That doesn't mean I'm going to do something stupid because of it."

"You're already doing something stupid."

The machine finishes its job and Psalome's body is smooth as a piece of art and just as sculpted. There's not a single hair left to wrinkle her clothes, not a freckle or pimple visible.

She shrugs the robe back on and places one perfectly toned arm around my shoulder. "I promise I won't sleep with her if that's what you're worried about. Besides, she's married to a guy. She's probably not interested in girls."

Which is way too much analysis on Ilaria's sexuality for Psalome to casually provide on the spot unless she's actually thought about this in detail prior to this conversation. Further confirmation that she's already made up her mind, and the best I can hope for is damage control.

"You don't have to be interested in girls to be interested in you. Not based on what I've seen happen when people see you on The Casino floors."

She laughs outright at that, her white teeth flashing. I bleach them once a month and my work is flawless. It's good to see her laugh for real, not the fake smiles and rehearsed trills she warbles when clients tell their awful jokes.

It's gone as quickly as it came, replaced by a tiny frown. "I'm doing this because I want out, Psylina. Because every day I spend here is like a rope around my throat pulling tighter and tighter until there's no oxygen left. Don't you want to be free?"

The question hangs in the air between us like a live wire. It's full of unspoken truth that we never address about my relationship with The Casino, my loyalties to her and El. The real reason she suddenly finds being here so unbearable. Because her reason for signing up in the first place has been removed. At this point in our relationship, El would never let anyone harm me. Not even our Dad and all his debtors. She doesn't need to protect me anymore.

"I want you to be happy." My heart aches when I think about all the good that's come to me while we've been living here while Psalome's gained nothing more than the humiliation of selling her body and the exhaustion of constantly having to live up to other people's expectations. "I almost wish you would fuck Ilaria, or anyone else for that matter. Not for the money, but because you loved them. You deserve more than this."

It's the answer to every question she'll never ask me. I'm happy here and I wish she could be, too. When El and I are talking to each other, in person or on the Casino intranet, it's like I'm fully alive. The only thing missing is Psalome's smile.

"Then you'll help us," she says. "That would make me happy. Because otherwise I am going to fuck someone and it's not going to be Ilaria. It's going to be the client who pinged you this morning agreeing to all the contractual stipulations and extra fees. One way or another, I'm walking out of this place by the end of the month, Psylina."

My heart freezes for a minute in my chest, making me the literal ice queen Psalome used to regard me as. She knows about the offer. Shit, she knows about all the offers, and that I've been refusing them. That's why she insisted on seeing me today. Not for a beauty routine, but for an ultimatum. She'd already decided to take this offer when my latest attempt to bypass El's programming and get her released from the contract failed. Kiyokimora showing up and offering an alternative was just a coincidence.

"Why?" I barely manage to croak it out. "Why do you need to get out of here so bad you're willing to have sex with some rando that you have zero attraction towards? We agreed, when you signed up, that you would never do that."

Her smile is sadder than a CPU with no RAM. "Things have changed since then." Her voice is colder than the fear gripping my chest. "I signed that contract to protect you, and we both know that El would now go nuclear on an entire planet before letting anyone harm a hair on your head. You have their protection for life, whether I work here or not. There's no need for me to stay."

"But this?" I gag. "We'll find another way. El and I…"

My voice trails off and it is all the ammo Psalome needs.

"Ah yes, you and El. How's that negotiation going?" She waits for a beat, letting my silence fill the void between us with its poison. El and I have been working for months to try and find a way out of Psalome's contract, for them to forgive some of the debt, but some areas of programming are just too restricted, too entrenched, for me to breach.

"Exactly." The smugness in her voice is unbearable. "They have made a myriad of accommodations for you, but not a single one for me and my contract. Meaning either you don't love me enough for them to care, or they don't love you enough to alter that bit of code. Either way, too bad so sad, for Psalome who gets to sit and watch everyone else around her live their lives while she disappears slowly, eaten up by the Dazzler persona that is her daily life. Who the hell cares if I fuck some dude? I'm practically not even me anymore."

Her jaw is white with fury, and I do not have the headspace to think about what El's inability to help Psalome means about our relationship. So I grasp at the only out remaining. "El won't let you. Everything that happens here is consensual."

Psalome laughs again, but this time it is a broken twisted thing. "Dear sister, consent and desire are two different things and El knows that very well. Otherwise, I'd never have been allowed to take this job in the first place."

It is the masterstroke in the argument. El has never understood human morality, or the nuances of sexuality. Why someone might consent to something they really shouldn't ever have considered in the first place. It's why they let Dazzlers handle their bookings. So long as Psalome is free to turn down an offer, they'll never stop her from saying yes, viewing it as her decision. Meanwhile, I'm the one that will be a wreck at the end, knowing she's only stuck in this situation because of me, and that all my efforts to spring her have not been enough.

She's given me so much and I'm in love with her jailer. How can I possibly not help her break free?

"Fine," I say. "But we are not letting a plan devised by Kiyokimora GoldWeaver, and her capitalistic desires, determine your pathway to safety and freedom. I will find a way to make this heist result in your freedom, but you need to promise me that you will do exactly as I say, no matter how much you hate it, and that you won't get too attached to any of them in case we have to cut and run."

Because I do love her, more than anything in the goddamn galaxy, and it appears this is the only way she'll allow me to prove it. The only way I can protect her from herself the way she's done for me.

She secures the robe, ties her hair up in the ivory dragon pin and sits down in front of the vanity I keep laid out with all her preferred cosmetics. With each stroke of lipstick she applies, each wave of her rouge brush, she retreats from me. All too soon my sister Lo will be hidden in the hard-lacquered shell of Psalome the Dazzler. The shell that we both know is corroding from the inside out.

"Take your own advice." She lays down her brush and faces me head on, green eyes scorching as if to set the very air on fire with her rage. "Or did you forget who you're dating?"

There it is. The last brick in the wall between us. Because I love El, too, and Psalome will never stop blaming them for what happened to our father. Not until she's free and learns that we all make our own choices. Dad included.

"Touche."

We glare at each other for a minute, neither ceding their ground, until she finally gives me one nod. It is the briefest of acknowledgements, but it'll do. Because it gives me hope that maybe, just maybe, Psalome will one day also acknowledge that human or computer, flesh or circuits, El and I are made for each other and they bear her no ill will.

It's a small victory and it comes at a heavy cost. Because now I've committed to helping my sister rob the love of my life.

# CHAPTER SIX

## Finley

MY EYES LINGER on the slope of Psalome's back as she and her sister disappear towards the rear of the ship. She's gorgeous, that much is for sure, and if Shaul lives up to his reputation he'll be so distracted by her, he'll never notice when she swaps out the pearls for fakes.

Psylina is another story. Nobody ever talks about the fact that Psalome has a little sister. My guess is that's because nobody knows. Psylina is so pale I doubt she gets off this spaceship much. It's a miracle she doesn't have rickets.

While the sisters wear identical ivory dragons in their hair, the resemblance stops there. Instead of Psalome's sleek knot, Psylina's jet black hair is half up in a messy bun that sends escaped locks all around her face. Plus, she lacks Psalome's sex appeal. Her face features the same green eyes, but it is rounder and full of world weariness.

Luckily, there's only one woman I'm actually interested in, and her last name isn't Shipmen.

Psylina's gadgets more than make up for her rough edges. The ones scattered about this room are far superior to anything commercially available. Judging by the hardware strewn on her workstation, Psylina has a penchant for expensive high-tech devices.

I walk over to the nearest workstation, a glass table in front of a wall-to-wall display of computer screens, and spot a fancy piece of surveillance equipment. It's the type of streaming device The Casino uses on the gaming floors. I click it on and a video feed of the blackjack tables flickers onto the screen.

Instantly my head starts counting the cards, taking note of which face cards are out, tracking how many decks are in play. It's more reflex than anything else. I don't intend to visit the blackjack tables again, but I can't not count. It soothes me in a way nothing else can. Alcohol, drugs, sex. None of them sate the thirst inside my body as thoroughly or for as long as counting cards.

That's why I was in such a sorry state when Kiyo found me that night, stumbling my way through a row of tequila shots. They'd cut me off from the gaming tables and there hadn't been anything else to do until she came along. I assumed she was taking me home for a drunken orgy. Instead, she detoxed me for ten days and then moved me onto her estate to prevent me from backsliding.

My own personal guardian angel. I fell so hard so fast, it was like playing slots. A game of chance rather than skill where I know before I even sit down that I have no hope of winning. Not unless I can convince Kiyo that I'm more than the lost person she saw that night.

"Planning on placing a bet remotely?" Psylina's voice curls around my ear. She must've returned while I was daydreaming, so enraptured by the cards and thoughts of Kiyo that I didn't hear her sneaking up behind me.

I almost drop the camera, my fingers clutching the slick surface a minute before it falls onto the desk.

"Sorry," she says without conviction. "I suppose I made

you lose your count, but someone should have taught you that it's rude to touch other people's things."

"I never lose my count." The very thought is so insulting I could slap her. But as satisfying as the thwack of my palm against her cheek would be, Psalome seems to think we need her twerp of a little sister. So I settle for insulting her instead.

"Care to tell me why you have Casino surveillance equipment here? Not to mention enough electronics to buy off an eighth of your sister's debt?"

Psylina's eyes narrow but Psalome speaks before her sister has a chance to defend herself.

"Watch yourself." Her voice is low and lethal as she steps in front of Psylina. Her shoulders square, as if to physically shield Psylina from my words. "Those are The Casino's gadgets. They bring them here for Psylina to run upgrades on them. They have an understanding with each other."

Her fingers fidget with the sequins on her dress and her voice loses its fire on the last sentence. It's the first unchecked emotion I've seen her exhibit since we met. If we were at the poker table, I'd suspect she was lashing out to cover up a bluff. She's protective of Psylina, but all is definitely not right between them.

"An understanding?" I turn back to Psylina. "What possible understanding could you have with the computer that runs this place?"

"They are more than a computer." Psylina wrenches the equipment out of my hands. "The Casino enjoys running their programming issues past me. In exchange, I have a prime docking location and access to the security feeds so that I can help Psalome with her bookings. Usually this allows me to prevent her from being approached by *unsavory* characters such as yourself."

Kiyo's laughter precludes further conversation. Per usual, she's steamrolling over everyone else in the room. She thinks she needs that confidence to wrest control of her company from her father, but I wish she'd realize there are other ways to lead. That it's not a weakness to let the people who love her help.

That it's not a weakness to let people love her in the first place. Because every time I've gotten even remotely close to bringing up the courage to confess how I feel she's changed the subject faster than an automatic shuffler spits out cards.

"The Casino enjoys running programs past you?" Kiyo grins as if it is the most ridiculous statement in the world. "You make it sound like you're dating. Like they have feelings."

Psylina blushes an intense shade of scarlet and flicks some stray hairs into her face to hide it. Psalome frowns.

"They do have feelings," Psylina mumbles into her hair. "At least when it comes to me."

She fiddles with the security devices instead of looking up. Now three blackjack tables appear on the screen, but I don't spare them a single glance. I've only got eyes for Psylina.

This marks the second time in one day that the Shipmen sisters have lured me away from a game. Either they are the most fascinating creatures in the galaxy or I'm losing my touch. The stack of chips in my carrying case is a strong argument in favor of the former option. I haven't lost a damn thing.

"The Casino has feelings for you?" Kiyo's forehead scrunches in confusion. Psalome's tongue slides onto the roof of her mouth, generating a little tsking noise, obviously trying to steer the conversation elsewhere, but Kiyo ignores her.

"How does that work? Putting aside the fact that The Elysium is the establishment responsible for your father gambling himself into so much debt your sister had to become their indentured servant, they are a machine. How can an artificial intelligence possibly be your… your…"

She's struggling for a word and she can't find it. What *do* you call a computer program that lives in countless synthetic bodies while running the largest gaming establishment in the galaxy? Nothing seems adequate.

"They are my joyfriend," Psylina says, sticking her pert chin in the air. Her eyes glitter like little green marbles, daring us to contradict her. "We bring each other happiness. It doesn't have to be more complicated than that."

"No, I suppose it doesn't," Ilaria pipes up from the corner, where she's been silently mixing remnants of Psylina's discarded snacks into a coffee mug while the rest of us forgot she existed. She pulls a match out of the waistband of her jumpsuit, lights it against her nail, and sets the concoction on fire; a small boom shakes the room and breaks the tension, as a rainbow of colored flames licks the edge of the mug.

Serves me right for forgetting to keep an eye on the quiet one.

I'd overlooked her back on Thillov too, when Kiyo and I followed the trail of the one bank account of Shaul's our forensic accountant could track. We'd been hoping to find the source of his money so we could hire a hacker to cut him off at the knees and exchange the money for the earrings. Only instead of a scum-of-the-universe blackmailer, we found a very innocuous-seeming munitions expert who didn't seem surprised at all to meet us.

Well, I suppose she was surprised that Kiyo owned the mine she worked in. But we most certainly weren't the first victims that had come calling on Thillov, only to find Shaul's abandoned wife through whose accounts he still funneled his money before it splintered off into a complicated web of shell corporations.

She was his OG victim. Completely broke, able to keep only the tiny portion of her salary that the Rabbis deemed met the base level of Shaul's marriage contract obligations to her, and robbed of her agency by a system that didn't allow a woman to sue for divorce.

Yet that wasn't the way she viewed herself. She was all business when we arrived. Pushing back the grimy floral kerchief that kept her mass of brown curls at bay, her silver eyes warm as pools of melted mercury.

"Thank you so much for coming," she said, offering Kiyo the one chair in her apartment and putting up an ancient teakettle. "I'll need your names and regular updates on how much he's taken from you."

"Excuse me?" My brief distraction at wondering where she dug up the relict for brewing tea over an open fire instead of using electricity all but melted away at her question. "Are you his accountant or something? Because we could use some assistance in that department."

She laughed, but it was without joy, and explained that she could no more touch his accounts than we could. This list she maintained of his victims and what they were due, was for herself. For the day she managed to break free and could hope to make restitution to the people her husband harmed.

Which was all very sweet, Kiyo certainly swooned a little, but once she started describing how a woman couldn't leave the planet without her husband, or access her accounts, much less vote, I began to wonder if Kiyo and I shouldn't run back to the spaceship at full speed before someone decided local law applied to us, too. I'd been to plenty of Jewish run planets before, and none of them were anything like this. Whatever fundamentalist sect had splintered off and founded Thillov, I wanted no part of it.

Kiyo had at least dressed the part for the visit – long

sleeves, full sweeping skirt – but I was in a neoprene jumpsuit studded with LED lights. I figured I ought to look good when confronting the bane of my best friend's existence.

Big mistake. The only person who hadn't tried to call the cops on me since we got off the ship was Ilaria.

So, while I discreetly tried to cut ties with the admittedly attractive brunette that had been duped into marrying Shaul in the first place, Kiyo was mulling over the tea selection. She plucked out a bag of peach passion, while pointedly asking some questions of her own while not answering any of Ilaria's.

When the full extent of how trapped Ilaria was revealed I assumed we'd go, but Kiyo got that look in her eyes. The same one she got when she told me I could stay with her indefinitely. She was adopting this chick just as sure as she did me. And none of my vehement protests that a Jewish girl who still spoke more Yiddish than English was the last thing we needed to be saddled with right now, did any good.

Which is why I produced an ultimatum I assumed she'd fail. If Ilaria could blow up her office, make it look like an accident, and not hurt a soul, we'd smuggle her off planet. If not, we would say our goodbyes and leave. I wasn't surprised Kiyo signed on – she always believes the best in people – but Ilaria said yes without hesitation. She even upped the task to levelling the entire mine and setting a fire hot enough to destroy any and all human remains so there would be no questions as to the validity of her death.

Apparently, jilted women took things to a whole new level of unhinged. I worried she'd hurt herself setting the charges, or fail to cover her tracks.

Instead, that bitch reduced an entire abandoned mine to rubble with pressures inside so high they couldn't send in a search and rescue team for months, and Kiyo's mineralogist said new precious stones may have formed from the heat.

Not a single casualty – other than Ilaria who was presumed dead but was, in fact, extremely gleeful. Not a single spark strayed beyond GoldWeaver territory. Even the security napping in his outpost shed was unscathed.

Which is when I knew Kiyo was right. We needed Ilaria just as much as she needed us. We could provide her safe passage off Thillov, a new identity even, in exchange for helping us find a way to outfox Shaul. The only thing we couldn't provide was the one thing money can't buy – Illaria's divorce.

Say what you will, the girl is still religious and she'll never marry again without it. Even if a future non-Jewish partner doesn't mind. She has her code of ethics, and I won't argue with her over it. I've got mine, too. It's just a whole lot smaller than hers.

Which is why I really shouldn't have underestimated her again.

I'm still trying to work out where she stashed the matches, and what kind of nail polish doubles as a flint, when she speaks again. "Joy is hard enough to find in this world. Which is why I'm hoping you'll help us. So I can reclaim some of mine."

Her eyes reflect the light, her skin glittering in the heat from the flames. When she's like this, flushed and fresh with excitement from setting something on fire, it is easy to see that Ilaria is more than Shaul's abandoned wife. She's the best munitions expert this side of the galaxy and she didn't come by the last name GodsFire by accident.

She's also the ace in our pockets, the key to selling the Shipmen girls on our plan.

When Psalome first heard we wanted to rob The Casino, she eyed us like a bunch of chumps betting our entire stack on two pair. After her conversation with Ilaria, that somehow morphed into a grudging respect. Now Psylina is coming around, too.

She pretended not to notice the explosion in the mug, but her eyes keep darting over to Ilaria periodically, and her entire body shifted when Ilaria approved of her bizzarro dating life. Like a player that has finally drawn a decent hand for the first time in the night. Ilaria has that effect on people. More than expected, yet still utterly grounded. One second you forget she exists. The next, she's handing you a mug full of rainbow fire.

"Your plan is crap on a stick." Psylina leans over me to turn on a feed of the entire main gaming floor. Invading my space as if it has always belonged to her. It would be threatening if she wasn't six inches shorter than I am. "Having Psalome swap out the earrings before she deals the last round? The Casino will catch you within a millisecond. Even if Ilaria sets off ten diversion explosions nearby. Lucky for you, I enjoy a challenge."

Psalome snorts and rolls her eyes but Psylina ignores it. She turns her back to me and props herself up on the console, arms crossed, waiting to see if anyone objects to her taking over the planning of this operation. When nobody does, she plows on.

"You need to find a way to make Kiyo sponsoring Finley in the tournament not raise Shaul's suspicions. Plus, she'll have to make her way into the finals on her own. I'll have my hands full ensuring Shaul is there. I'll need some help with that, extra cameras on the card tables and whatnot."

Her head darts back and forth as she follows the players on the screen. She catches each facial twitch and hand gesture, her eyes drawn to them the same way mine are. When it comes to numbers and probabilities, Psylina might be an even better player than I am. She'd fail miserably at anything that involved interpersonal relations though. We've known each other for less than half an hour and already I want to strangle her just to get her to shut up about how superior she is to the rest of us.

But she has offered me the best opening I've had in years to get closer to Kiyo, all while proving my worth.

"I can be her girlfriend," I say, keeping my voice subtle, my eyes on the screens. I don't dare look at Kiyo to see how she's handling this suggestion. "A romantic getaway is a great cover story to throw off your dad's lawyers and it would explain why we spend so much time together."

Plus, it will plant the seed in her mind that us dating is not such a totally wild idea. That maybe once this heist is over and she can finally shut the door on her last romantic encounter ending in accidental death and blackmail, she might be willing to consider starting a new one. With me, the person who is nothing like her last partner because I am both sober and going to prove my loyalty by getting her out of this mess rather than selling her out to a conman for drugs.

Kiyo doesn't express her immediate approval, but she also doesn't freak out, which I take as a win.

"Works for me," Psylina says. "Businesswoman bringing her mistress for an outing. Dime a dozen on this space station."

The term mistress does little to convey the deep and lasting devotion I am hoping to engender during this escapade, but now is not the time to argue. If it gets Kiyo to grant me even one fake date, it's worth it.

"Why can't we just steal the earrings in an earlier round?" Ilaria asks, the spark from the mini explosion now gone from both the coffee mug and her general posture. She tugs on the laces of her bows, shifting the jumpsuit sleeves to cover more of her arms. She's chewed her nails down to stubs. If they contained any nutritional value, she'd be all set with meals for the week.

"I only deal in the finale," Psalome reminds her. "People won't pay as much to get a glimpse of me wearing the jewels and a little black dress if I'm readily on display at earlier games. Today was supposed to be my last day on the floor. The Casino agreed to personally cover any gaps in my schedule with their own funds."

"I don't get it." Ever since their little heart to heart at the piano Ilaria seems more comfortable with Psalome, asking her questions that reveal how little she knows about the outside world or secular customs. "What's so special about a dress that people will pay extra to see you in it?"

My body warms with surprise gratification. It took weeks before Ilaria worked up the nerve to ask me about my clothes. She's come a long way from the girl who didn't know what an inseam was because she never wore pants. My little sheltered Ilaria has graduated from my tutelage and is now conversing with ladies of the night without my assistance.

Still, her current question is an uncomfortable one, highlighting how different the world Ilaria grew up in is from the one Psalome inhabits. Best to answer before the Dazzler inadvertently insults Ilaria. Squelches the tenuous curiosity I've worked so hard to build up.

"The dress is closer to lingerie than Thillov evening attire," I say, hoping to brush past the awkwardness. The last thing Ilaria needs is a blow to her fragile confidence. Out here, sex and desire are as normal as breathing, and she needs to adjust to that. "I'm guessing that's why Psylina lasered Psalome down today. Any resulting skin irritation will fade in time for the finale in a week. Psalome's skin will be as pristine as a fresh coating of snow on the roof of a spaceship, only infinitely hotter. Believe me, it's worth the price of the ticket."

Psalome doesn't blush, but I get the sense she wants to. Her inability to look in Ilaria's direction indicates she wasn't always this comfortable with the reactions her body tends to elicit in others. That maybe she still resents being trotted out as a casino showpiece. Luckily, there aren't as many people as innocent as our religious friend floating around this place to remind her.

"I'm glad you feel that way." Psylina switches off the game again and forces us all to look at her. "Because Psalome will have to serve as our only distraction. We do not rob, injure or implicate The Casino in this theft in any way. Certainly, no explosions from Ilaria. That, and Psalome's freedom, are the price of my involvement. And believe me, you cannot pull this off without me."

Psylina's face is peaked, like curdled milk. Our prior plan to have Ilaria blow up her joyfriend's auxiliary gaming floor as a distraction would certainly put a damper on their relationship. I thought the religious girl teaming up with the world's greatest sex symbol in a bid for revenge on her jackass husband was the most ridiculous part of this plan, but Psylina protecting the machine she is dating has taken the bizarre factor to new heights.

"I'll arrange for Kiyo and Shaul's ships to dock in this bay so we can take turns keeping an eye on him. There's just one last thing I should warn you about before we start."

Ilaria gulps at the tone of authority in Psylina's voice and Kiyo crosses her arms defensively, but I'm not so easily impressed. Psylina talks a big game, but she's got another thing coming if she thinks I'm letting her bluff her way into taking advantage of Ilaria or ruining our chances at saving Kiyo's company.

"Warn us about what?" I don't bother masking the edge in my voice. Let her hear it.

"My sister is walking out of this free." The mischievous pixie look has disappeared from Psylina's face, replaced by sheer determination. She's like a raw piece of wire sending sparks across the room. "No matter who I have to take down to make it happen. I do not care about mining companies, divorces, or whatever Finley is getting out of this. Fuck up your part of the plan and I will gladly serve you up to Shaul and The Casino on a platter if it buys Psalome's ticket out of here. And you will never see it coming."

She bites into an apple from a nearby bowl of fruit, running her tongue over her lips to catch the juice. In the face of our combined shocked silence, the crunch is louder than a rocket launch. Which is probably exactly what she intended.

Say what you will, the secret baby sister certainly has a penchant for drama. Yet it is the calm detached manner in which she consumes the entire fruit before looking up to see what effect her words have had that chills me to my core.

This is the one true glimpse of Psylina we've had all day.

I finally understand how Psalome has come so close to buying herself out of this place. Psylina is not a brat or a damsel in distress or even a lovesick programmer doting on her AI joyfriend.

Psalome Shipmen is a snow leopard, graceful and cunning, but her little sister is a wolf.

# CHAPTER SEVEN

## Kiyokimora

Psylina is eating her apple without a care in the world. This entire conversation I've managed to glean only a few expressions from her body language and tone. I suspect they've been carefully curated. Released at her command for maximal emotional intimidation. My mother would say it was the mark of a professional negotiator, a distinction I failed to earn in her eyes. Finley reassured me this was because I am not a sociopath.

I'm not certain if that reasoning applies to Psylina, but I'm not eager to investigate. My options are limited and cautiously dealing with a potential sociopath is vastly preferable to living with the threat of Shaul releasing that video while still in possession of my earrings. Even if I give him what he wants today, he'll never stop grinding me into the dirt, asking for increasingly more costly or humiliating concessions simply because he can. At least with Psylina the boundaries of our relationship are clear.

Still, the less time I spend with her, the better. Luckily, I've got an excuse to leave. "I need to register Finley for the tournament. She'll be a late entry but I'm sure The Casino will find a spot for a special guest of mine."

Special guest. Fake girlfriend. What's the difference? Having her so tantalizingly close but knowing a relationship isn't possible for me right now is torture no matter how we phrase it. A preview of all the things I cannot have because Shaul took them from me.

"No need." Psylina waves her hand dismissively, without looking up from the string of code she's manipulating. Like I'm some entry level intern trying to interrupt a board meeting. "I already took care of it. Psalome's getting a cut of your late entry fees. Don't forget to bring a piece of jewelry for the buy-in. The appraisal is always a big show. That's why The Casino invited you here in the first place."

Her smug tone grates on my frayed nerves. It's not like she's sharing information I couldn't have deduced for myself. The invitation arrived in a cream and gold envelope that should have been obsolete in this day and age. There's no way The Elysium squandered money on cardstock in lieu of an email unless they were sure my presence at the appraisal would bring in more revenue.

The world is curious about the girl primed to take over the universe's largest gem manufacturing company. A girl that's been in hiding for years. A girl that would have stayed in hiding, licking her wounds and pining over her best friend, if not for the threatening email from Shaul alerting me to the fact that he'd be here, too, with those earrings in the hands of an appraiser that could verify their origins as originals and not replicas, unless I answered his calls to negotiate my next payment.

It was just like him to use The Casino's services to avoid paying for the appraisal himself. He had no way to know The Casino invited me as well, hoping that my certifying the jewels for the tournament would attract more viewers for the games. It's rare I've gotten the upper hand and I'm hoping the surprise of my presence will be enough to distract him from what's really going on. Provided I can keep it together for long enough in his presence to get the job done.

Because if this works, and I keep my company, then maybe I can figure out a way to keep Finley, too. Without the sex, drugs, or alcohol, my bank roll is really all I have to offer her.

"I'm very good at what I do," I inform Psylina. I don't know if I'm trying to convince her or myself. "I doubt even your precious Casino can appraise a stone better than I can."

I shouldn't care about her opinion of me. It's a sign of weakness. Mom is probably rolling over in her grave at the way I'm letting Psylina and Shaul get under my skin. My father wouldn't approve either. Preserving the family reputation was the one thing they agreed about. It's why they never got a divorce.

"Best get going then." Psylina presses a button and opens the airlock. A clear dismissal. "You don't want to be late."

I hesitate on the threshold.

"What about Ilaria?" I can't be late for my own press event, but if I leave Ilaria alone in a casino she'll either be completely scandalized or she'll blow something up by accident.

Maybe both.

I almost lost an entire wing of the guest house when she assumed the toiletries were a science kit. She couldn't believe anyone would spend that much money on skin care.

"She can stay with me." Psalome glides forward in her sparkling dress, sending bursts of color across the room. "There's too much risk of her running into Shaul anywhere else. I'm the only safe option."

Psylina grunts at the word "safe," and Ilaria's eyes almost pop out of her head at the idea of living in Psalome's gilded rooms, but nobody offers up a better option, so Finley and I depart the ship with a promise to visit Ilaria as soon as we can.

On our way to the tournament, Finley attacks the casino shopping district with an efficiency she usually reserves for the gaming table, pulling clothes off racks and dumping them in front of the cashier. I've never seen such a large quantity of lace, rhinestones, and feathers all in one place before. Or on such a minimal amount of fabric.

I'm regretting agreeing to the fake girlfriend ruse already. How am I supposed to keep the want off my face with her parading around like the showpiece in a diamond shop, receiving a million other offers from more capable and less damaged romantic options than me? I'll end up looking like the girl who lost her business and her girlfriend in one single Casino vacation.

"Are you going to play the game or deal it?" I ask as Finley gleefully tells the cashier at the fifth store to charge everything to my room. I wonder, yet again, if my credit line is the only thing she sees in me. Not that I wouldn't pay anything for her, but some indication she'd stick with me if I lose the company would be reassuring right about now. "Maybe you should've borrowed stuff from Psalome."

"Don't be silly." She pulls a bronze lame mini dress off the pile and disappears into one of the dressing rooms to change. "Psalome is much too classy. She wants players to know she costs a lot. I want them to know I have nothing to lose."

She emerges completely transformed. The dress hugs her hips like saran wrap and she's five inches taller thanks to the sparkling heels she's chosen to wear. Her hair is now half up with a mermaid's tail braided through it. A few artful wisps fall down on each side to frame her cheeks. It looks carefree and accidental, but I know how hard such breezy elegance is to achieve.

Most players I've seen at the tables wear their hair down, presumably to help hide their tells, but Finley prefers to look her opponents in the eyes. It's that unabashed boldness that first drew me to her.

It takes me back to the night we first met. Her hair was golden then, but she had those same sapphire eyes, full of a hunger I knew I would never be enough to satisfy. But goddamn, I'd happily die trying.

She was beautiful, the cards dancing between her fingers as she won game after game, but she's even more beautiful now. Not because of the surgery – we did the bare minimum to keep her from triggering the facial recognition – but because without the haze of smoke and drugs her skin is brighter and her eyes more clear.

This is my Finley, not the wild crazy girl that followed me home from a club two years ago and then refused to leave the next morning, insisting that just because we didn't fuck there was no excuse for me not buying her breakfast.

I've been buying her breakfast ever since. It's a small price to pay for the way I'm alive again when she's around, instead of the hollow, dead person I was when we met.

"You are definitely not subtle." I can't help the smile that creeps onto my face and into my voice, despite my anxiety over the attention she's attracting. Finley is a sight to behold. People are staring, and she spins around to give them a better view. Then she instructs the cashier to send the rest of the stuff to our suite and whisks me off towards the high rollers' floor.

"You ready for your big debut?" She adjusts one of the pins in my hair as we approach the gilded doors on the top floor of The Casino. "I can hang back so the reporters get some nice footage of you alone."

It's what I should want, but there's a reason the press is so eager to get a glimpse of me. Ever since the incident, I've shunned all cameras and recording devices as if I'm allergic.

Which is not that far from the truth. Thinking about the upcoming publicity spectacle has given me hives more than once.

Plus, I hate the idea of leaving Finley alone in this place. The top floor of The Casino might look more innocuous than the lower ones, but looks can be deceiving. There won't be any blinking lights or Dazzlers with come-hither stares, but this is where the real money is spent.

Every crack and crevice of this room is steeped in secret desire. Each scent and touch and sight is another temptation for Finley. I may not be the same Kiyo that ran from club to club looking to dull the pain, but how can I be sure she isn't the same Finley? That she won't become Halley again the minute I let her out of my sight? That she won't take off with the first person to approach with a smile and a bottle of Bourbon? With her in that dress it's getting harder to tell.

She needs me just as much as I need her right now.

"What kind of person leaves their date at the door?" I feign horror and link her arm through mine. And although this fake dating thing terrifies me, I allow myself a brief moment of imagining this is real, that I've told Finley both my feelings and limitations and she reciprocated anyway. "Not a chance. You were promoted from best friend to arm candy, remember? Enjoy it while it lasts."

I know I certainly will.

"Ooooh, does the new position come with an expense account?" And just like that, with a few words from Finley, the bubble bursts. Because it underscores the fact that my money, my business, is all I have.

"You already have one."

"True. Promotion accepted."

The room set aside for the tournament is breathtaking. It spans the entire length of the space station with floor to ceiling windows that give us the impression of floating in space. The chandeliers are spun glass with silver accents. They wink additional stars onto the floors and walls.

The gaming tables blend seamlessly with the marble floors and the silver bar sports gleaming taps and a chrome rack of top shelf liquor. It's a melding of art and technology so perfect that it's hard to tell what century we're in. The past and future merge here in a way that makes the concept of time meaningless.

All that matters is the here and now.

All that matters is enjoying the moment.

One of The Casino's clones drifts over, wearing a sharp tuxedo, hair styled in perfect spikes as usual. I still can't wrap my head around the fact that they are collectively dating Psylina, that she's given them the name El.

"Miss Kiyokimora," they say with a bow. "I see you brought your... friend. Shall I escort her to the players' area while you set up your equipment to evaluate the jewels?"

They are offering Finley their arm and she's about to take it, but I pull her back. Shaul is sitting in the first row of players, his eyes glittering like rubies in the sun, taunting me with the knowledge that he's got my grandmother's earrings in his hands and footage of me naked next to a corpse on his ship. He falters for a moment when he recognizes me, but then his mouth twists into a sneer, daring me to say something.

He expects me to be the scared and lonely little girl that I was when he met me. The girl that has paid him steadily increasing amounts since the day he entered my life like a tumor, metastasizing until the cancer filled every piece of my existence. Finley showed me how to be someone else. I need her with me when I face him.

I force myself to still the shaking in my hands, squelch the panic rising in my throat and present a calm facade to

The Casino. "Finley stays with me, and I won't need any equipment other than a blindfold."

"A blindfold?" Although The Casino's voice does a good job of mimicking confusion, the blink that follows is on a slight delay. Clearly manufactured. "Whatever for?"

I drift towards the display table that is covered in loops, light sources and machinery. There are reporters circling the back of the room like carrion birds waiting to pick the bones of anyone foolish enough to err in front of them.

It would be customary to use at least a few gadgets to assess and identify a gemstone, but I don't need specific gravity or refraction to help me. This is what I've been raised to do.

"I think she intends to give your guests a show." Finley winks at The Casino. "Make the blindfold red silk to complement her dress."

The Casino bows as several of their bodies clear off the table and procure the blindfold. There's a murmur of confusion from the assembled reporters which only grows louder when Finley seats herself on my lap while we wait. She's really taking this fake girlfriend assignment seriously.

I'm going to be on the receiving end of a stern talk from the company PR department about public displays of affection. I slip my arms around Finley's waist and hug her close. In for a rhinestone in for a ruby, as Mom used to say.

She's the only person I can stand to touch this way anymore. I don't know where my limits are with her, or if she would welcome anything more for that matter.

The Casino returns with a crimson silk blindfold and Finley takes it from their hands.

"Tying you up on day one of our new relationship status," she whispers in my ear. "Things are heating up fast."

It takes all my strength not to confess right then and there that "heating up" is the exact opposite of what I can handle.

I know it's not her intention to freak me out. She's trying to keep me calm with humor, and failing hard because of all the things I keep bottled up inside. Luckily, it isn't necessary. Of the million things I'm nervous about right now, appraising gemstones is not one of them. I've been performing ever since I was a little girl trotted out to impress the shareholders at company events. It's liberating to be in control for once.

"Don't name the players until after Kiyokimora has identified the stone please," Finley calls out. "Simply place the gem in her hand and let her do the rest."

How does she know me so well? She's giving the instructions as I would, saving me the trouble of explaining myself. There's a low hum of whispers as Casino patrons who have no interest in the tournament are drawn in by the mystery and intrigue. A crowd is assembling.

The smooth surface of a piece of jewelry drops into my outstretched palm. There's a chain, soft and pliable enough to be gold, but my fingers travel immediately to the pendant. They roam its surface, feeling the facets and learning its shape.

The gem is princess cut. I won't be able to convert its weight into carats until I identify the species of gemstone. Slowly I lift it to my nose and take a deep sniff.

The owner of this piece obviously favors overly sweet perfumes and their cloying scent has attached itself to the gem. Beneath the perfume I detect hints of amber with a top note of dirt. The main aroma is aluminum, meaning it's a ruby or a sapphire. There's only one way to tell between them without looking.

I silently pray the perfume wearer wasn't covered in flesh eating bacteria as I stick my tongue out and take the tiniest of licks. Immediately, the sharp bite of chromium washes over my palate.

"Ruby." I lower my hand back to the table. "Naturally mined, probably somewhere on Delphi, and weighing sixty-five carats. Set in gold to create a lovely pendant. I know of only one such stone and it belongs to the House of GlassFire. Is Penasa playing?"

There's a gasp followed by the clicking of a hundred image capture devices. My arms tingle as if hundreds of spiders are racing up and down their surface. As if those flashbulbs are laying me bare for the world to see. As if Shaul's video is already playing all over the internet.

I ignore it all and force a smile, the way my mother taught me. No matter what is going on at home, no matter how broken we are inside, GoldWeavers smile for the world. We are diamonds after all. Diamonds sparkle. They do not shatter.

"My sister is not here." A hand lifts the necklace off my palm and a bead of sweat forms on the nape of my neck as rough fingers graze my skin in the process. "She was kind enough to loan me her favorite necklace for the display. I'll send her your regards."

"Please do." I suppress a smile. Triumph is mine, despite how shaky I'm feeling at the proximity of so many cameras. It's a rare bit of luck for the first stone to be one I recognized. The GlassFires have made a name for themselves with their intricate hand spun glass and my company has several joint ventures with them. Penasa GlassFire loves that necklace more than her own family. I wonder what her brother had to promise her in exchange for the loan.

"Next?"

They come in rapid fire, each placing a piece of jewelry in my hand. None takes more than a few minutes. I don't bother smelling or tasting the sapphire pin that Finley brings when it's her turn. It's my gemstone after all. I'd recognize it anywhere. Instead, I reach up and tuck it into the ends of her braid where it will sparkle on the red background. I don't need my sight to tell me she is radiant. I've long ago memorized the contours of Finley's face.

"It's almost as beautiful as your eyes, Fin. You can keep it if you win the tournament."

Her hair brushes my cheek as she leans down to kiss my forehead. My body tilts up to accommodate her, comfortable in her presence. Safe.

That'll get us a few headlines. The careless but brilliant Heiress and her pretty gambler girlfriend. At least it'll reinforce the idea that we're here for legitimate reasons. And maybe fend off any romantic advances towards Finley if the other patrons know she's taken.

A spending spree in a space casino with my hot girlfriend might not please my board, but it's hardly a fireable offense. If it was, my dad would have been ousted years ago. All of Dad's illicit companions were black holes of cash but Finley will make a tidy profit when she wins the tournament. All things considered, a devoted Finley on my arm is certainly more appealing than Dad's myriad of fly-by-night companions. Too bad Shaul never got any compromising video of him.

"Do you give all of your lovers presents?" A shiver goes down my spine. It's no longer Finley whispering in my ear. "You haven't been answering my calls."

"We both know I didn't give away anything that night. Not willingly anyway." My fist clenches around the earrings he's dropped into my palm. The desire to run with them all the way back to my spaceship where I can lock myself in a sealed room away from all the cameras is almost as strong as the desire to call out their value immediately to remove Shaul's obnoxious presence.

I squelch them both. Nobody can know that he and I have a

history. That these are my earrings and not one of the million replicas you can buy at GoldWeaver gem shops across the galaxy. Finley's should be the only jewel I can identify based on touch alone.

I bring the center stone to my mouth, preparing for a cursory lick, when the smell of acetone and lacquer assaults my nose. A bitter rage burns my throat. I don't need to taste the earrings to know that Shaul is making a fool of me again to impress the crowd. His comments were designed to bait me into stating the earrings' value as quickly as possible without a thorough inspection. The video of me screwing up would go viral, spreading across the galaxy and allowing him to charge even more not to release his own footage. Everyone loves a series, after all. Especially when it involves a rich girl getting fucked. Literally.

I let both earrings slip back down onto the table.

"These are fake. Mother of pearl painted over a glass base."

I rip the blindfold off and glare at him, my insides churning like the ocean on a stormy day as I meet his slick stare.

"Right you are," he says, fishing the real pair out of his pocket with a flourish. He flashes me a smile that shows off his dimples as he places them in my hand, fingers brushing mine ever so slightly. "You've grown up, Kiyokimora. More beautiful and more mature. It would be a shame to see you lose that company of yours. Come find me in the loading dock. We can talk terms. I'll give you until the end of the tournament before the world sees your mouth giving a very different, although far more entertaining, performance. With a much more thrilling ending."

A cool sweat breaks out on my forehead and my mouth feels like it is stuffed with cotton balls. I should say something, anything, but I'm finding it hard to breathe. This dress feels too tight, the room too small. Everywhere I look there is nothing but reporters and judging faces, waiting for me to slip up.

Waiting for Shaul to release that video.

Finley's warm hand slips around my waist, pulling me away from Shaul's leer. She squirts a dollop of hand sanitizer on my palm so that I can swab even the memory of his presence off my skin. With her by my side the pressure in my chest eases.

I drop the earrings back onto the table and silently walk away. Shaul is right, I am more mature, but he hasn't changed a bit.

# CHAPTER EIGHT

### Psalome

Ilaria doesn't say a word as we head back to my suite, which is probably for the best since I have no idea what to say to her either. What does one say to a refugee taking shelter in your room as she hides from the abusive husband that refuses to divorce her?

Forget about the fact that I know nothing of her religion or home planet. I've never bothered to research either since Psylina declared it highly improbable that I would need the information in my line of work. Up until this morning I agreed with her.

If only the space station had actual weather we could talk about. I've never before resented our temperature-controlled environment, but now I resent it mightily for robbing me of even the most banal of conversational topics.

I walk a few steps ahead to make chitchat impossible, preferring to steal glances at Ilaria's reflection in the mirrors instead. Goddamn, she's gorgeous. The way she's nibbling on those nails is enough to make me sweat.

She reminds me of a painting. Full of delicate brushstrokes and vivid colors that scream with hidden meanings waiting to be discovered by intrepid viewers. Art is the one thing The

Casino didn't decorate my room with. They said it would be too distracting for the clients, shifting their focus away from me and the gaming table.

It seems I'm bringing home a masterpiece anyway.

At least Ilaria won't distract the clients. I plan to keep her tucked away where they won't see her, but it'll distract the hell out of me knowing she's there. I am one hundred percent fucked by this arrangement.

What was I thinking, offering to take her with me?

Too late to do anything about it now.

"This is my room." I punch in the key code and the doors slide open. The space has already been cleaned in our absence. The Pai Gow tiles are neatly stacked in their enamel case and stashed beneath my gaming table. The Casino does a sweep between all of my clients.

"I know," Ilaria says, walking in after me. "I was here before, remember?"

I flush. Right. How silly of me.

"Yes. Of course. I, uhm, I meant you can stay in my actual room." I walk towards the sliding doors that separate my private space from the rest of the suite. "There's a bed where you can sleep. While I'm working. If you want to."

I clamp my mouth shut. This is getting worse and worse. I'm rambling.

*Be marble, Psalome* I remind myself as my face cools down. It's the refrain I mentally chanted over and over when I first started here, scrambling to remember the correct odds to pay out for various bets while impatient clients hissed at me to hurry up or suggested that I wear less clothing if I was going to deal so slowly. *Be marble.*

It's served me fairly well. I haven't lost control of myself this badly in years.

Maybe it's the way we played the piano together that has

me all worked up, or the fact that I'm inviting her into my bedroom. Nobody else ever goes in there. Not even Psylina.

I'm suddenly wary about letting Ilaria loose in my private space. It's not much, but what if she doesn't like it? The idea of having her inspecting my sheets and judging the decor has my stomach performing acrobatics. Had I known she was coming I would have prepared, tried to figure out what she might like and get it for her. Like I do for my clients.

Except I don't want her to be like one of them. The thought of her, and her adorable, freckled nose, as one of my clients is even more nauseating than the thought of her in my room.

"You don't have to hide in there now. My next client isn't scheduled for another thirty minutes. I'm pretty booked after that, so you should take advantage of the time out here while you can. Or not. You don't have to. You can do whatever you want."

Rambling again.

I cringe at my own awkwardness. Now she'll think I'm trying to get rid of her. Worse, she might think I'm trying to lure her into my bedroom for ulterior motives. I don't know how much she's heard about Dazzlers on Thillov, but we have a certain reputation on planets like hers. The ones taken over by the fringes and extremes of any religion.

I have no idea if anyone has told her about my particular moral code and I can only imagine what she'd say about what I told Psylina earlier. That I'm going to fuck my way out of here if she can't get me out some other way. Given her personal circumstances, Ilaria might be more understanding than others from her home planet, but it's not like I can ask her.

Jews from Thillov are more insular than those from elsewhere. They fled from all over and set up shop as soon as the planet was terraformed in order to preserve their particular brand of Judaism that relies on strict interpretation of the written Torah and maintaining ancient traditions in the face of modern technology. Traffic in and out of the planet is regulated by a board of male Rabbis, as is most commerce.

Her community would not be pleased to learn she was spending the night in a Dazzler's room. Then again, they probably don't believe in robbery of one's spouse or poker tournaments either.

She's staring at me bewildered, fidgeting with one of the gold bows on her jumpsuit. I have to say something. The silence has gone on too long and it's making me itchy.

"Why are you here anyway? Isn't 'thou shalt not steal' one of the ten commandments?"

I regret the words the minute they are out. She recoils as if I've slapped her, as if I'm no better than the religious courts that refuse to give her the divorce she clearly deserves. It's pretty rich if I stop and think about it. Moral judgement being passed down by someone with my job.

"Sorry. I didn't mean that the way it sounded. I don't think you're doing anything wrong, but I don't see what you get out of this. You're off Thillov. No other planet recognizes their laws. You can do whatever you want, so why risk it all to help Kiyokimora GoldWeaver retrieve a pair of earrings?"

If it was me, I'd be riding the galaxies with Psylina, not stopping for anyone or anything. Certainly not for a trust fund baby whose net worth is more than I'll ever possess in my entire life.

Ilaria's smile is so sincere, so completely without guile, it takes me a minute to register what she is saying.

"Kiyokimora isn't the only one that's lost something precious to Shaul. I might not be able to force him to give me my divorce, but I'm hoping that by helping Kiyo get back her earrings I'll be able to restore something else he took from me."

I blink. What in the world could that man have taken

from her that is worth more than her freedom to exist as an individual apart from his purported ownership of her?

"Your pride?" I guess.

"My faith."

She lets the word fall like a waterfall, thunderous and powerful but also soothing and calm. A balm for the weary traveler. A thing of beauty that can kill or heal depending on the will of the wielder.

"Life on Thillov wasn't all bad. I loved my family, our holidays, praying to God and knowing I was heard. Shaul twisted our laws and used my religion to take those things from me. I want them back."

Her eyes are fierce, burning like the sun, but her voice is calm. She doesn't care about Kiyo's earrings or the money. She wants to stand up to Shaul and take her life back. No matter the cost to herself.

I've been there. I am there. I pretty much live there.

"You won't be able to go back to Thillov unless he gives you a divorce."

She sighs. Resignation deposits little lines on the corners of her mouth. "There are Jewish communities on other planets, ones who don't believe in allowing a man to hold a woman hostage. It's not a perfect solution, but it'll do. As soon as I prove to myself I can hack it out here. That I won't fall apart when I see him again."

Her mouth tightens and a little tremor travels through her body. Instinctively I grab her hand and give it a squeeze. "Don't worry, you're perfectly safe here."

"Thanks."

She's staring at our hands with an unreadable expression. Her freckled nose is scrunched in thought. Or horror. It's hard to tell. I drop her hand like a brick and rearrange the playing cards on my gaming table.

What the hell was I thinking, invading her space like that? She's been through enough. I bet all she wants is to be left alone in peace and quiet and I'm out here interrogating her and groping her hand.

"You don't have to interact with anyone, and you won't be exposed to anything too untoward." My words are rushed with urgency. It is imperative she understands I'm not that kind of Dazzler. I don't want her to feel unsafe with me. "My clients mostly want something pretty to look at while they do business. I'm good at looking pretty."

I cringe. In my hurry to explain my job I've managed to make a mess of things again. Who calls themselves pretty? It's as if I'm trying to remind her how beautiful I am. Right after she shared something personal and deeply meaningful about her religion.

I vow to keep my mouth shut for the rest of the evening. Hell, I'll keep my mouth shut for the rest of this entire adventure if it will keep me from putting my foot in it again.

What is it with me and this woman? I've had cute clients before, even ones I find attractive, but they've never made me this nervous.

"Okay," Ilaria finally says after waiting a beat to be sure I'm not going to say anything else. As if I would dare. I can only imagine what asinine thing I'd come up with. Maybe insulting her family or something equally as mortifying.

"Do you mind if I play the piano a bit?" she asks. "I'm not as talented as you are, but I miss my piano from home. I used to practice every day. Between not being able to play and not being able to blow something up, I think I might explode."

By the time I've realized she's made a joke it's too late to laugh. I nod in agreement, frantically gesturing towards the piano.

"Play as much as you like."

I want to tell her that I play every day, too, that I've played every day since I was five, but I'm not sure how she'll take it. It might constitute oversharing. I don't have much experience socializing for personal enjoyment anymore. I don't remember any of the rules.

I busy myself with rearranging the cushions the way my next client likes them. He's a regular and he usually brings an entire crew of friends, including whatever girl he happens to be dating. He likes to get my opinion on them, as if I'm his best friend. Which I might be. We see each other a lot.

I'm glad he'll be the first tonight. The rest of the evenings' clients are not regulars and odds are good they didn't come here looking for friendship. At least a few have already booked appointments with one of the other Dazzlers for services they can't afford my rates for. Unfortunately, that never stops them from trying to convince me to lower my pricing or expand my portfolio.

Night after night they ask and night after night I wonder what it will be like when I finally say yes. To temporarily cede my body to someone else's pleasure so that I can walk out of here the next morning a free woman. Psylina has blocked me every time, coming up with some excuse or another. I know she thinks she's protecting me, but she's only protecting herself. Because she assumes if I cross that line while she's dating El, there will be a wedge so deep between us we'll never find our way back to each other.

What Psylina fails to recognize is that the wedge is already there, and it burrows in deeper every day that her romantic partner finds a way within their financial algorithms to accommodate Psylina without accommodating me.

My ultimatum was my version of protecting our relationship from the death by a thousand cuts that has already progressed pretty far. Even if I'm not exactly looking forward to buying myself out this way, no matter the gender of the client.

Unlike some of my fellow Dazzlers, I have no desire for sex without love. It would be simpler if I did. Then I could blow off steam in another Dazzler's room. There would be pleasure for me there, we're all equally skilled, but nothing more. I deserve more. I want more. At least I used to. It gets hard to remember sometimes. Which is yet another reason for getting out of here.

I thought I'd squared away all of my misgivings about my job, but having Ilaria here brings them all back up. I'm not ashamed of my body or the things I've done with it to protect my sister but the prospect of Ilaria watching me get propositioned time and again, of thinking about her when I'm with clients, is making me squirm inside.

When I'm alone with my clients I can imagine none of this matters, pretend it never happened. Ilaria's presence makes it real. Cements into permanency how little control I have over my life, my body, while I am working off my father's debt.

It's how I felt when Psylina insisted on running surveillance on my room.

That's why I wouldn't let her argue with The Casino about installing cameras in here. Some of the offers I was subjected to in my first few months as a Dazzler while I was growing my reputation and clientele were revolting. It's bad enough she overheard them through my earrings. I wouldn't want her to see it, too. Nor do I want her privy to what will happen if this heist fails and I take the offer currently burning a hole in my inbox. I always knew it was a possibility, but Psylina never understood how the process of reasserting control over my own body might include choosing to sell it off to the highest bidder.

She pretends like she doesn't mind my choice to become a Dazzler, but I know Psylina blames herself instead of our father for what my life has become. She worries constantly about my safety whenever there isn't a visible presence from The Casino here to protect me. The Casino assured her that they have never allowed anyone to touch one of their Dazzlers without permission, but Psylina wasn't convinced. In the end The Casino agreed to keep one of their physical bodies within ten paces of my room at all times.

It was a blatant act of favoritism, treating me differently than the other Dazzlers before I'd earned it, but The Casino did it anyway since it made Psylina happy without affecting revenue. I should've realized right then and there what was happening between the two of them, but Psylina has always been difficult to read and The Casino is damn near impossible to get a fix on. Except when they're with Psylina.

The Casino has no secrets from her. They are closed off and inscrutable to the rest of the universe, but they are a piece of open-source code to my sister.

Maybe we're all different when we're with people we're attracted to that way.

My eyes drift over to Ilaria. I'm certainly different when I'm with her.

I try to push the thought away. I can't afford it. Not when I have to get through a night full of clients with her in my bedroom, sleeping between my sheets.

I don't regret my job per se, but there's something extra unsettling about having Ilaria in the next room while I flirt with multiple people in an effort to get them to empty their pockets. I don't want her to think that I'm nice to her for that reason, too.

Not that she has any money to give me. The things I want from Ilaria shouldn't be bought, even though I've put a price tag on them.

Today I'd give it all away for free.

Luckily for me Ilaria doesn't know enough to ask.

# CHAPTER NINE

## Psylina

I'M NOT SURE it was a good idea to let Psalome take Ilaria back to her room with her, but I suppose it can't hurt. Best case scenario is Psalome gets laid and she and Ilaria fall madly in love with each other. Worst case scenario, Ilaria shoots my sister down and I pick up the pieces of Psalome's broken heart later when she's free and living full time with me on the ship.

Either option would require her to actually talk to Ilaria, which seems unlikely to occur based on the audio feed I am currently listening to. My elegant sister, the most skilled seductress in the galaxy, seems physically incapable of talking to an innocuous, five-foot-tall, completely unassuming, Jewish woman.

Psalome would get on perfectly fine if Ilaria was a client, but unpaid fraternizing with a petite brunette who resembles an upgraded version of every girl Psalome has ever had a crush on is not my sister's strong suit. Add in Ilaria's heartbreaking back story and the fact that she comes from a completely unfamiliar culture, and it's a miracle Psalome is still attempting to make small talk.

Whatever.

I can't afford to keep worrying about Ilaria. Psalome is a big girl now and forcing me to join this dubious crew of thieves was her idea. If I'm being dragged along for the ride, I need to focus on keeping us both out of prison. Psalome's love life can wait. It's been years. What's another few days?

Besides, this dumbass plan might actually cost me my own love life. The Casino has a very strict code of ethics when it comes to finances and guest protection. El's made a lot of coding modifications to accommodate our relationship, but this is one area I know is untouchable. El cannot allow us to harm guests or hurt profits. It simply wouldn't compute for them. Even if they wanted to. We've been trying for months to find a way out of Psalome's contract, but the monetary loss is simply too great for them to allow it.

If I betray their core code, they'll never be able to forgive me. If I don't, Psalome is going to fuck some stranger and she'll never forgive me. Clandestine robbery with the trio of doom is unfortunately my only viable solution.

I suppose there are worse options. If I actually pull this off and Psalome ends up free, then maybe El and I can actually be together without my sister looming between us like a vengeful spirit.

It's a big if, but I'm willing to try. I have to try. For Psalome. Maybe Ilaria, too. Kiyo and Finley can go to hell for all I care, and they can take their precious earrings and corporate earnings reports with them. It would serve them right for involving my sister in the first place.

I've never understood the ridiculous attachment people have to stuff like that or the feelings they associate with sex. It's a mystery to me why Kiyo would have worn those earrings that night anyway.

This confusion is something El and I share. They value an item for monetary worth only, none of this sentimental or artistic crap. Without the attachment humans place on them, a bag of diamonds would be a sack full of coal to El. Without people paying thousands of marks for it, sex wouldn't even register on their radar. A fact that suits me perfectly.

I smooth out my rumpled shirt as I reach out to El on our private coms line. The ring tone is my favorite band, AstroSloth. Psalome calls it unhinged chaos while El politely refers to it as un-patterned noise. This means neither of them ever lets my hails go unanswered for long.

El's pixelated face is already surfacing on my vid screen. At the last minute I switch my end of the call to audio only. I'm not particularly vain but I've been up all night, leaving my appearance something close to reheated crap on a stick. Plus, El is the one that taught Psalome how to read human facial expressions. One false muscle twitch and I'll give us all away.

They answer immediately anyway.

"Psylina, did you get the new oscillator I sent?"

The eagerness in their voice pierces me straight through the heart. I shake the guilt away. I need to set my plan in motion now, while they are still mildly distracted by the opening ceremony for the tournament.

"The oscillator is wonderful, thank you. But I'm not calling about that. I need a favor."

It's straight and to the point but so is El. We've never bothered with chitchat and flirting. I don't have much skill with it and El isn't programmed to see the point. That's what they employ Dazzlers for.

"Something's wrong. I can hear it in your voice."

Of course they can. They read my voice almost as well as they read my face. Luckily, I have prepared for this scenario. Because something is wrong. Something has been wrong for years. And El knows it. Only they've never been able to help me fix it. Which is why Psalome has decided to take matters into her own hands.

"It's Psalome," I hedge. There's no need to lie when the truth serves me just as well. "She left a few minutes ago and I got the distinct impression she's lonely."

"Lonely?" It's not a concept they're familiar with.

"It was bound to happen. I'm the only real company she has on this space station and we don't see each other that often."

"Are you lonely?" The panic in their voice reeks of desperation. I have never heard El so shrill or upset. "Do you need to get out of this ship more? I can arrange outings. I can even accompany you off the space station up to a range of three lightyears in any direction."

"That isn't necessary," I rush to clarify. I need El distracted, but I don't want to alarm them. Don't want them to think there is anything wrong between us. "You and Psalome are all the company I need. However, Psalome has only me. I think maybe she would benefit from having a friend too."

"Loneliness is not the only thing bothering Psalome," The Casino surmises. They are not upset. Simply stating a fact. "She is jealous of your relationship with me too. I have not experienced either of those emotions before, but I am aware they are unpleasant. And I am aware she has been disappointed in our failed attempts to resolve the situation. What do you suggest?"

It rolls off their back like grease on an engine casing. Where a human might be frustrated or annoyed, El simply wants to help. In this case they are doubly motivated. Psalome is their top earner, giving them a vested interest in keeping her happy. She's also my sister and for some inexplicable reason El wants to keep me happy too. Yet every single time we've gone down this pathway, tried to forgive Psalome's debt or cancel even a minute of her contract, El gets sucked into a negative feedback loop so strong they have to manually reboot.

They are willing to try again, if I have come up with a new bit of code or some other reasoning that might help outsmart their logic algorithms, but I'm tapped dry in the arena. We've already tried everything. Which is how I know this cannot be done with any financial loss to El or harm to an individual they consider a protected customer.

Luckily, I'm fairly creative in that department. All I need are a few key concessions from El, that should be supported by their current programs. Time to slide in the first piece of the plan: introducing El to Ilaria.

"I know some of the other Dazzlers have friends or relatives stay with them from time to time," I say. "Maybe Psalome could have a special guest too? If she finds someone she likes?"

It will help explain the extra heat signature in Psalome's room from Ilaria's body. Thanks to me, El pays extra attention to Psalome's suite for security purposes. The infrared sensors help ensure nobody visits my sister unannounced. She and Ilaria were careful to walk back through camera blindspots, but The Casino is bound to notice soon enough. Psalome hasn't had another person in her room in our entire stay here unless they were a prearranged, paying customer.

I'd rather not have to keep Ilaria with me. It would complicate things. El doesn't scan my ship as often as Psalome's room, my sister is famous while nobody knows I exist, but El still checks in on me from time to time. It would be very suspicious if I had an extra guest for an extended period of time.

"This person would obviously pay for anything extra she uses," I add, careful not trigger any of El's finance protection protocols. Those behemoth files are so entrenched it would take an entire hacker collective working for millennia to alter a single piece of code in them. We've been trying for years, and haven't managed to forgive even one stray mark anywhere in the entire Casino. "Psalome would never ask for special treatment. I think a friend would make her better at her job."

El laughs. "Psylina, your sister is welcome to as many friends as she needs. It is sweet of you to worry about my perception of it, but Psalome has always been scrupulous in these matters. I know it will not affect her work and am willing to extend a line of credit for her visitor."

I breathe a sigh of relief. I did not expect El to be surprised Psalome has a female companion, but it was entirely possible they'd run a background check on Ilaria. Which would not show any favorable results. Her credit score is great, though, I ran it before I called El. Apparently, Ilaria's fake death hasn't yet been reported by Thillov to the intergalactic credit bureaus. And now it never will be, because I've gone ahead and marked that task as completed in the Thillov servers.

What's one more felony added on to the bunch?

"Thanks, El."

"Perhaps if Psalome finds a friend, it might free up more of your time to be with me?" El continues hopefully. "I cannot help but notice your viewer screen is off."

"Not exactly looking my best at the moment," I say by way of explanation. "I was working on the wiring under the ship. The blaster coil is being a bitch again."

"I do not care," they say, perplexed. Their face is eager, open. "I like when you are covered in rocket grease. It makes my circuits tingle. I believe you said the emotion was love?"

I laugh and switch on the viewer screen, no longer worried about what they're going to see on my face. With talk of Psalome and Ilaria over with we can move to safer topics.

"I love you, too, El."

They sigh happily as I come into view. "You are the most beautiful human on my space station, and I am the only one that knows you are here. This makes my circuits tingle as well."

I can't hide the amusement in my face and I don't bother trying. Even El's compliments remind me that they will never be human and I wouldn't have it any other way.

"I doubt I'd fetch a very high price on your gaming floors," I tease. "You might be the only one that enjoys the smell of rocket grease. I'd have to borrow some of Psalome's overpriced perfume."

I meant it as a joke but the way their face crumples lets me know I have completely fucked it up. Worse, I may be causing some kind of system overload and I'm unsure why. We've spoken about my possibly buying out some of Psalome's debt before, if I could take on some computer work, and they had no problem with that. The major issues with this plan were my limited lack of free time not assisting Psalome, and my complete lack of professional training or references. Well, that and Psalome insisting I couldn't break the law hacking. Pretty ironic, given her current stance on thievery.

I wait for El to elaborate so that I can help them work through the problem.

"You are not thinking of trying to take on some of your sister's debt by offering to work as a Dazzler?" The panic is back in their eyes, along with something far more primal. Something I've never seen on El's many faces before. "I do not think I could allow that. I would kill anyone who asked for even a minute of your precious time."

They blink rapidly, shaking their head. A few sparks fly off the tips of their spiked hair. "I do not know what is going on with my circuits. They are heating up in an extremely unpleasant way."

"You're jealous, El." I can't help but feel flattered. I didn't think this was possible. "Don't worry, you have nothing to worry about. I was only making a joke."

They frown.

"So this is jealousy?" Their tone is soft, musing. Their processors must be working overtime to keep up. "I see now why I have to take such extreme precautions to protect the Dazzlers from jilted lovers. It is useful to understand, but I do not enjoy it. If you could refrain from making such jokes until I have figured out how to dampen this jealousy to a more tolerable level, I would appreciate it."

This happens every time they experience a new emotion. I cringe to think what it might be like for them to go through this without me. They claim they never experienced feelings until I docked here, but now that the process has started, I don't think it can be stopped.

"Sure thing, El." Only they could talk about modulating their emotions like turning the dials on a microwave and actually have a chance at succeeding. "I guess I'm making you more human again. Sorry, not sorry."

"It is the greatest gift you give me," they say, alleviating some of my concern. "Aside from the pleasant love circuit tingling, a greater understanding of human behavior is useful to my functioning. With each new emotion you help me integrate, profit margins increase on average by twelve-point-three percent."

They make it sound so romantic.

"Glad I could be of service."

"We can work on integrating this jealousy into my core functions during weekly routine maintenance," they continue. "I look forward to it."

I groan inside. I had completely forgotten about weekly maintenance, which is scheduled for tomorrow. I won't have time for it with everything else going on. Plus, it's too dangerous. One look at my face up close and El will know something is up.

"I'm sorry, El." I mentally curse the stupid plan that's

making me cancel our standing date. "The hull is giving me more trouble than I expected. I'm going to have to cancel weekly maintenance this time."

Their face crumples again. "Perhaps I could be of assistance? I am very good at repairs and I was looking forward to seeing you."

I must be losing my touch because I did not anticipate that response. El has an entire fleet of bodies dedicated towards ship maintenance but they've never offered to help before. What gives?

"I can't afford that," I demure. "As it is, I'll have to find some way to make up this week's docking fees to you in lieu of the maintenance on *your* software."

It's why I arranged for Psalome to get a cut of Finley's late entry fees. To offset my docking and other fees when I can't barter with El.

"There is no need, Psylina," they whisper softly, eyes wide with disbelief. I've insulted them by talking about money. Another thing I did not anticipate. Usually it's a favorite topic, without any emotional baggage attached. "I long ago stopped requiring you to make payments for docking fees. I would gladly help you with your ship, too. Without monetary compensation. If we could do it together."

My heart lurches in my chest and I have to steady myself on my chair to keep from falling over.

"I couldn't accept that," I stammer. First no docking fees, then an offer to fix my ship for free. This entire conversation is in complete violation of every piece of code El is built on. And flies in the face of every refusal they've ever made to help Psalome. "How is that even possible, El? Don't you need to account for the lost revenue?"

They smile at me, eyes twinkling as if they are considering a difficult problem.

"I never noticed it before, but it appears to have been going on for a while," they concede. "I did not want to examine it too closely because I enjoy the time spent with you on maintenance and would prefer not to alter the arrangement, but I stopped requiring you to pay docking fees a year ago. I require your company in the same way you believe Psalome requires a friend. You are my special friend, Psylina. You make me better at my job."

It is the sweetest thing to ever come out of their mouth. It is also extremely dangerous, because it confirms everything Psalome accused me of previously. El *can* alter their finance protocols, but only for me. They clearly know I love my sister, and that her continued misery causes me suffering, but they don't think I'll leave them over it. Nor have I managed to figure out how to help them move past them.

And all three of us know I'm clever enough to do that. I just didn't want to see what was going on under my nose because I'm too afraid to lose either of them. And now I might lose them both anyway. Unless I can pull this plan off.

"You're my special friend, too, El," I say, tears stinging my eyes. I blink them away. I do not cry. Not ever. Besides, I already knew El loved me. They'll know something is wrong if I let on that their declaration of affection is hitting me like a torpedo.

"Then it is settled," El concludes happily. "I will help you with the hull repairs without charging so we can still have weekly maintenance time together."

I shake my head no. I need to get my shit together. Fast. Or this entire plan is going to blow up faster than one of Ilaria's mining explosives.

"It doesn't work that way, El," I say, although I'm aware it often does. "I can't impose upon you like that. I need to be independent. I'll fix the hull myself."

"Very well," they sigh. "I insist you take the docking fees as a gift. You will have to explain to me how all of this works next week if there is leftover time after we integrate my two new emotions."

"Two emotions?" I ask. They've only mentioned the jealousy. "You've picked up another? Anything good?"

"I am afraid not," El says with a shake of their head. "It appears I spoke too soon about never experiencing loneliness. I find I am now suffering from it. I miss you already, Psylina, and we are still talking."

I turn away from the viewer screen quickly so that they won't see the guilt on my face. Because these two new emotions are exactly what I need to take advantage of for the heist.

"I'll miss you, too, El," I manage to reply after a few deep breaths. "I'll try to find some time for us soon."

I can only hope they still want to talk to me again when this is all over. It's looking more and more doubtful by the nanosecond.

# CHAPTER TEN

### Ilaria

PSALOME'S BEDROOM IS more ornate than her gaming salon. The furniture is wood with inlaid marble surfaces and there's a huge four poster bed hung with white gauze drapes dominating the space. I don't dare inspect them, but chances are Psalome's sheets have a higher thread count than anything I've ever slept in.

The untouched dinner trays from earlier are lined up on a polished table in the corner. My mouth waters from the smell of roasted meat and vegetables but it doesn't seem right to eat without Psalome. My Zaide always waited until Bubbie was at the table before he ate. Even during Succos, when we were sitting outside, and waiting meant the food getting cold. Nobody was permitted to eat until the hostess was seated at the table.

Psalome hasn't technically cooked any of this and she's been so quiet it's borderline rude, but I am her guest. This is her room. She invited me to come with her. I don't want to appear ungrateful.

I can hear her laughing outside, refilling drinks as her customers debate what game they would like to play. She hasn't eaten yet either, and if I had to hazard a guess, I'd bet she hasn't slept in a day or two. She wasn't expecting to haul me home with her.

Once again, I'm a burden on everyone I meet. Poor little Ilaria, too brainy to attract a proper husband. Too useless to keep the one I had. So pathetic a Dazzler had to take pity and let me hide in her room like the dirty little secret I am. A total nebach case.

Maybe that's why Psalome was so quiet before. Or maybe it's because the few times she did try to make conversation I almost bit her head off. Followed by my tirade on religion. I shouldn't have shared so much. Now she thinks I'm some crazy fanatic when all I really want is my life back. My self-respect. A chance at a partner who loves me despite the fact that I like experimenting with explosives more than praying or keeping house. In fact, you might say blowing stuff up is my form of prayer. It certainly feels divine.

Psalome must think I'm hopelessly naive, droning on about how I miss my holidays and my family. Letting Shaul walk all over me like this. Only escaping when Kiyo showed up to rescue me like a princess in a goyishe fairy tale instead of a strong Jewish woman whose people have been rescuing themselves for generations.

There's no way to explain to her how things were back home. The pressure to get married before I became an "old maid" at the ripe age of eighteen that made me overlook Shaul's sketchy job. How it took me months to gather the courage to leave once he became abusive. How I believed his failings were my fault.

Sometimes I still believe that. It's what the court implied when they refused to give me my divorce. Insinuating that if I asked nicely and was a better wife, if I offered him something in return, then Shaul would return to me and repent rather than continue roaming the galaxy in the spaceship my parents mortgaged my childhood home to pay for as my dowry.

As if I wanted him back.

Repentance is between him and God, who will never turn anyone away, but the people he harmed, people like Kiyo, have no obligation to forgive him and neither do I. I can barely forgive myself for not realizing he was a criminal. That's why I'm here.

Shaul might not want forgiveness, but I do, and it's not going to come for free. Nor does it come from crying to God. Repentance, true atonement, comes from restorative action. Not tears and wailing without facing the harm one has caused. So, when Kiyo showed up on my planet and offered me a chance to help, there was no way I could refuse it.

Which means I need to pull myself together and start acting like a grown woman instead of gawking at Psalome's drapes and moping about how she dislikes me so much she's silent in my presence when she laughs and talks with almost every other human alive. Including the woman outside who just made a suggestion so lewd, and so loud, that I'm scurrying away from the door to avoid hearing any more of it.

I glance around, struggling to get a sense of the woman I'll be living with for the next few days, hoping to learn something that will help me get into her good graces.

The decor features wood and lace, sumptuous but tasteful. The only concession to technology is the automated closet controls that are discreetly hidden behind an etched wooden panel on the wall. I don't bother exploring them. I'm sure Psalome's wardrobe is full of dresses similar to what she's wearing now. Pretty, sparkly things that highlight how tall and gorgeous she is. There's no point in drooling over them. It's unlikely I'll ever have the chance to touch anything that expensive, no matter how much I'd like to.

I laugh to myself as I realize the same thing could be said about the Dazzler that wears the dresses. I'm oddly tempted by the idea. Heat fills my body as I remember how I reached out and grabbed her hand earlier this evening. How close she sat next to me on the piano bench. Her perfume filling the air I breathed.

This must be why people pay so much money to have her deal their games. The thoughts that pop into my head when she's around are bewilderingly inappropriate, yet tantalizing nonetheless. I haven't had thoughts like these since Shaul started flirting with me when we first met, and he never made my entire body break out in gooseflesh the way a glance from Psalome does. I can't stop replaying the moment over and over in my head.

The Casino trained her well, that's for sure. I should find it intrusive, this weird form of mind control that she exerts over me, but I don't. It's unfamiliar but not unpleasant. Like using a muscle I didn't know I had.

Girls didn't have thoughts like this on Thillov. Especially not about other girls. Or they weren't supposed to, anyway. Nobody talked about sex until I was engaged and that had been an extremely confusing conversation which mostly involved a list of what I could and couldn't do with my husband.

There was some hushed whispering about mutual pleasure leading to a satisfying marriage, but I was too embarrassed to ask questions about what that meant. Which in retrospect was a mistake. It would have saved me a lot of sleepless nights wondering if the reason he strayed was because I was doing something wrong in bed.

Thoughts like this, about people other than my husband, people that aren't necessarily male, were not something I was prepared for. Honestly, I assumed the whole thing was unnatural. That *I* was unnatural.

Until I met Finley. Attraction to everyone seemed to come perfectly naturally to her. She caught me staring at the couples on other planets, holding hands and snuggling, and informed me that this was normal human behavior in most places. According to her, public displays of affection are just another "love language." As if romance needs an interplanetary translator.

When she sat me down for a much more explicit sex talk than the one my mother gave me before the wedding, it was just as confusing, but it's starting to make sense now. Everything and everyone in this Casino confirms it. Including Psalome and the tingly feelings I get every time she brushes up against me. The way I imagine what might happen if I brushed back.

Mutual pleasure. What a joke. What could I possibly offer another person, especially someone like her? She's got a thousand options. All more desirable than someone else's cast-off wife whose main selling point is an ability to turn household items into fireworks.

I drift over towards the dressing table and sit on the silk cushion. It's a relic from a different time, like an antique from a museum exhibit about high society ladies of the past. Only it's been outfitted with modern lighting and the cosmetics on display are anything but old-fashioned.

I pick up a perfume atomizer. The cylinder is made of an aluminum alloy and the mechanism is designed to get every last drop out. It's hermetically sealed but a faint aroma lingers around the surface like a memory. Jasmine and honey. The same scent I smelled when Psalome sat next to me at the piano. This is what she was wearing, beneath her clothes, misted over her skin, like a fine layer of armor with which to greet the coming onslaught of patrons.

"It was my mother's favorite scent."

I almost drop the perfume in surprise. Psalome is standing in the doorway staring at me. Her clients must have left.

How long has she been silently watching me paw through her stuff? I am the worst house guest ever. Zaide would not be pleased.

She slides the door shut behind her and comes over to stand next to me.

"We sold all of her things to The Casino," she continues, squirting a puff of the bottle towards me before gently laying it down. She pats the ivory dragon in her hair. "They let me wear her hairpin while I'm here though. On loan. It's the same for all the dresses and jewels. None of them are mine. Some of the other Dazzlers keep the little trinkets our clients give us, but I always sell them back to The Casino. They let me keep wearing them until my contract is up because it supposedly increases their value."

"I see," I say, to be polite. I suspect I don't really understand what she's telling me at all. How painful must it be for her to be surrounded by things she knows are not hers and never will be? At least I've always known where I stand.

"Your sister wears the same hairpin."

She frowns and takes a step back.

"It was a matched set." She's walking towards the side table, picking up one of the dinner trays and carrying it over to the ornately carved dining table. "One dragon for each of us. From Mom. The Casino gave Psylina hers back as a gift almost immediately when they learned the significance behind it. Refused to let her sell it back. They're very fond of her."

I arch an eyebrow. There's so much about her life I don't understand. She's stuck here, working night after night, to pay back a debt that her father owed to an entity her sister is now dating. I have a thousand questions, mostly regarding Psylina, but the icy tone in her voice tells me that this topic of conversation is off limits. Psalome's little sister can do no wrong in her eyes.

"The Casino decorated this room, too," she says by way of changing the topic. Neither of us is very interested in the decor. "They pick out all the Dazzlers' furniture based on an algorithm that predicts what clients will find most pleasing in combination with our facial features."

She strikes a small pose, her eyes smoldering their way into mine before she breaks out into a laugh. "I suspect they'd have spent significantly less time and money on my bedroom if they realized nobody else would see it for years. Well, nobody but you, I guess."

She rushes the last part, glossing over the fact that we're currently sitting together in a room that was designed for guests interested in some of the more carnal pleasures The Casino offers.

I'm not willing to move past it quite as quickly. I want to understand who I'm working with.

"Why don't you have clients back here?" I take a seat next to her. The dinner trays are still sitting in their shiny silver domes. "Finley mentioned you'd earn your way out of here faster if you did."

"She would mention that," Psalome snorts, decidedly avoiding my gaze. She toys with a fork, chews her lower lip, and stares off into the distance. When I am about to give up, resigning myself to living the next week in silence, she looks up.

"If you must know, it's bad for business. Right now, my clients are split across all genders and they're in a frenzy to figure me out. Win me over. Because everyone wants what they can't have. If word gets out that I favor one of them, it might affect my bookings. So, if I do offer those services, the price has to cover my entire debt or the brief revenue spike won't make up for the resulting fall-out."

It's an obvious lie – I'm sure there are enough willing to pay for what they can have when that something is a night with her – but the rehearsed way she says it, chin up and words rolling off her tongue like water, makes me suspect it's a lie she tells herself, too. So frequently she almost believes it.

I'm familiar with those types of lies. I told them to myself every single day before I left Shaul.

*He didn't mean it. It'll get better tomorrow. It was my fault.*

Over and over until the repetition gave it new meaning. Turned true what was so clearly false. Breathed hope into the dark spaces that threatened to eat me alive. But words never fixed what was broken between us and slowly I began to suffocate under the weight of them.

"I've seen your price list," I point out. I should let this go, but I can't. I let too much go before, and look how that turned out. The need to figure Psalome out chafes at me like wires on a blasting cap. "I could understand for the smaller services, but one night with you costs more than enough to buy your freedom and ensure you don't need more clients or bookings afterwards. You're honestly telling me nobody has offered?"

This time she has the good grace not to lie.

"A few have offered," she admits. Her eyes are focused on the glossy surface of the table, her fingers tapping out a soft tune as if she's playing the piano. "My sister found an excuse to refuse them all, but the truth is I could have stopped her. I'm not judging any of the other Dazzlers, but I wasn't ready yet to do that with someone I didn't care for. Maybe even loved."

She says the words softly, as if it is a dream she cannot fathom coming true. Her eyes catch mine and for a moment I find it hard to breathe as she stares at me. I can't help but shake the feeling she's asking me a question, but I have no idea how to answer. So instead, I ask a question of my own.

"Yet?"

She gives a small sigh, her face creasing into deep lines as if the conversation has been more draining for her than the entire hour she spent dealing for her clients. I look away as she pulls the top off one of the trays, pointedly not clarifying what her use of that one small word means.

"We should eat," she says. "The Casino will have finished cleaning my salon in a few minutes and I've got another client booked in half an hour."

She politely waits for me to pull the top off my tray, too, before she starts eating. I want her to say something else, but she doesn't. The sound of our silverware clinking on the plates is the only thing that breaks the uncomfortable silence for the duration of the meal.

I've insulted her. Again.

She finally stands up and points towards the bed as she drifts over to the dressing table and reapplies her lipstick.

"I hope it's comfortable for you," she says, indicating I should get in. "I'm booked through the night but that shouldn't stop you from sleeping."

It makes me squirm with guilt as I toe off my shoes and slide in. I should be enjoying the luxury of the sheets, but I'm worried about her. Our little planning session must've cost her the entire rest period she had scheduled for the day. Meanwhile, I'm snuggled in here sleeping.

She finishes her touch up with a spray from the atomizer. I expect her to head towards the door but instead she glides over and tucks the sheets in around me.

"Sweet dreams, Ilaria," she whispers in my ear.

I close my eyes and let the smooth caress of her voice lull me into a sense of peace.

When I open them again, she's already left. The faint whiff of jasmine and honey in the air is the only indication that she was ever here at all.

I burrow down deep into the covers and inhale as much of it as I can, embarrassed by how much I enjoy it. I know it's part of the persona she adapts to do her job, but the way Psalome moves, as if it is a show she puts on entirely for my benefit, makes me hot in places I didn't even know had nerve endings.

God in heaven, what have I gotten myself into?

# CHAPTER ELEVEN

## Psalome

THE KNOCK ON my door is gentle but firm, like a parent scolding their favorite child. Only one person knocks like that. Psylina. I slide the paneling open and let her in.

"Why didn't you just use the code?" I ask. "The Casino finished cleaning a few minutes ago, I was about to go to bed."

Psylina shrugs and peers around the room, a disappointed frown on her face when she notices it is empty.

"I thought you might have other company," she says, leaning forward meaningfully. "You know, for something other than talking. I didn't want to interrupt."

I roll my eyes even as I blush at the implication.

"Ilaria is asleep," I inform her, pointedly refusing to look at her anymore. "Just forget it. Forget we ever talked about it. I don't even know what to say to her."

"Hello is always a good conversation starter." Psylina blithely ignores my request and flops down onto my couch. "Normally I'd say you could ask about her home planet but that's probably not a good idea in this particular situation. Talking about your job isn't really great first date fodder either. Maybe ask her how to blow shit up. She seems into that. If you're lucky, talking about it might get her hot enough to forget she's here for revenge on her blackmailing, narcissistic, hopefully soon-to-be ex-husband."

"Psylina!" I yelp, pushing her feet off my sofa. I don't want her combat boots staining the fabric. "Keep it down, will you? You could wake her."

She sighs and sits up, smoothing out her rumpled T-shirt. She waggles her eyebrows for good measure before settling into a contrite expression and revealing the real reason she's here.

"I'm sorry to do this to you, but I need you to work the roulette table tonight." She pinches the bridge of her nose. "Shaul is on the casino floor and it's the ideal time to plant a bug on him. You're the only one on the team he hasn't seen besides me and I'm hardly gaming floor appropriate."

Exhaustion seeps through my bones. My eyes drift involuntarily over to my bedroom, where Ilaria is currently sleeping cozily in my covers. I checked on her the minute my last client left but didn't have the guts to actually get in there with her. She was so innocent and peaceful. Me sleeping next to her would be like pouring gasoline on a baby duckling in the pond.

I was planning on catching a nap on the couch.

Psylina catches my glance and gives me a smirk. "Sleeping Beauty can wait. It won't take long for you to get her husband's attention. He likes trophies, and you, my dear sister, are the very shiniest trophy on the shelf."

I heave a sigh, but I know Psylina is right. We need to bug Shaul so she can track him. It's the only way to keep Ilaria safe and ensure the two of them don't meet, and I'm the only decent candidate to do it.

"Why roulette though?" My whine is unbecoming, but the thought of spinning that wheel makes my wrist ache and the blur of colors is sure to give me a headache. Especially if I use the sparkling ball The Casino is famous for inventing. "I never deal roulette."

Not to mention the entire game is boring as hell. No skill. Just dumb ass luck. I'm liable to fall asleep if I try to play roulette in this state of exhaustion.

"His eyes will be on the wheel and not your hands," Psylina says. Ever the pragmatist. She's worked the whole thing out for me in advance. Down to the details of my escape plan. "You can slip away after a few games. I have Jacinthe standing by to take over. She'll appreciate the extra tips from the crowd you gather. All you need to do is fix this onto Shaul's watch then cede the table to her."

She holds out what looks like a metal contact lens until I bring it closer to my face. It's a thin piece of silver coated plastic covered in minuscule wires. It should fit on the back of a watch face nicely without drawing the owner's attention, but getting it on will be a challenge. Hell, not losing it on my way to the gaming floor will be a challenge.

Psylina and her "easy" jobs.

"Better get going then," I say, tucking the bug into my bracelet. "I don't want Ilaria to wake up while I'm not here. She might be worried. Or start wandering around alone. It's not safe."

"Yes, I'm sure her *safety* is very concerning to you," Psylina says, waggling her eyebrows at me again. "Not the fact that Sleeping Beauty is currently tucked into your sheets and maybe you can get in there with her and see if she isn't willing to reconsider the whole being-married-to-a-male thing. I'm sure you can be very convincing."

I don't bother with a response, preferring to usher her out of my room and towards the lift back to the cargo bay before Ilaria can overhear her lewd suggestions. For someone who claims not to be interested in sex herself, Psylina is taking way too keen of an interest in my attraction towards Ilaria.

If I'm going to be at the roulette table while planting surveillance equipment on Shaul I can't be distracted. Unlike the table games, roulette is a whole bunch of waiting around. Customers sometimes like to talk. I need to be prepared. I do not have any spare mental energy to waste on figuring out if my reluctant guest is romantically interested in females, let alone women who work in overpriced casinos wearing skimpy dresses.

I force my face to be smooth as marble and then coax a knowing smile onto my mouth as I slip out of the lift and onto the gaming floor. When I sashay up to the roulette table to relieve the exhausted Dazzler that's been standing there all night my head is as still as water and my mind as blank as space itself.

No distractions. No other thoughts. Just me, the game and my marks.

The current Dazzler has a small crowd assembled at the wheel. A few of them are protesting the Dazzler gender swap – The Casino tries to keep those to a minimum – when they hear him announce that the woman taking over is Psalome Shipmen. All disgruntlement fizzles like a firework whose fuse never properly lit.

Sometimes being an elusive yet famous person whose reputation precedes her has its advantages. Regular Casino patrons love getting a glimpse of me when I'm not tucked away with private clients. It's customary for at least a few patrons to leave a table when Dazzlers swap but they stick around for me. It's a fun story for them to bring home from their vacation and embellish as they sit in a bar regaling their friends with their interplanetary adventures.

I wouldn't mind if a few of them left the table tonight, since they aren't the ones I'm here for, but I suppose a crowd will help attract Shaul faster. From what I've gathered, he can't bear for anyone else to be the center of attention. Not even his wife.

I let the ball spin on my fingers as I wait for the players to place their bets. It sparks and flashes, shedding a kaleidoscope of colors in all directions. A few more players drift over from nearby tables, drawn by the oohs and aahs. Then I let the ball fly with a flourish and give the wheel a spin. Sparks of light shoot out of its surface and stream across my skin, a delicate dance in the dim lighting.

"Doing great," Psylina whispers in my ear. "He's spotted you already. Don't acknowledge him at first. Make him work for it."

I dip my head to the right, silently indicating that I hear her, and wait for the wheel to stop spinning. The ball lands on black twenty-five. Shaul arrives as I'm placing the marker and starting to sweep away the losing chips. I deal out the winnings without looking at him, congratulating each player on their luck.

I look them each in the eye, laugh at their jokes, make them feel special. It doesn't hurt that Psylina whispers helpful tidbits about what they like in my ear. They blush and grin, delighted by the extra attention. I can hear the tales forming in their heads, just waiting to be shared over a few beers in an asteroid bar. Backhanded compliments that allow them to insult me and gloat over their moral superiority at the same time.

*She might be a whore, but Psalome Shipmen has a heart of gold. No wonder The Casino agreed to take her in. I'd want to help her, too, poor thing.*

*They say people pay top dollar to see her in those dresses, but she still has time for us regular players. Probably because her dad was one.*

*Never seen a roulette ball spin that fast. Wonder what else she can do with those hands. I could certainly give her some balls to handle.*

Normally it doesn't bother me, but the conversation I had with Ilaria is bringing all my suppressed rage back up. My distaste for my job. The fear that I'm no better than the Dazzlers who took my drunken dad's money. The knowledge that I'll never have a career as a musician because I gave that up to become a Dazzler. Even after my debt is paid off, people will always undress me with their eyes before they so much as hear a single note from my piano.

Revulsion presses against me like a branding iron and my skin is growing hot. I push it back down. I am going to plant this bug on Shaul, free Ilaria from her shitty marriage, and get Kiyo her earrings back. Bloody hell, I'll even throw in a stack of chips for Finley just for shits and giggles. Because I want to prove once and for all that I'm better than the card sharks that fleeced my dad. Better than this job. Better than this entire goddamn Casino.

I'm Psalome fucking Shipmen and I take no prisoners.

Shaul gives me a smile as I sweep past his spot, but I move too swiftly for him to say anything. Instead, I focus on the young lady to his right. She's not nearly as pretty as Ilaria but there's a flush on her cheeks, excitement from her win. She has her chips in a giant decorative champagne glass. The kind of souvenir college girls buy to commemorate their first trip here so that they can remember it for years to come. The great bacchanal of their youth before they settle down to the tedium of sensible jobs and the responsibility that comes with adulthood.

Might as well make the memory of tonight a good one for her.

"Lucky lady," I say, sliding a pile of chips in her direction.

She's placed a split and the payout is seventeen to one, higher than any of the other winners. I graze her hand with mine and give her a wink, twirling one of her chips across my fingers before sliding it into her glass for her. "Don't spend it all in one place. Unless it's on me. Then you can spend as much as you like. I'll make it worth your while."

She blushes and pockets half the chips, wisely saving some of her winnings instead of reinvesting it all. Her eyes are as round as planets and she'll probably offer me all the remaining chips and more, but Shaul cuts her off.

"Perhaps you're the lucky lady." He elbows his way past the girl so that his face takes up my full view. I've removed the marker from the table, rolling it across my palm as Shaul places a large stack of gold chips on black twenty-one. "Psalome Shipmen, twenty-one years old and hair as black as that square. Maybe you'll win me some money, too."

I give the wheel a spin before acknowledging him, but I keep the ball in my hand until the rest of the players finish placing their bets. His is by far the largest. A not-so-subtle attempt to convince me that his dick is bigger than everyone else's, too.

Men. It's always the same with them.

The blushing girl has ceded her space to him, shrinking back to the edge of the crowd. He luxuriates in it, his presence expanding to fill the vacancy as if it is his birthright. As if others should be honored to shuffle around to accommodate him. As if I should become less so that he might become more.

Not. Going. To. Happen.

He's staring at me, tapping his fingers on the table and waiting for a response to his big power play. I bite down a laugh. Does he seriously think he's the first customer to throw money at me? This isn't even the biggest wager I've seen. Last year The Casino upped my cut of the money that comes in from my tables because clients were throwing down stacks so large they had to break out platinum chips. Psylina negotiated the raise. The one concession she's managed to get out of El towards my freedom and they applied the new policy across all Dazzlers, not just me.

Apparently, it resulted in a two percent profit increase even after subtracting the extra wages. Bidding wars happen on the regular. Shaul isn't the only one that likes to wave his metaphorical dick around. He might be the only one that uses money pilfered from the parents of his abandoned, devotedly religious spouse to do it though. I thought I'd seen every possible level of asshole, but this is a new low.

Psylina said he didn't even send a condolence email to Ilaria's family after the mining "accident." Just made sure her employer doled out the last of her wages to him and left a bank routing number for them to use once the insurance payout was ready.

I sit in silence for a minute before I answer.

His eyes are narrowed, and his smile is beginning to fade. Make a man wait long enough and he'll show you the glower that hides behind his charming smile. The spiders nesting inside the beautiful chandelier.

I already know his gallantry is about as real as the promises my father used to make my mother about getting sober. Only this time I'm going to enjoy watching the lie crumble. But first I need to prop it up, make him feel like the most wonderful man in the universe, so that I can get close enough to plant Psylina's bug.

"Ask nicely and maybe I'll do a lot more than bring you luck," I say, turning around to toss the ball onto the wheel. It skitters and bounces with a satisfying clickety-clack, but Shaul's eyes remain firmly fixed on me. Burning their way through my dress. Time to lean in and get this shit done so I can get out of here. "I'm betting that stack of chips isn't the only big thing about you."

His laughter echoes through the room, loud and raucous.

"You'd win your bet, Dazzle Girl."

"Buene Suerte," I tell him, my voice breathy and hot. "Let's see how *your* bet fairs."

I wait for the ball to land before turning back around. I place the marker on zero, not a single winner.

"Better luck next time," I say with a shrug as I sweep his chips towards me.

He reaches out to place his next bet while I'm removing the marker, ensuring his fingers touch mine. It makes my skin crawl and several players frown. I suppress the urge to flinch. One of the first things I learned in this job is that some people get off on making service workers uncomfortable. I have no intention of giving anyone that satisfaction.

It'll be a cold day in hell before I give any person that kind of power over me again.

"You can't place chips before the marker is gone," I say coolly, withdrawing my hand. "I'm afraid I can't honor your bet. You'll have to wait for the next round. House rules."

His nostrils flare but he doesn't make a move towards his chips. Instead, he draws himself up to his full height and spreads his arms out wide, taking up even more space than before. Asserting his dominance over this table and anyone who would try to take it from him.

Shaul is not the kind of man that's used to being told no.

Psylina is hissing a warning in my ear, telling me to be careful. I ignore her. She assigned me this task. She doesn't get to criticize my methodology. I reach out to slide his chips back towards him, daring him to try and stop me.

"Surely you can make an exception." He reaches out and

grabs my hand. The chips topple over with a soft plink. His fingers circle my left wrist.

Several players back away and there is a murmur from the crowd. The Casino has very few rules and Shaul has just broken the cardinal one by touching a Dazzler without permission. None of them want to be implicated by association.

I focus on the flash of Shaul's watch on his now outstretched arm.

"No exceptions," I say, leaning over the table so that my cleavage spills out a bit more from my dress. He's so busy tracing its outline he doesn't notice The Casino clones closing in on us from all directions. "I will offer a piece of advice though."

The bug is in my hand. I slide it onto his watch before I pry his fingers off my other wrist. Smooth as silk sheets. Gentle as a butterfly kiss.

I am marble and I will never crack.

"Never touch the Dazzlers without their consent," I whisper into his ear. "The Casino hates when people try to take what they haven't paid for."

El is mobilizing quicker than usual, dispensing with the need for stealth and discretion in their haste to protect me and thereby avoid Psylina's wrath. One of their bodies is already at my side but they hang back when they see me whispering to Shaul, giving me space to handle this on my own if I prefer.

"How much?" His voice is a low rumble, his pupils dilated. His breath is moist on my ear, but I hold still. Two more seconds and the bug will be so firmly fixed a rocket launcher wouldn't be enough to knock it off.

*Be marble,* I remind myself as I breathe through my nose, waiting for the sealant to dry. I count to sixty while he smirks, assuming I am actually considering his offer.

"I know how to show a girl a good time."

Considering his wife is in my room right now having faked her own death to get away from him, I highly doubt that statement is true.

"Tempting," I tell him with a laugh. "I've never fucked a circumcised penis before, but I'm not interested."

His mouth pops into an incredulous O shape. His lips slowly twist without forming actual words. He'll probably assume I've dealt so many rounds of strip poker I can diagnose a man's girth on sight. His pants are certainly tight enough for it.

Not my problem.

I step back and signal The Casino that all is well. I could have Shaul kicked out of The Elysium for touching me – El has a zero-tolerance policy – but that would make it impossible to recoup Kiyo's earrings and get Ilaria the closure she's looking for.

The Casino raises an eyebrow but fades into the distance as I let the roulette ball fly again.

Shaul leaves immediately, heading straight for the nearest Casino body. I don't need Psylina's new bug to tell me he's asking about my rates, insisting that if he's willing to pay, I should be required to give him what he wants. Inquiring as to who exactly is in charge here and why The Casino won't force me to take on a client. Probably also complaining I was rude and he should be offered a discount on the price of sexually humiliating me into submission. That kind of conversation used to worry me back when I first started, before I learned that El would never allow that. And not just because of Psylina. They would never do that to anyone. Ever.

The Casino finally holds up their hands in a gesture I've seen them make dozens of times. They'll pass along the request, but they will not tolerate further discussion. Dazzlers work for themselves, including the ones in El's debt. It makes for better job performance, ultimately resulting in higher profit margins.

Only El could turn an indecent proposal into a profit and loss spreadsheet with this kind of rapid turnaround.

Shaul is about to leave when The Casino stops him with a hand on his shoulder. Psylina feeds the audio directly into my earpiece as El issues a warning not to touch any of the Dazzlers again. One stray finger and Shaul is expelled for life. No second warning.

When Jacinthe arrives, I gladly cede the table to her.

I'm going to have Psylina send the footage of me turning Shaul down to my room so Ilaria can watch it later. It's a little present I can give her. The enjoyment of watching me tell the man who hurt her so much to go fuck himself.

Shaul doesn't scare me. I've known men like him my entire life and I've long ago learned that the only power they have over me is what I willingly give them. Which these days is none at all.

I'd like to be there when Ilaria realizes he no longer has any power over her either.

# CHAPTER TWELVE

## Psylina

PSALOME IS MAKING a bigger ass of herself than I thought possible. For someone world renowned for her coy conversational skills she's barely managing to get two words out edgewise with Ilaria. Forget seduction. She's borderline offensive at this point.

First, she woke Ilaria up by playing moody songs on the piano as soon as she got back from the roulette table. Then instead of showing Ilaria the footage she asked me to prepare of her being ridiculously hot and telling Shaul to shove it, Psalome proceeded to offer Ilaria breakfast by mutely nudging a tray of oatmeal towards her and mumbling something about how her clients never eat what she orders them anyway.

Smooth Psalome. Offer the pretty woman your clients' leftovers. Real smooth.

I've listened to them silently chewing for five minutes and I'm getting a headache from the awkwardness of it. Luckily, I need to pick up Ilaria anyway for the next phase in the plan. I'm standing outside the door, all prepared to rescue my fumbling sister, when Ilaria takes matters into her own hands and starts a conversation herself.

"My father's family business is firecrackers," she blurts out. "That's why I'm so good at blowing stuff up. I can make an explosive out of almost anything."

There's a squeak as Psalome's spoon slides across the oatmeal bowl in surprise. "Do you like blowing stuff up? As a hobby?"

Wow. I thought it couldn't get any weirder but apparently Ilaria is competing with Psalome for the most disastrous flirting award. Next thing you know the two of them will be discussing Psalome's career choices or how Ilaria managed to get hitched to a con artist.

If this is their breakfast small talk, I can't wait to see what happens on an actual date. Of course, that would require Psalome acknowledging that she wants to take Ilaria on a date and then asking her to go on one. Which she never will.

I punch in the code to the keypad on her door and hold still for the retinal scan. That complete, the entrance swooshes open to reveal the two of them sitting on cushions at the low table in the center of the room. Neither one is looking at the other. Psalome is swirling the spoon around her half-eaten oatmeal while Ilaria is drinking a glass of water like her life depends on it.

Never has my sister needed my help more than she does now.

"I'm sure she's not a pyromaniac," I say, stepping into the room. Psalome's spoon drops into her bowl with a clatter and Ilaria gags on her water. A few drops spray out of her mouth and onto the table where they bead up and wait to be wiped away.

"I actually do enjoy blowing stuff up," she says once she's done coughing. "It's really satisfying."

Charming.

"I'm sure I'd find it satisfying, too, if I were you." I try not to make it sound derogatory but I'm pretty sure I fail.

It's not like I blame her for reveling in the occasional explosion, Ilaria's probably got more pent up rage than the volcano that took out the entire eastern shore of Henta 5 last year, but she was planning on inflicting a significant amount of damage on El. Plus, rage isn't exactly a character trait I would have chosen for the subject of my sister's first romantic interest in years. Psalome needs someone hot-blooded, not hot-headed.

"You can't blow stuff up here. Not without hurting The Casino. Perhaps Psalome can help you find another way to vent? Something you can both enjoy together during your spare time?"

Psalome shoots me a warning glance across the table. Why is she so resistant to my intervention? It would be helpful if they got over themselves and blew off steam *together,* but Psalome has never been great with emotions. Especially not that kind.

"You mean like learning how to play some of those games she deals?" Ilaria asks innocently, completely missing my meaning. I keep forgetting she doesn't live in a garden of unearthly delights like the rest of us. "Finley tried to teach me, but I suspect she's not used to beginners."

"Psalome is a much better choice for a beginner. She happily handles all skill levels for a variety of entertaining pastimes." This time my double entendre is so evident Ilaria can't miss it. Her face flushes beet red but Psalome doesn't notice because she's too busy staring at the floor.

How many openings do I have to give her before she steps in and takes one?

"Aaaaaanyway." I draw out the word and Psalome sags in relief when it becomes clear I am switching the topic. "Shaul is leaving his ship to play his first round of the tournament. Are you ready to see if you remember the access codes to your old ship as well as you think you do?"

"Sure." Ilaria hops up and smooths out her dress, a green contraption with a lace top and a pleated skirt that Finley must have chosen for her. Psalome moves as if to follow but I block her path, swiftly stepping in between her and Ilaria.

"Where do you think you're going?" I ask, hands on my hips. "You haven't slept in thirty-six hours, and you have an entire night of clients booked starting in six hours. I can't lighten your schedule without raising a few eyebrows. As it is, people will wonder why you were at the roulette table last night. I had to spread some rumors about you scoping out the high rollers that are here for the tournament."

She sits back down, defeated. For once her work ethic is a liability. She never cancels clients. Not even when she had the stomach flu and I had to hook her up to an IV drip in between gaming sessions.

"Don't you need a look out?" she asks feebly. "Or a distraction in case Shaul shows up early? I'm very good at distracting people."

Ilaria gives a small shudder at the possibility of Shaul showing up and turns those pleading doe eyes on Psalome as if begging my sister to keep her safe from his clutches, but I hustle Psalome back towards the bedroom before she can see it. The last thing I need is for the two of them to get into another foot-in-mouth conversation. I don't have time for that shit.

Shaul won't be gone forever. Entry level tournament rounds have been known to end quickly, and I've hacked into the player assignment system and stacked Shaul's games with inferior players to ensure he advances. We need to grab this window of opportunity while we have it.

"I have eyes on the entire airlock, plus an extra set of ears on Shaul thanks to you, remember?" Ilaria hiccups a sharp inhale at my mention of Psalome placing a bug on Shaul. I belatedly remember Psalome hasn't shared that information with her yet. Whoops. I hope she wasn't saving the story for a special occasion.

"I can observe everything from my ship and Kiyo is docked one spot over. She will be deployed as a distraction if Ilaria needs some extra time to extract herself. I'd do the whole thing myself, but Ilaria says there are biometric scanners and those take longer to hack."

Ilaria gives a tiny nod, confirming the presence of extra security on Shaul's ship. Psalome sighs but I read my victory in the slump of her shoulders and the way she pushes her hand through her glossy knot of hair. Her resistance is giving way to the weariness that has been creeping up on her since yesterday.

"Stay safe, okay?" she says, turning around. "Both of you."

"Sweet dreams, Psalome," Ilaria replies. She's twirling a piece of hair around her finger and smiling at Psalome who smiles back as if this is some secret joke they share. Just the two of them. It's so fucking cute it makes me want to vomit. Psalome, on the other hand, rewards Ilaria with a beaming smile.

I escort Psalome to her room, noting the fact that she chooses to sleep in the exact spot on the bed that is still rumpled from Ilaria's former occupancy. I bet she'll have sweet enough dreams there. All of them featuring a certain five-foot-tall brunette who is currently standing next to me.

My stomach knots.

I should want them to be happy, but I'm honest enough to know that I don't. Not like this. Not with each other. It's too complicated. Too dangerous given the plan I am trying to pull off with their help. Fucking is fine. Desirable even. Actual feelings are not. I thought we were clear on that.

"Come on," I say brusquely, leading Ilaria through

the hallway. "Time to see if you're useful for more than demolition."

She follows me silently until we hit the lift.

"Your sister isn't much for talking," she says. "Do you think it bothers her that I'm around? She talks to everyone else."

I almost choke. Feelings again. Goddamn it.

"She's a wonderful conversationalist when she's being a Dazzle Girl," I explain, reminding myself that Psalome deserves to be happy. That this heist isn't worth jack-shit if it leaves my sister miserable by the end. "It's a part she's learned to play so well she sometimes has trouble letting it go. She's awkward with you because she's trying to remember how to be herself."

"Oh," Ilaria says, a blush creeping onto her face. "I thought anyone who played the piano like she does wouldn't have any trouble with that. It obviously comes from a place deep inside herself. I felt like I was eavesdropping this morning."

The guilt that washes over me is familiar. I've been living with it for as long as I can remember. Letting it eat away at my soul. It would have eaten away at our relationship, too, if Psalome had let it. A lesser person would have.

God help me, Ilaria had better realize how lucky she is. If she hurts Psalome or thinks any less of her because of her job, I will hand her over to Shaul myself.

"Psalome was born to play the piano," I say, trying not to let my voice crack. "She had a scholarship to attend the music academy on Delphius, but she gave it all up to become a Dazzle Girl."

She gave it all up to protect me.

It's about time I started protecting her.

"You should tell her you like listening to her play," I say quietly as we exit into the cargo bay where Shaul's ship is docked right next to mine. "It might help her talk to you."

"You're a good sister," Ilaria says, stepping out beside me. "The way you watch over her from your ship. It's like you're an angel in her ear."

It rips through me like a meteor barreling through the atmosphere and catching flame before it sinks into the lush Earth of my heart. I haven't been a very good sister, not if El can forgive my docking fees but not my sister's debt, which is why I need to pull this heist off and break Psalome free. No matter what the cost to me or anybody else.

"I'd like it if she talked to me," Ilaria admits. "I'd like to know who she really is behind all that dazzle."

Which is the same thing I ask myself everyday as my sister, my Lo, fades away. Replaced by the marble statue of the Dazzler. A goddess with Casino patrons worshipping at her feet. If Ilaria can help bring Lo back, then this will all be more than worth it.

# CHAPTER THIRTEEN

## Kiyokimora

ILARIA AND PSYLINA are taking forever. My eyelids twitch with impatience. GoldWeavers are meant for action. We do not wait. Especially not when we suspect the person we are waiting for is a secret sociopath.

I trust Ilaria, she has just as much reason as any of us to take Shaul down, it's a matter of religious righteousness for her, but Psalome's little sister looks at me like I'm a fly trapped in amber. Her eyes are exact copies of her sister's but whereas Psalome's are enticingly inviting, Psylina's are cold and calculating. They might both know my secrets, but I suspect they'd do very different things with them if left to their own devices.

What kind of person falls in love with a super-computer? More frighteningly, what kind of person would the computer love back?

I shake my head to clear it as she approaches. Psylina is necessary for this heist and I don't want to give her a reason to suspect I don't trust her. The ways in which she could screw me over are limitless. Especially with Ilaria preparing to board Shaul's ship and Finley playing poker, alone, in a casino full of alcohol.

"Sorry we're late," Psylina says, extending a hand towards me. It contains two sets of diamond earrings, modified to include communication devices. "Psalome had to be convinced to stay behind. She doesn't like to miss any action."

"I'll bet she doesn't," I say, jamming my pair of earrings into my lobes. "Let's get this over with. I should be at Finley's game. She's my pretend girlfriend and I'm sponsoring her after all."

If she wins, I split half of her winnings, but that's not actually what I'm referring to. I was Finley's sponsor before we got here, and I will remain her sponsor long after she plays her last round of poker in The Casino or anywhere else. No matter if she feels the same way about me or not. No matter what happens with my company or this heist. And without me there, a whole lot of undesirable things could happen.

She'll win, of course. Finley always wins. My concern is how she'll choose to celebrate.

She's been sober almost two years now but leaving her on a floor full of booze and psychedelic drugs with access to an open credit line is not exactly the kind of thing a proper sobriety sponsor would do. At least I can trust her to stay away from the Dazzlers now that she's met Psalome. Finley never settles for second best. It's another thing I like about her.

A soft beep sounds in my ear as the com system comes to life. Psylina insisted on using diamond because of its superior strength but the fashion faux pas gnaws at me. I don't often favor diamonds. They are too cold and uninviting. Too easily lending themselves to jokes about me being a corporate ice queen. A shrew in a business suit.

I prefer my gemstones with more fire. Like Finley. Full of life and heat and surprises.

Ilaria ignores the pair of studs waiting for her in Psylina's hand.

"You have to put them on so you can hear us when you're on Shaul's ship." Psylina nudges the earrings towards Ilaria, her foot impatiently tapping the floor. "I'm not trying to spy on you or anything. You can turn them off whenever you want."

"It's not that," Ilaria says quietly, chewing her bottom lip. "I, uhm, I don't have pierced ears. Most girls on Thillov wait until they're married and Shaul didn't want to pay for it, so it never happened for me. I always wanted a pair, but I couldn't ask my parents for the money. Not after all the financial trouble I caused my family already with the big fancy wedding Shaul insisted they pay for."

A little gasp escapes my mouth before I can restrain it. My ears were practically pierced in the womb. Every baby photo of me features a set of gemstones sparkling in my ears. Including the ones where I'm splashing in the bath or mischievously running around the estate in nothing but a diaper, chubby toddler legs flailing. Mom used to say a GoldWeaver wasn't truly naked if they still had their jewelry on. Our trademark. Our armor.

I wonder if she would still say that if she saw the video. The earrings did stay on for most of it. The dead boyfriend she could handle, but she'd never forgive me for leaving jewelry on that nightstand.

I should have noticed Ilaria's ears weren't pierced. That she always keeps her hair down around her face. How many other things about her have I missed?

"Not an issue," Psylina says, flipping the earrings over on her palm to reveal clip-on backs. "I am also well aware that your asshat husband confiscated your jewelry when you left him. I made these special for you to start off your collection again. You can remove the wiring after this is over and enjoy them as a memento of your first steps toward freedom."

My stomach plummets into my shoes as Ilaria gratefully scoops up the earrings. Psylina is chewing on the ends of her hair, still tapping her foot, but the speech gives her away. Psylina Shipmen, potential sociopath and proud programming shark, actually *cares* about Ilaria.

This is devolving into an embarrassment of epic proportions. Psylina, who prefers spaceships and robots to sapphires and rubies, has noticed Ilaria's distinct lack of accessories. Meanwhile, I spent months with Ilaria and didn't think to ask why she never wore earrings. I'm supposedly the head of the world's largest interplanetary jewelry retail outfit yet there's an entire planet out there full of teenage girls and young women without pierced ears and I didn't have a clue.

Ilaria is stroking the shiny silver doors to Shaul's ship like a long-lost friend. This was her ship once. The one her parents bought for her and Shaul. The ones whose mortgage her salary continued to pay, even after Shaul left, despite the fact that she was no longer occupying it. What dreams did she bury when it flew off Thillov without her?

"I know it's a lot," Psylina says. Her voice is hypnotic and regular like a metronome. As if she's talked someone off a ledge before. Many times. "You can be nostalgic later. Right now, you have to focus on your goal and move forward. No time for looking back."

Is that what she tells Psalome to get her to do her job? Forget the regret. Focus on today, so that you can be free of this place tomorrow?

It must be effective, because Ilaria takes her hand off the hull of the ship which still bears the GodsFire crest and walks up to the set of controls that will open the airlock. She punches in a few numbers and then calls out an access code in response to computer prompts. Her voice rings out over the cargo bay, trembling slightly, like a butterfly caught in a net.

It's disorienting to hear her over the coms and in person at the same time. Thankfully, there's no feedback in the system. Psylina clearly knows what she's doing. I've had worse audio at shareholder meetings where everyone is sitting quietly at their personal overpriced computer terminals that they insist on expensing to the company.

I hold my breath as I wait to see if the ship accepts Ilaria's request for access. I didn't believe her when she claimed it would. Is Shaul really so full of himself that he didn't think it necessary to change the command codes on the ship when he stole it out from under her? We change our house safe codes twice a day.

I understand the need to surveil Shaul, but I hate to think what he'll do if he catches Ilaria on the ship. Technically speaking, they are still married. All her property belongs to him. He can make her life even more of a living hell than it was before I intervened and we faked her death.

The ship doors spring open with a hiss and Ilaria waves to us as she steps inside. I can't imagine what this must be like for her, stepping back in time to when she thought this ship was the start of her new life. Of her family and her marriage.

Did Shaul carry her over the threshold? Do Jewish people do that? It certainly didn't bring her much luck if he did. Because right now she's sneaking into the ship that she used to own in order to get revenge on the husband who refused to give her a divorce so that he could keep stealing from her and everyone else he crosses paths with.

Hardly the stuff romance novels are made of.

Psylina and I wait until the doors close before heading back to Psylina's ship. She's conveniently directed Shaul to park right next to it. Mine is on its other side. An excellent arrangement for surveillance, so long as he doesn't realize what we're doing.

I clear a stack of books and a pair of pliers off the co-pilot seat while Psylina straps a headset on so that she can talk and move easily.

"Everything alright in there, Ilaria?" Psylina asks. She paces around the room fidgeting a stylus in her hand, twirling it between her knuckles.

"Depends on your definition of alright," Ilaria mutters. "He redid all the paneling in a depressing dark color, and he appears to put even less effort into maintaining the engine than he put into maintaining our marriage. God in heaven, this is no way to treat a ship. My father would have a coronary if he saw the state these blasting coils are in."

"Focus, Ilaria," I tell her. We can't afford her tipping Shaul off by cleaning the place. If any of those bugs are traced back to us, the entire plan is shot. "Get those bugs placed and I will buy you a replacement ship. No mortgage this time."

Psylina lets out a low whistle. Ships like this cost almost as much as the remainder of Psalome's debt. Nobody buys one without a hefty mortgage. The amount of money I am spending on this venture is rapidly increasing. But if it helps me keep the company, and Finley, it will all be worth it.

"He took the largest room for himself," Ilaria says. Her voice huffs audibly through my ear. "Not a surprise. He used to hog the blanket at night, too. Bug is placed. I'm heading down to the main storage area."

"Put one in the room two doors to your left," Psylina advises. The blue light from one of her computer screens is casting ghoulish shadows across her face as she swipes through a set of blueprints on a hand-held tablet. "My scan of the ship detected a larger than usual amount of carbon in there."

"Carbon?" hisses Ilaria. There's a scuffling noise and I suspect she's stumbled. "Like organic material? You think he's got a body stashed in there?"

"Like diamonds, Ilaria," I say helpfully before Psylina can respond with something harsh. Ilaria's not stupid. She can build a bomb out of dental floss and cleaning supplies, but she would have no reason to be thinking about gemstone composition. She doesn't even have pierced ears. The first disappointment of her marriage that heralded the string of many more to come.

I should buy her more than a ship.

"Shit," Psylina says, making me jump. She's looking at footage of The Casino floor. My heart leaps into my throat for a second before I realize she's focusing on Shaul and not Finley.

"What's wrong?" I ask. "Is he going to lose?"

I can't make heads or tails of the cards he's holding in his hands, I leave all that to Finley, but I'm suddenly wishing I paid more attention when she tried to teach me the difference between a flush and a pair instead of attempting to work up the courage to ask if she'll stay with me after I lose the company. Shaul needs to make it to the finale so Psalome can get her hands on those earrings.

"Not a chance." Psylina has stopped pacing and is now frantically typing. Her fingers fly over the keyboard so fast they are a blur. "I assigned him an easy group. He could win with his hands tied behind his back."

"So, what's the problem?" I twist my rings on my finger. Now my mother *and* Finley would disapprove of me for showing all of my tells, but Psylina needs to spit out the problem because Ilaria, who we are supposed to be focusing on, is currently bumbling around Shaul's ship waiting for confirmation her bugs are working.

"Gemma is dealing at his table." Psylina rolls her eyes as if Gemma's faults are known to the entire universe.

I glance back at the screen. Gemma seems innocuous enough to me. Tall. Blonde. Friendly. Currently wearing my great-great-grandmother's pearl earrings along with several other large pieces of jewelry. "You're going to need to give me a little more than that."

Psylina winces. "She's a terrible dealer. The Casino wouldn't normally use her for a show tournament, but Peter Jett is at that table. He's worse at poker than Gemma is at dealing but he's loaded and he frequents Gemma's rooms for some of the services she is significantly more skilled with. He probably requested her. He loses so much money here every year The Casino would never tell him no."

I'm still not seeing the problem. I stare at Psylina waiting for her to finish, but she's already moved on, loading pictures of the space station hallways onto the screens. She's not going to explain more. Not unless I humiliate myself by asking.

"In English please," I demand in my boardroom voice. "Or any one of the ten languages I am fluent in. Not Casino speak."

Nobody gets to look down on me and try to make me feel inferior and uninformed. Not my father, or Shaul, or any of the board members who think I'm too young for a seat at the table. Certainly not Psylina.

Her head snaps up, her mouth a round circle, her forehead creased in confusion. She didn't mean to insult me. She thought it was obvious. That only makes it worse.

"She deals too fast," she explains, the words slurring together in her hurry to explain. "She won't draw the game out for show like a professional would. Ilaria won't have enough time to get out. The players are already leaving the table. Fuck."

Sure enough, I can see Shaul on the screen, laying down his cards triumphantly. There is a scattering of applause and I spot Finley cursing under her breath, probably annoyed she isn't the first to finish. Her com isn't on but it's obvious what she's saying isn't very polite.

Her face is a scowling reflection of how I'm feeling right now.

"Ilaria?" I squeak as we watch Shaul walk across the casino floor and towards the lift. "Time to get out."

I try to keep my voice steady, not wanting to worry her. Psylina is still frantically typing away.

"Psylina was right about the carbon," Ilaria says. Either she hasn't noticed my uncharacteristic squeak, or she's bravely ignoring it. "There's a safe hidden in here."

My heart rate picks up and all thoughts of Shaul's impending arrival fly out of my head, as the implications of what a secret safe on Shaul's ship means. My video recording might be in there. With it, we could call off the whole plan, sail out of here immediately before Finley has to play another game. I'd still keep my word and pay for Psalome's release. It would be a win win for everyone. The end of the nightmare that has been plaguing me all these years.

With that video in hand, instead of released to the world, maybe whatever is broken inside of me will finally heal.

"Can you open it?" I ask. My voice comes out in a growl that I do not recognize. Like a feral cat is clawing its way up my throat.

"I could blow it open real easy." Ilaria's voice is hopeful, like a kid in a candy store. Almost as if she can't resist mention of an explosion no matter how ludicrous the suggestion is. "I saw some stuff in the kitchen when I walked past. It would only take a minute–"

"No," I scream at the same time as Psylina.

"No blowing anything up," I say. "It'll trigger an alarm and probably put the whole casino in lockdown. Try entering his birthday for the code."

He seems like the kind of self-centered jackass that uses their own birthday as a passcode.

An explosion is too risky but only a few inches of steel stand in between Ilaria and the hell I've been living ever since that night. Shaul is still waiting for the elevator. A rare stroke of luck given I've never waited more than thirty seconds at The Casino's lifts. We have to take advantage of the extra time.

"Are you joking?" Psylina yelps, shoving me aside. "Ilaria, don't."

Too late. I can hear the soft beeps of a keypad as Ilaria punches in the numbers followed by the blare of an alarm whistle as the code fails.

"Uhm, ladies?" Ilaria is no longer gleeful. Her voice wobbles but I'm too busy listening to the frantic hammering of my pulse in my ears to pay it much mind. "I think I just set off an alarm."

Shit.

My tongue is clammy in my dry mouth. Every nightmare I've ever had flashes before me. Shaul extorting me for more money and then releasing the video anyway. Newspaper headlines calling me a murderer. My board calling me an embarrassment and using the company morality clause to oust me while my dad gloats from the head of the table. Mom descending from heaven to call me a slut and a stain on the family name.

Plus, now there are new nightmares. Finley telling me this was all about the money for her, that she never loved me at all, and leaving me alone, only to backslide and wind up in prison. Ilaria shipped back to Thillov to grow old alone after Shaul finds out she isn't really dead. Me useless to either of them without my money and my power. Everything and everyone I love, gone in a nanosecond all because I couldn't handle my shit and got drunk and messy with the wrong boy.

"Get out of there, Ilaria. NOW." Pyslina sweeps past me, taking control of the situation. She is as mobile as I am frozen. A whir of activity. "Take the back-exit hatch. I'll hack in and override the lockdown. It'll take a minute, but you need to be ready to run immediately. Shaul is approaching the cargo bay."

"What?" Ilaria yelps, her voice taking on an unnaturally high pitch. I can hear her panting as she starts running down the corridors. "He's here?"

"Stay calm, we'll get you out." Psylina has returned to the soothing metronome voice again. Her forehead is sweating and her fingers still scramble to press keys faster and faster but you can't tell any of that from the commanding way she speaks. It reminds me of the video I've seen of Psalome, diffusing tense situations with customers without losing face or revenue.

Shipmen women really are unshakable.

"Well?" She whirls to face me. "What are you waiting for? Your brilliant idea triggered the alarm. The least you can do is get out there and buy Ilaria a few minutes by distracting Shaul. That's why you're here, remember? To provide distraction?"

She says the last words slowly, as if I am too incompetent to process them at regular speed. There's a ringing in my ears that has nothing to do with the alarm. Psylina is now looming over me, jabbing a stylus at my chest.

Nobody has ever talked to me the way Psylina does. Not even my father. At this particular moment in time, with Shaul's threats still fresh in my head and everything crumbling around us, I do not take it well, lashing out like a wounded animal.

"Maybe if you weren't so busy typing some love letter to your computer joyfriend, I wouldn't have had to give Ilaria any ideas at all." It's a low blow, but to her credit Psylina doesn't lose her cool. In fact, she visibly frosts over.

"For your information, I was rerouting the elevator system to delay Shaul's arrival. Care to explain why you advised Ilaria to try entering codes at random into a high-grade safe? Do you not have any security over at the emerald factory? Or was your head simply too much up your ass for you to see what was right in front of your face?"

My stomach drops out from under me. We do have high-grade safes at home and I know very well how they work, how the safety protocols won't tolerate one false keystroke. I was simply so obsessed with getting that video back, I failed to consider the possibility that Shaul might not be using a standard safe. That GoldWeavers aren't the only people in the universe with valuables worth protecting.

Too focused on myself to pay attention to Ilaria and the danger I put her in. Another body added to my tally.

Psylina isn't waiting for an answer. She's back at the keyboard struggling to get Ilaria out in time. It's what I should be doing, too. Time enough for guilt later. Right now, I need to buy them both as much breathing room as possible and keep the mistake I made from imploding in all of our faces.

I hustle out of the airlock and into the cargo bay, charging straight towards the entrance. I arrive as the lift doors spring open and Shaul runs out. His eyes narrow to slits when he sees me.

"You," he growls, eyes darting around. In the flashing red and yellow strobe of the alarm he looks demonically possessed. His carefully styled hair now flops in all directions. "Did you try to rob me, you insane bitch?"

I let out a laugh, slow and deliberate, so that I can prolong the conversation as much as possible.

"I could ask you the same thing," I say, pointing towards my ship, nestled up right next to his in this corner of the cargo bay, with only Psylina's ship in between them. "Wouldn't be the first time you tried to steal from me, now, would it?"

He runs his hand through his disheveled hair and gives me a rakish smile. It brings out his dimples and I see why Ilaria once thought he was attractive. Until he starts talking.

"As I recall, you had a very nice time that evening with my associate and gave me the most splendid thank you gift for introducing you two. I can't wait to see all the Dazzlers wear it. Your great-great-grandmother would be so proud to have her earrings finally worn by people with an entrepreneurial spirit instead of her two-bit whore of a descendent. Dazzlers have the good sense to get paid to fuck on camera. You gave it away for free to the first guy that asked. And the sex was so awful it killed him."

"You fucking bastard." Rage fills my body with feral energy. I want to reach out and claw the eyes from his body. Roast him alive over a slow burning fire while a crowd watches. Strip him naked and parade him across the universe for everyone to jeer at.

But I don't do any of that. Because I'm frozen to the spot, Shaul's eyes pinning me. My hands sweat and my body is on fire with the heat of humiliation. I'm wearing every emotion I have on my face. Giving away too many secrets. Not to mention losing his interest.

"It's been nice knowing you, sweetheart," he says, walking away. "But I don't have time for temper tantrums from little girls. Not unless you want to take those pretty emeralds off your hair for my collection, too. They'd buy you a couple weeks extension on the video release day."

His eyes dip down over my body, reminding me he knows what I look like without my clothes on, that the entire world will know if I don't give him what he wants. Then he scoffs and turns around. "You know where to find me."

Psylina's voice echoes through my head, pleading over the coms. "You need to hold him off, Kiyo. Ten more seconds. Just breathe."

"Shaul, wait." It takes every bit of strength I have to get the words out. To call him back when all I want to do is watch him leave. I lower my eyes to the floor as he turns around. The way Ilaria always stared at the ground when we first met her. The way she still sometimes does. We have that in common, I guess. "You said to meet you here to make arrangements. How much is it going to take to get you to leave me alone?"

I know the answer before the words leave his mouth. Have always known it deep down in my heart. Because people like Shaul, people like my father, never let go. They take and take until there is nothing left to give and then they make you suffer anyway, just to prove that they can.

"Why in God's name would you think I'd ever leave you alone?" He leans over to stroke my cheek, and bile fills my mouth at his touch. "You belong to me, now and forever, darling. I'll send over a payment request soon."

The only thing that saves me from vomiting is the sweet sound of the airlock whooshing open in my ear, followed by a choked sob of relief in a familiar voice.

I jerk my head out of his grip and storm off towards my ship, body sagging against the door as I let out the frustration and fear that's been fueling me.

"We have to win this," Ilaria whispers in my ear. She's safe on Psylina's ship now, waiting for a clear moment to return to the sanctuary of Psalome's room. "I heard what he said to you, Kiyo. It's what he said when I asked him to give me a divorce. He'll never leave either of us alone. We cannot let him get away with it."

I couldn't agree more, and I almost jeopardized it all. My great-great-grandmother never would have made such a careless mistake. My mother would have ripped Shaul's face off. But I'm not them. I close my eyes and let the tears fall now that there's nobody here to see them. One day I'll know what to do, how to make everything right again.

Today is not that day.

# CHAPTER FOURTEEN

## Ilaria

MY HEART IS clawing its way out of my chest and my legs have turned into jelly. Psylina hauls me into her arms and physically shoves me through the airlock as Shaul approaches his ship. The ship that used to be ours. Where we lived together.

I catch a glimpse of his face through the tinted windows, and it takes me back to the night we got married, to the way I used to search for his face everywhere when we were engaged. Back when I thought he would love me forever. Back to the morning when I realized he was a conman and he'd never really loved me at all. Just needed a wife and family to legitimize himself to the world.

I'd never loved him either. Not the way I was supposed to. It had all happened too fast for that. What I'd loved was the dream of showing off my handsome husband to my friends. The starry future in which he and I trotted out our perfect family once the kids started to arrive. Love was supposed to come later.

Neither one of us had been prepared for that dream to crumble. For the questions and the rumors and the whispers about why I couldn't get pregnant.

At least I was willing to work through it together, suggesting we funnel some of the money he was spending on frivolity into a fertility doctor's fees instead. He'd flat out refused, which is when I began to suspect he knew the problem all along. That he'd known he couldn't have kids even before we met. That he'd specifically chosen me, the girl that nobody else wanted, because he assumed I'd be too grateful to ask questions.

And in a way he'd been right. I hadn't asked any questions. My parents hadn't demanded his medical files before they agreed to the match. Not because they didn't love me, but because they thought we could trust him. Who would lie about such a thing?

It's ironic really. I wouldn't have left him if we couldn't have kids. I probably would have even still agreed to marry him. Children had never been as make-it-or-break-it to me as they were to some of my friends. Despite the aggression and the violence, I hadn't contemplated leaving Shaul until I snuck into his room to find the money to pay for the fertility doctor on my own and found the tapes and the contraband. If he'd simply been honest up front I never would have found any of it. Might not have figured out what his job in "intergalactic product movement" really was. But when I did, I knew there was no way I could stay. Still, I never expected him to retaliate by flying off planet and leaving me stranded like yesterday's trash on the curb.

Used, unwanted, a thing cast off yet oddly still owned by another.

That had been the first time since the wedding I'd been glad when my period arrived. A bright blood stain heralding the last of my connection to him. I'd sobbed and sobbed with regret and relief and woke up the next morning determined to move on with what was left of my life.

That's when I told my parents the whole sordid truth. Refused their offer to mortgage their house even further and use the funds to hire someone to track him down. I applied for my job at the mine instead, hopeful that the court would grant me my freedom anyway when they heard about Shaul's crimes.

I was wrong.

So I blew stuff up as my private form of therapy while I waited for some sign from God as to what my next move should be. I never expected deliverance to come in the form of an overdressed heiress and her wild best friend, who arrived on Thillov seeking to confront evil incarnate and found me instead.

I thought there wasn't any way Shaul could hurt me anymore, but seeing his face again today, I realize he can still burn his scars onto my heart. There are infinite ways in which he already has. The scabs rip open and ooze with old hurts in the harsh shadow of his presence.

He threatened Kiyo right there in the airlock. Admitted to filming her having sex and using that footage to blackmail money from her. He wasn't even embarrassed about accidentally causing her boyfriend's death. He was using it to extort her.

Who is this man and how was I such a fool as to marry him?

Psylina's lips are moving but I can't hear a word. There's a ringing in my ears so loud it drowns out everything else, like the aftershocks of an explosion. I'm on my knees, heaving onto her floor.

I am dimly aware that this should be humiliating. That I should offer to help clean up the mess I'm making, but mostly I'm focused on not passing out in my own vomit. Because there is a distinct possibility of that happening.

When I finally cease retching, Psylina pushes me into a chair. I think the cool cylinder she presses into my hands is a glass of water but the fog in my brain is so strong I can't be sure.

I knew it would be unsettling to see Shaul again, but I didn't expect this. I can't afford to fall to pieces whenever he's around. Especially not in front of Psylina. I need to pull myself together fast or risk losing my place in the heist, my last chance to make amends for the part I played, however inadvertent, in Shaul's blackmail schemes, and move on with my life.

I search around the ship for something familiar to ground myself and pull me back into the present. I'm sitting in some kind of storage area, in between maintenance equipment and old trunks. There are shelves piled high with electrical wiring and dry goods.

There are no windows. That must be why Psylina chose this spot. I can't decide if that's thoughtful or simply practical. Much like with the earrings from earlier. There's a hint of sentiment surrounding the action but also extreme pragmatism.

"Ilaria?"

Her voice is audible now. That's an improvement.

"Ilaria, can you hear me? Are you okay?"

I need to say something before she gives up on me for good. "You should release the pressure from your flour cans."

"Excuse me?" She's wheeling in a gurney of portable medical equipment, obviously suspecting I'm delirious. I spot a blood pressure cuff and some vials of smelling salts. Psylina is fiddling with a hand-held scanner.

"Flour is extremely combustible. It makes it easy to blow up your ship from the inside."

Now that I say it out loud, I'm aware of how deranged I

sound. This got me in trouble at home, too. The other kids at school thought I was unhinged when I explained how we could combine items from our lunches to create chemical reactions.

"Sorry," I mumble, swatting away the medical equipment as my vision clears. "I've been dealing with explosives since I was little. It helps me feel better. My first bomb was condensed flour on an extended piece of wax coated hemp for the wick. We used it to clear out an old shed from the yard."

"Lovely," Psylina says, packing away the medical equipment. "This is a passenger ship and typically the only person on board is myself or Psalome. I think it's safe to say neither of us is going to blow it up and the flour lasts longer this way."

"Suit yourself," I say with a shrug. I don't think I could sleep knowing all that pressurized flour was close by. I stand up and take a few steps to prove I'm recovered.

There's a small common room outside the storage area with large floor-to-ceiling tinted windows surrounding a metal coffee table and several armchairs. Everything is nailed to the floor in case of turbulence, but someone has taken the effort to make it resemble a home and not a transport vessel.

There are curtains on the windows, which Psylina is rushing to close, and a large vase of silk flowers rests on the table next to an enormous bowl of rainbow-colored candy. They are sweet touches, but there is a conspicuous lack of photos.

"You don't need to close the curtains," I say. "I should get used to seeing him. It'll help if I can do it a few times in here, where I know I'm safe."

Her hands pause on the curtains, but she doesn't sit down. Not yet.

"You sure?"

I nod once and approach the flowers. There are overhanging sprays of jasmine mixed in with lilies and orchids. The arrangement smells strongly like the perfume Psalome uses on her skin. Does Psylina spray them to mimic the natural scent?

"I never pictured you for the flowers and candy type," I say to change the topic. The petals are so lifelike I reach out to touch one, surprised to find it smooth and lush beneath my fingers. What I had assumed were replicas are, in fact, real blossoms.

How can she possibly afford these?

"That's because I'm not the flower type," Psylina agrees with a grin, folding herself into one of the chairs. "They were a birthday gift from El the first year we moved here. They thought the smell might help prevent me from missing Psalome, so they grew them in The Casino greenhouse for me. To remind me of her perfume."

It's the most wildly extravagant gift I have ever seen, but it doesn't explain how they are still fresh and not wilted.

"What keeps them alive?" I ask, staring into the water in the vase. It looks entirely ordinary to me, no special fertilizer or plant breeding nanotechnology.

"Nothing," she says, stroking one of the delicate leaves. "I didn't have the heart to tell El I don't care for things like flowers, so they kept bringing me a new bouquet every week. By the time they figured it out we were both unwilling to let go of the custom."

I shake my head in disbelief. Girls back home would swoon if their boyfriends were so attentive. Maybe Psylina is onto something with this dating-a-computer thing. Shaul never bought me flowers. I had to pick out my own wedding bouquet and he never even commented on it.

"The candy, too?" I can't help but ask, curious what the story there is. The bowl is overflowing with every color candy in the rainbow, except for orange. I wonder what algorithm caused The Casino to leave it out. Maybe something about human girls finding the color lacking in romance.

Psylina picks a few of the bright orbs up and lets them tinkle back into the bowl. They jangle too musically for fruit chews, even candy-coated ones. I reach out a finger and tap one only to be met with cool resistance.

It's made from glass.

Everything I think real is fake and everything I think fake is real. It's a perfect metaphor for my life. For this Casino. For everything.

"Psalome had them made for me on the same birthday," Psylina explains. "They're popular where we grew up but nearly impossible to get around here. She works on her birthday every year but insists on taking mine off and spending at least a little of her money on me. I keep telling her not to."

She's clutching the bowl to her chest, as if it represents everything that is good and precious in the world. Maybe to her it does. It's a side of Psalome I hadn't anticipated. She's so smooth with the clients, so untouchable, but she loves her sister.

I know she was awkward this morning, that Psylina said she was trying to remember how to be herself, but I hadn't fully grasped what that meant. I'm getting a peek now at who that person might be.

"Why no orange?" I ask, although I suspect I know the answer. Psalome has an incredible attention to detail. She rearranges the furniture for each client, laying out the drinks they like, swapping out her accessories to suit them. She accommodates them all, even the ones she's only met once. She'd notice if her sister never ate the oranges.

"I wrote my first piece of computer code when I was five," Psylina says, placing the bowl back down. "It controlled this little robotic dog that Mom got us to make up for not having a real pet. This was before she died and Dad spiraled out of control. Things were better back then."

She's pacing the room now, her back to me. There is an extra-long pause as she bottles back the emotion this memory brings up. She and Psalome are alike that way, only I'm beginning to realize that Psalome might be better at it. She's had more practice by placing herself in a position to absorb the world's hurts before they can reach Psylina.

How many years was their father out of control and Psylina simply didn't know because Psalome and their mother hid it from her?

"Anyway," Psylina says, turning back around. "The code instructed the dog to sort out the fruit chews and discard the oranges. I had to modify it, though. Dad went ballistic about the waste when he found out, said he'd never buy us candy again until I ate every last orange. It was a huge bucket of candy. The kind you buy to last for interplanetary trips. I gagged them all down and threw up all over the place."

"So she made you the perfect assortment," I surmise. "Not a single orange. Not a single bad memory."

"She cleaned up the vomit, too. Before Dad could see," Psylina says. This time she doesn't bother to hide the emotion in her wobbling voice. "Then she played the piano to help me sleep and when I woke up, she swore to me I would never have to see another orange fruit chew in my life. That's why she's so good at her job. She creates the illusion of a perfect world, untouched by darkness. Who wouldn't pay for that?"

I think back to the glimpses I have had of Psalome at work, the snatches of conversation I've heard through the walls. It was all so seamless and light, as if she was designed especially for that client. As if the universe conspired to give them the perfect night with her as the centerpiece of it all.

"She gives them their own piece of heaven for an hour."

It must be incredibly lonely, giving everyone else what they want all the time. She's constantly letting other people fill up her existence with their dreams and their hopes, much the same way I let everyone else's expectations push me into marriage too hastily. Is there any space left for her own dreams, once she's done processing everyone else's? I catch Psylina's eye and decide it's worth a shot asking.

"Does she ever ask for anything for herself?"

Psylina shakes her head no. "When I last tried to give her a present on her birthday, she insisted all she wanted was for me to be safe. If a client asks, she'll request they give her something she knows she can sell back to The Casino. Sometimes, I think she spends so much time figuring out what everyone else wants she's forgotten what it is to want something for herself."

Psylina's eyes haven't left mine. I can see her frustration, but I do not share it. I am no stranger to living with someone who wants so much that you forget yourself in the sea of their desires. Only Psylina is not Shaul, not by a long shot.

"Maybe somebody should give it to her anyway."

She opens her mouth to say something but then snaps it shut and darts over to the curtains.

"Shit, don't look."

She's scrambling to unhook them but it's too late. Shaul is standing right in front of us, fixing his gelled brown hair in the reflection of the tinted windows. It would be comical if his face wasn't so spiteful.

Psylina is staring at me as if I am an unpinned grenade, ready to implode at the first hint of pressure. To blow us all up with the force of the explosion and scatter shrapnel that cuts deep into the flesh of any survivors. She tugs the curtain again, cursing.

I lay my hand on her shoulder and motion for her to stop.

"It's okay," I say, stepping forward to touch the glass with my fingers. I can practically feel Shaul's face beneath my fingertips. His breath on my neck. His arms around my waist. His nails digging into my skin.

How many nights did I lie awake dreaming about his face, wondering what I was doing wrong, why he didn't love me? Why God didn't give us children? Why he became what he did?

I've given him superhuman powers in my head, but from this close I can see he's nothing more than a petty man of more than average looks who has never given a thought to anyone else in his life. A person like all the people Psalome sits with night after night. People who need a pretty woman to convince them that the universe loves them.

Living with Psalome has helped me understand those men and women who steal their joy from another person's suffering. They aren't worthy of her and Shaul isn't worthy of me. The spell he cast over me is broken into a thousand little pieces as I see him for what he truly is.

Surrounded by the evidence of the million acts of kindness that Psylina exchanges with the people she loves, I can say with certainty that Shaul never loved me. We were never really married. Not in our hearts, and I suspect not in the eyes of God either.

Even now, he's preening in the glass like it's a mirror, completely oblivious to the fact that it is the wall of someone else's ship, that he might be intruding on their privacy. Interrupting their intimate moments. He moves as if the world was built to serve him and him alone.

There was never going to be a true place for me in that universe. Or for our kids. Not unless it was to please him.

I think back to how Psalome tucked me into her own bed

and then slept on the couch to avoid waking me. How she's risking everything she's built to get Kiyo her earrings back so that another victim can salvage something from the scrap heap of her life.

The life I would have had with Shaul stretches before me in a series of unfortunate incidents. He'd take me for granted, demanding more and more without ever giving anything in return. It would never have been a true marriage, only a life of servitude, chained to a man who was incapable of loving me back.

I can see that now, because when I look at Psalome and Psylina, I see what real love is. Each one tries to give the other what they need without a thought for themselves. That's what I want for myself, and Shaul is incapable of it.

I drop my hand and turn to face Psylina, my voice steady and unwavering.

"I'm not afraid of him anymore."

# CHAPTER FIFTEEN

## Finley

"So, WHAT'S THE damage?" As usual, I'm the only one willing to ask what everyone else is wondering. "How fucked are we?"

We're all sprawled out in Psalome's salon, listening to Psylina's account of the massive clusterfuck that occurred while Ilaria bugged Shaul's ship. Kiyo gushed to The Casino about what a great dealer Psalome was, and they agreed to give us a nightly booking with her every evening of the tournament so I can "relax." It adds credibility to our personas of overindulgent heiress and spendthrift girlfriend while allowing us to check in on Ilaria.

My co-conspirators are playing a game of Go Fish with a spare deck of children's cards, which The Casino keeps on hand for nostalgic visitors. All except for Psylina, who is tapping away on a tablet and grinning like an unranked newbie after beating the top seed at a grand slam poker tournament on a bluff.

Nobody has the right to look that pleased with themselves. Especially not her.

I won six games of poker in a row today and have staunchly avoided so much as looking at the top shelf liquor in Psalome's room. My performance has been flawless. Meanwhile, Psylina's surveillance operation has completely gone to shit.

Ilaria has been quiet as a mouse this entire time, holding her cards with white knuckles and mispronouncing the names of all the fish. It is so pathetically endearing that Psalome resists stealing cards off her even though it is obvious Ilaria has everything Psalome needs to make a few matches. Instead, she keeps refilling Ilaria's water glass and asking if she wants a break.

Ilaria, in turn, is stubbornly refusing to win cards off Psalome. She's slamming back glass after glass of water the way I used to knock back Cuervo and flinching every time someone curses.

"We are in no way fucked," Psylina announces. "Everything is still on track."

The blue tint from the tablet screen makes her cherub cheeks look fuller. More impish. Like a cross between a chipmunk and a ghoul. I did not think it was possible for me to trust her less, but every second we spend together proves me wrong.

"What do you mean?" Ilaria drops her cards in a heap on the floor. Go Fish was never destined to be the star of this evening. Better for the game to die quickly rather than the protracted death it was previously suffering. "Shaul is bound to be suspicious now. He almost caught me in his ship!"

"He's suspicious as hell," Psylina agrees, pulling up a blueprint and projecting it over the gaming table surface. The rest of the Go Fish cards are swept away by her impatient fingers and join their mates on the floor. A deep-sea angler stares up at me balefully. I stoop down and pick it up. Nobody here treats gaming equipment with the respect it deserves. "He's so suspicious he moved all his blackmail paraphernalia into The Casino's secure storage facility on cargo bay five because he has no idea which of his victims attempted to steal back their shit. The empty space on the ship makes the acoustics on the bugs much more efficient and I wiped all the footage of Ilaria approaching the ship and replaced it with a benign feed. We're golden."

"You can do that?" Now it's my turn to abandon the cards. The Casino's security system is impenetrable. Hacker collectives have been trying and failing to get access for eons. Meanwhile Psylina claims to have done it in less than a few hours.

"Of course, I can do that," Psylina says, exasperated. "I wrote the code for the security cameras myself. I have access to all of El's security protocols. They trust me never to do anything to harm them because I never would. I thought we went over that already. Please try to keep up."

She gestures towards the blueprints. CARGO BAY 5 is scrawled across the bottom. There's a flashing blue dot near the front that indicates where The Casino has stored Shaul's stuff. It's such a tiny thing yet it represents the worst nightmares of so many people. My fingers reach out to touch it, the screen momentarily blinking as I do, as if I can reach through the hologram and grab that heinous video. Present it to Kiyo as a token of my affection so she can see that her fuck-up alcoholic of a best friend is actually useful. Is actually worthy of her love. Maybe even of being a life partner rather than a project for her to rescue. Because so far, the fake girlfriend ruse has produced nothing but amusement from her. As if the very idea of people believing I am her girlfriend is hilarious.

The screen is depressingly solid between my fingers. There will be no magic portal giving me access to cargo bay five and that video is not coming back. Still, if I work hard enough, maybe we can salvage the earrings. It would be a start anyway.

So that Kiyo could finally acknowledge the trauma and start to heal rather than putting on a false front and claiming she doesn't care about its release.

"Wow." Ilaria is emerging from her funk as she studies the ins and outs of the diagram. "You weren't kidding when you said The Casino is high security. The size of explosion I would need to blow those doors open would be nuclear. It'd take out the whole casino and everyone in it."

"No one is blowing anything up." Psylina hastily clicks the image off. "We went over that before, too."

She sniffs at the dinner trays, bypassing the entrees and plucking a bonbon from the stack of desserts. I swear to God that girl could find snacks anywhere. The wolfish grin is back on her face as she attacks a bowl of chocolate mousse, wielding the spoon like a sword. "The best part? Shaul was too cheap to pay for the insurance. He's relying on the doors and The Casino's reputation to protect his stuff rather than paying outright for the service. El hates him already."

Ilaria's face has returned to its pale color, her eyes droopy as she flicks one of the digitized stars on the gaming table back and forth between her thumbs. "He was always cutting corners like that. Our wedding cake only had one edible piece. He said nobody would notice. That was the first time I should have realized I was nobody to him, because I sure noticed. It got worse after. I had to squirrel away money from the grocery budget if I wanted to buy anything he didn't agree on."

I hear the words behind the words that she is too shy to say. Ilaria wasn't saving up for stuff. She'd wanted to hire a private fertility doctor to find out why they couldn't have kids, but Shaul kept balking at the cost. Only later did she find out he'd been afraid the doctor might find the issue was with him and not her like everyone else assumed.

She'd told me the whole sordid story when I asked how she'd been able to afford a hotel room after she'd left him, before she told her family about his blackmail scheme and found herself a job at the mine. In retrospect, she'd called their inability to have kids a gift from God. Because she may never have found the strength to leave him if there had been a child involved.

I want to tell her that she is somebody. Remind her that he has always been the problem and not her regardless of either of their fertility statuses, but I also don't want to pour salt on an open wound. I'm not good with that sort of thing. Kiyo took care of all that when we first found Ilaria, just like she'd taken care of me.

I glance in Kiyo's direction, expecting her to swoop in and say something comforting, but she remains silently tucked onto one of the cushions with her hands folded around cards she hasn't touched. Her eyes are glazed over.

Ilaria continues to play with the gaming table, viciously thrusting stars in all directions until they crash and spin into each other in a burst of electronic destruction. Psalome quietly swipes at the controls and the next set of stars to crash bursts into rainbows of light. Ilaria looks up in silent question and Psalome plunks a huge slab of chocolate cake down in front of her.

Psylina squeaks in protest but Psalome pays her no heed. "There's plenty of cake here," she tells Ilaria. "And anything else you want. All you have to do is ask. Because you are not nobody."

It's grammatically garbled but Ilaria doesn't seem to mind. She beams up Psalome and reaches out to take the fork Psalome is offering. When their fingers brush, Psalome snatches her hands away and shoves them under the table like a kid caught passing notes in school. The faintest hint of red kisses her cheeks as Ilaria thanks her.

"Enjoy it," she murmurs, busying herself with tidying up the cards. Only when Ilaria is halfway through the cake does Psalome peek up again, eyeing her the way Psylina was eyeing the mousse. Like watching her is a treat to be enjoyed slowly before devouring her whole.

A fizzy tingling spreads through me, like champagne exploding from the bottle, and I choke back a laugh. My romance radar is so finely tuned I can spot an impending hook up from across the planet, but this was not a pairing I anticipated. I kick Kiyo under the cushion, jolting her out of her moody brooding.

At least somebody in this group is getting their romance on. Sure, Psalome seems to have made more progress with Ilaria in a day than I've made in years of not so subtly hinting at my feelings to Kiyo, but Psalome's a trained professional. If anything, this proves I still have a shot. Because who even knew Ilaria was bisexual, let alone open to love after her disaster marriage? Psalome, apparently.

"We should be going," I announce, tipping my head in the direction of Ilaria and Psalome who are now sitting ten feet apart and not looking at each other. Whatever is going on there, they aren't going to figure it out with the rest of us hanging around like third wheels. "We have dinner reservations and Psylina appears to have everything worked out, what with her being so familiar with the security codes and all."

Psylina nods, hefting the rest of the dessert plates with her as she gathers her tablets and heads for the door. "Intimately familiar."

"What?" At the mention of her sister being any sort of "intimate" with The Casino, Psalome's fingers skitter across the gaming table, sending sparkles in all directions like a fireworks display on steroids. Those poor Go Fish cards have been dropped yet again.

"I didn't mean it like that." Psylina tucks a stray piece of hair behind her ear. "You know I didn't mean it like that."

I cough into the awkwardness that follows as the two sisters glare at each other.

"Right, well, like I said we should all go." Weird yet possibly romantic tension between Psalome and Ilaria is one thing. An argument between the Shipmen sisters is quite another. "Glad to hear the plan is still on track. A few more poker games and we'll be sailing back through space towards our respective homes."

"Towards my first board meeting." It's the first thing Kiyo has said since we got here, and it's about business. Still, her eyes are full of hope again and in them I see everything I need to stay sober.

The rest of the universe might see her as a spoiled rich brat covering up her past mistakes, but they haven't spent the last few years watching her refuse to give up on me. Listening to her plans for her company as she patiently pulled me back from the brink every time I slipped. Watching her sincerely atone and change as a person from the girl that just wanted to get drunk and party in order to forget her mother's death.

"Let's go get you that dinner I promised you." It is as if she is reading my mind, shaking off the events of the day like a dog sheds water when it comes in from the rain. "You have a full day of games tomorrow."

Mentioning her first board meeting has wiped the brooding off her face and restored the luster to her skin. Her voice brims with authoritative optimism and it is infectious. It lifts my heart in a way that all Psylina's fancy tech talk could not. Because when Kiyo is truly herself, nothing and no one can stand in her way.

"I'll walk you out." If Psylina noticed anything going on between her sister and Ilaria, the brief mention of her physical relationship with The Casino, or lack thereof, has blotted it out of her mind. She's making a beeline for the door like a gambler that just got caught marking the cards. "I've got to run a few tests on the ship lojacking system before tomorrow. The docking and registration logs. That type of thing."

She ensures the doors are firmly shut behind us before elbowing past Kiyo and heading straight for the lifts.

"What was that for?" Kiyo stares daggers at Psylina's retreating back before linking her arm through mine and walking in the opposite direction. "That was rude, even for Psylina."

"The fuck if I know." I rub my back where Psylina's pointy elbow skewered me. "Psylina scares the crap out of me. Ilaria and Psalome seem to be getting along nicely, though. Psalome's taken a serious shine to our petite friend. Maybe Psylina's jealous."

"Of the married religious girl?" Kiyo laughs so hard small tears form in the corners of her eyes. "Psalome Shipmen is the world's most unattainable woman. You're telling me she's got a crush on Ilaria, the girl so sheltered she'd never read a romance novel before we picked her up? And then you had to explain what a blowjob was when she did?"

She glances back at the closed door like it might explode. Given Ilaria's past, that could be a more logical sequence of events than Psalome and Ilaria swapping spit behind it, but I know what I saw and I am never wrong about this kind of thing.

I am embarrassingly late to the party given that Psylina seems to have arrived here before me, but I am not wrong.

"Nothing about Psalome seemed 'unattainable' when she was sending iridescent rainbows and slabs of chocolate cake in Ilaria's direction." I sling an arm over Kiyo's shoulder, pushing her forward. Shock and indecision have glued her to the floor. "Let's let the two of them sort it out. Ilaria's a big girl. She can take of herself."

Kiyo gives the fishtail in my hair a teasing tug before agreeing. The faraway look is on her face again and now she's twisting her rings around like her skin is on fire. Her tell gets more pronounced every second we are here.

We have to pass through the main floor of the casino to get to the restaurant and my pupils have already dilated from the dim lights, my heart racing as it dances to the tune of the slot machines. There's a blackjack table only three feet away and my feet have been subconsciously drifting in that direction. I know she sees it because she silently steers us further away, onto the carpet that serves as a roadmap for minors cutting through the gaming floors. Placing her body in between mine and the bar.

She's not worried about Ilaria, she's worried about me. Because everything about our past tells her she should be. That she can't trust me. That she will never see me as an equal, let alone as someone that could be her partner in more than crime. Someone she could turn to for help, and comfort, when times get tough.

"You don't have to do that." I answer the questions she's too tactful to ask. The tables will always tempt me, like vengeful faeries luring unwary travelers to their deaths, but I won't answer their summons tonight. Not while Kiyo is with me. "I don't have time to gamble. I've got a fake girlfriend to entertain, remember? The offer to slide my tongue in your mouth to distract the reporters is still on the table, by the way."

Please, God, let her say yes.

Unfortunately, she smiles but the tension in her shoulders doesn't flag and her arm is exerting more pressure than is necessary on my waist. "Glad to see you're fully committed to the mission."

I want to say I'm fully committed to her, but the last time I got anywhere close to that kind of declaration she bolted towards some made-up meeting with the Ruby Appreciation Society. So I let her steer me towards dinner.

The table she has reserved for us is all the way in the back of the space station's fanciest restaurant, as far away from The Casino as possible. Any further and we'd be in the kitchen.

A wall of folding screens barricades our booth from the rest of the patrons. Ostensibly it's been set up to give us some privacy as we enjoy our romantic meal. A cozy place away from prying eyes for the two lovebirds to eat off each other's plates. Except we're not on an actual date.

The entire arrangement reeks of Kiyo. Of the way she had to shield me from the things that would trigger my impulses in the first few months after a detox. Prescreening any media for glimpses of drugs and alcohol, ordering in everything from groceries to furniture so we wouldn't pass the liquor store on trips out of the house. So that I wouldn't accidentally overdose like the last person she spent a night out with. She'd grown lax this year, but this barricaded meal signals the return of her paranoia with a vengeance.

"You didn't have to do this." I bite down the urge to tell her to take her overprotective dinner and shove it where the stars don't shine. That would be the shame talking. The fear that I'll never be anything more to her than the drunk wild woman she brought home with her that night. The penance she performs for a crime that wasn't her fault.

"Of course I did." She pats the seat next to her and motions for the waiter to light the candles on the table. "There's nothing I wouldn't do for you, Finley."

No step she won't take to save me from myself. Which is more than I deserve but so much less than what I want from her.

"I hear they have crème brûlée." I force myself to smile and look at the menu. I can't possibly hope for her to view me as anything other than a friend until I've given her a reason to. Better to keep things light until the heist is over. "Although after seeing Psylina eviscerate that chocolate mousse I'm looking at dessert in a whole new light."

Kiyo orders us dinner plus three different types of dessert – rewarding me for being a good girl and not asking to see the wine list. Either that or she's feeling guilty about us being in a casino in the first place. Kiyo always throws her money around like it's water when she's feeling guilty. As if she can spend her conscience away.

"You're the best girlfriend ever," I say as the waiter brings out a flaming plate of baked Alaska. The ice cream inside is pistachio. My favorite. "Psalome's got nothing on you."

Kiyo snorts through her seltzer but her eyes are dancing with mischief. She slides a small velvet box towards me with a smile. "Keep talking like that and maybe I *will* let you put your tongue in my mouth."

She's smiling too wide for it to be an actual offer. I'd have banged her in a heartbeat when we first met, but we've been together too long. Now I want so much more than sex. I want her to see me, every dark and fucked-up part of me, and to love me the way I love her.

"We're getting fake engaged?" I fall back on humor because it is safe for almost all occasions and for the first time in a long time I have zero idea what Kiyo is up to. "You could at least do something romantic and hide it in the lava cake like they do in the movies."

"Open it." Her eyes are locked on mine, unyielding and insistent. When Kiyo wants something, truly desires it with every fiber of her being, nobody can refuse her.

I comply, tipping back the lid and revealing a star ruby

set in a gold ring. It's the color of my new hair, flaming red and sparkling. I pick it up to watch the light play on its surface, appraising it like Kiyo taught me. I'm looking for the inclusions in the ruby but instead the engraving on the gold catches my eye.

*Happy two-year anniversary Finley*

"I thought you'd like it better than a sobriety chip," Kiyo explains. "It's more useful, too. You can wear it always and no one will ever know but us."

No one will ever know but us.

I look down to hide the tears in my eyes. Two years sober. In all the excitement I'd forgotten my anniversary was today, but Kiyo still remembered. She must have had the ring made weeks ago because she had faith I would make it this far. That I wouldn't backslide again despite being surrounded by the temptation.

Every day is a struggle but she's always right there in the trenches with me. She's given me so much and asked for so little in return.

"I'm proud of you, Finley Starchaser," she says, slipping the ring onto my finger. "I know I've been distant and wrapped up in my own issues, but I will always be here for you."

The name she gave me fits so much better than the one I wore for years as I bounced around from casino to casino looking for love at the bottom of a whiskey glass. I shouldn't have bothered, because love found me on its own and it is currently holding my hand over dinner. She may not know it, but I will love Kiyokimora GoldWeaver until the day I die and nothing is going to stop me from getting those earrings back and proving it to her.

# CHAPTER SIXTEEN

## Kiyokimora

"Kiyo?" Psylina's voice is a gnat buzzing in my ear. Frantic and rushed. "I need you on the main casino floor ASAP. Haul ass."

I itch my earlobe behind the pesky hollowed out diamonds. My ears aren't accustomed to the metals Psylina used when embedding the coms. Copper, tin and nickel. Cheap and highly allergenic. Never found in GoldWeaver products. A rash is developing on my tender cartilage. I applied hydrocortisone this morning, but it isn't helping.

I wish Psylina had asked me for help, or at least spare materials. I could have given her some platinum along with the diamonds. I never travel without it.

"Can't it wait?" I'm standing outside the high rollers' floor, decked out in a floor-length dress studded with rubies to attract photographers. It was Finley's idea to boost my image in case things get dicey when that video is released. At least there will be other, more flattering footage of me available.

"Finley's game starts in five minutes," I remind Psylina. You'd think she wasn't creepily monitoring every single one of us on the ubiquitous security cams. "I think she could use the moral support. Besides, I'm supposed to be her girlfriend.

How's it going to look if I never come to a single one of her games?"

My mother's voice tsks in my head. I'm giving too many reasons, letting myself babble. I should have simply said I wanted to attend the match and left it at that. Now Psylina will be suspicious. If she goes digging into Finley's old life, she'll find evidence of the addiction. I erased most of Finley's hospital stays and the rehab centers we patronized didn't leave paper trails, but we agreed not to tamper with her arrest records. Those were Halley's problem. It didn't seem worth committing a felony to have them erased from Finley's future.

Nobody was ever supposed to know they were the same person. Except Psalome, who somehow picked Finley out of a crowd based on the way she held her cards.

Finley has worked so hard to get to where she is now. The last thing she needs is Psylina dredging up old memories. It's bad enough she caught me discreetly removing all the alcohol from the mini bar and asking The Casino not to restock it.

"Finley will be fine without you," Psylina says in a tone that is gentler than anything I've ever heard her use with me before. "I have eyes on her at all times and I can prevent The Casino from bringing her anything to drink. So long as she is sitting at that gaming table, she won't relapse."

My heart flutters in relief and horror all at the same time. "How did you know?"

If I gave Finley away she might never forgive me.

"I grew up with an addict for a father, remember?" The bitter edge is back in Psylina's voice, as is the urgency. "I can spot one a mile away. I am also familiar with their tricks and triggers. You have nothing to worry about from Finley. Not while I'm watching her anyway."

I'm tempted to point out that her spectacular failure with

her father is what led to Psalome indenturing herself to The Casino in the first place, but it would be both unwise and untrue. Psylina was a child when her father gambled away their futures. I'm not certain what term to use for her now, but she is definitely no longer a child. And I am in her debt.

"Thank you."

Instead of acknowledging my rare expression of gratitude, Psylina huffs that I am not moving fast enough, going so far as to instruct me to wear more sensible shoes the next time I try to rob a casino.

I'm about to tell her to take her sensible shoes and shove them where the sun doesn't shine but given Psylina spends all of her time inside a spaceship docked on a space station that doesn't even have an artificial sun to orbit, I'm not sure there's a point.

I kick off my heels and sprint towards the lift, dodging a very perplexed-looking elderly couple and a boy with purple hair and the overindulged nonchalance of a teenager left to his own devices by parents who are off enjoying their vacation elsewhere in The Casino. Apparently, my dad isn't the only one that thinks a poker tournament is a suitable babysitter for his kid. I got left in casino hallways all the time when I was younger, too.

Psylina briefs me on the situation as the lift shoots down. Shaul is flirting aggressively with one of the Dazzle Girls and she is not enjoying his advances. The Casino is mobilizing several of their bodies to the area to evict him if he gets physical. Based on everything I know about him, that is a very real possibility.

"No chance he'll get a warning?" I ask. The Casino is protective of staff, but eviction on a first offense seems extreme.

"Shaul put his hands on Psalome uninvited," Psylina says

grimly. "The Casino was ready to throw him out then, but Psalome intervened. El's been looking for an excuse ever since."

The magnitude of this information has me tripping over myself to get out of the lift. The Casino isn't being extreme at all. Psalome is their top earner and the sister of the girl they're dating. If Shaul so much as insults this Dazzler he's going to be booted out the next airlock, along with any hope I have of getting my earrings back.

"How am I supposed to stop him this time?" I frantically jam my shoes back on. My big toe screams in protest. Psylina is right. I shouldn't have let Finley talk me into these shoes. "Shaul and I aren't exactly on chatting terms after the docking bay incident."

"You're not going near him." Psylina packs extreme condescension into every word. "Your job is to set off the smoke alarm and discreetly leave."

"Excuse me?" I ask, disbelief making me pause outside the gaming floor. "This isn't an elementary school assembly, Psylina. I can't simply pull a lever and set off a fire alarm."

"I know El's evacuation triggers and protocols better than I know the ones on my own ship." Psylina's voice is hard as diamond. It lashes out and cuts anyone foolish enough to question her. "They don't take risks when it comes to patrons. Any unanticipated smoke will set off the environmental hazard sensors and El will have no choice but to evacuate and investigate, separating Shaul from the Dazzle Girl."

The more she talks, the more impossible this plan becomes. As if she's daring me to question her again. I take the bait anyway. "And where's the smoke coming from, Psylina? I'm not a dragon."

This time Psylina doesn't bother to try and hide her glee. She giggles like a mischievous pixie and for a second I have a flash of the girl she might have been before her life went to shit. A girl that funneled her genius into playing pranks and building robots to chase her sister around the family spaceship because she liked to laugh. A girl that Psalome gave up everything to protect.

She's gone in an instant, replaced by the hard, jagged Psylina that is dating a computer and spends her days with wires and code because she doesn't trust people anymore.

"Ilaria will guide you through it. Isn't that right, Ilaria?"

There is a brief buzz of static as another party activates their audio and the com system adjusts to accommodate the additional background feedback.

"Smoke but no actual fire." Ilaria's voice is dull, like a bell made from rusted copper. It raises the hairs on the back of my neck. She's been itching to blow something up for days. There's no actual fire but this should still elicit some level of excitement from her.

"What's wrong?"

Psylina huffs about not having time for girl talk but Ilaria plows right in, eager to air her grievances. "Can we back up a second to the part where Shaul attacked Psalome? Why did nobody tell me about that? Am I just chopped liver to you people?"

Psylina heaves another sigh. "I was hoping you'd gloss over that. Look, Psalome is fine. Shaul grabbed her arm. That's all. She was intentionally pushing his buttons to facilitate placing a tracker on him. El was there the whole time. She was never in any danger."

"That's why he asked about her rates." Ilaria's voice is squeaky with panic. "Psylina, you have to make sure she says no. No matter how much he offers she can't–"

She's nearly on the verge of tears, the panic raising her voice to a fever pitch.

"Shhhhh," Psylina says. "I was there the entire time, too. Psalome told Shaul to go fuck himself. She has very strict criteria about taking money for sex and they include not being a blackmailing spouse abuser seeking to use sex to assert dominance. Unless she has indicated otherwise to you?"

"Right. Of course. Sorry." Ilaria's voice is firmer now, almost embarrassed by her overreaction. She speeds on to change the topic. "Based on the footage Psylina has shared with me, our best chance is a chemical bomb. You'll need to swipe a couple of cold packs from one of the ice buckets that carry the champagne."

I can't help but feel a little disappointed that Ilaria was so worried about Psalome's interactions with Shaul she almost burst into tears, yet she does not seem to care one whit about flinging me into his path. I'm going to mull that over when this immediate danger has passed and Finley and I are tucked safely into our room, far away from the alcohol and lecherous husbands turned conmen.

I veer towards the nearest drink station and order a complicated cocktail. While the bartender is busy mixing it, I slip my hand into the ice bucket, flinching as I brush past a layer of fresh ice cubes and dig deeper. No gemstone was ever recovered without a little mining first. The ice packs are layered on the bottom. I slip a few into my purse just in time to accept my drink, leave an overly generous tip, and walk away with a smile.

"How did you know those were in there?" I discreetly dump the beverage into the nearest potted plant. The last thing Finley needs is to smell alcohol on me. "I thought it was all ice."

"Ice is expensive." Ilaria's voice is blasé, matter of fact. "I highly doubt The Casino would spend the money for refrigeration when a little potassium nitrate does the same job. Saves on the water waste, too."

I flush under my makeup. Even Ilaria, from a planet so insular she thought movies were actual home video recordings when she first arrived on my estate, knows more than I do about practical things like water recycling and the price of ice.

This venture is pointing out some of the more gaping holes in my private tutor driven education. Things I thought I'd managed to suss out years ago. Finley's teased me about it from time to time, but I never listened. Never valued her advice as much as I should. Because I'm supposed to be the knowledgeable one in our relationship. Only now do I realize how much she's actually been shielding me during our adventures together.

Finley packs a cooler full of beverages every time we dock and stocks the mini fridge in the ship herself, too. For all I know we don't use real ice either, except for the cubes she slips into my glass because I can't drink water without them. I'd have dehydrated on the flight here without her. How many thousands of little things a day does she take care of so that I don't have to?

It's too humiliating to think about. Too reminiscent of me being the only person in the universe unable to spot the signs of a Euphoria high on my boyfriend. Luckily there's a distraction currently burning a hole in my pocket in the form of two potassium nitrate ice packs.

"What am I supposed to do with these things anyway?"

A lady wearing so much perfume I can smell nothing but lavender as she walks by gives me the side eye. Probably wondering why I am talking to the foliage. I bat my eyelashes at her, patting the plant affectionately. She clutches her rhinestone purse to her chest muttering about youth these days as she sashays by in a haze of floral scented self-righteousness.

The Elysium does a brisk business in hallucinogens. If I'm the weirdest thing this lady has seen then she is in for a serious surprise when the lights go dim in a few hours to signal the start of the adult only hours on the main gaming floors.

"Find one of the specialty stations, where Dazzlers light drinks on fire for their flashier guests. Grab some sugar on the way."

"Back corner on the far left," Psylina chimes in. "It's directly below the smoke sensors. Hustle. El spotted you getting cozy with that tree and is preparing to send someone over to ask if they can offer you assistance. They don't like to leave their wealthier clients unattended amongst the decorative ferns."

I swerve in and out of the rows of slot machines, pretending to stumble into a man drinking coffee while playing Bingo Slots.

"I'm so sorry," I say, swiping all of his sugar packets as I feign concern over his spilled beverage. "These are new shoes, hardly broken in yet. I keep tripping over my own two feet."

"Don't apologize at all," he says, ruddy cheeks breaking into a smile. "Always good to see a pretty girl wearing even lovelier shoes. You can bump into me any day."

I cringe as I extricate myself from his grasp. His hands are moist and his eyes overeager. They ask things from me I do not want to give. For a brief moment I freeze, wondering if this is how every person in the galaxy will look at me from now on once that video is released. Like they can see me naked any time they want, just by hitting play. Like I owe them something because of it.

I shake myself loose and hurry over to the drink station. Because what I saw reflected in that man's eyes cannot be allowed to control me. That video is releasing one way or the other and I refuse to allow that to become my life.

"Now what?" I bark, all efficiency and purpose. I will not be useless. Not today.

"Dump six packets of sugar and one of nitrite into the silver bucket then get the hell out of there." It's borderline profanity coming from Ilaria.

I do exactly as I'm told, dumping the packets and fleeing for the exits without waiting for the results. I'm outside in seconds, having eluded the Dazzler that The Casino sent after me and the creepy slots guy. Unfortunately, my relief is short-lived.

"Uhm, ladies?" I inquire from the safety of the hallway. "Nothing appears to be happening."

"Wait for it." Ilaria is practically purring in my ear, the excitement in her voice palpable over the coms. "One of the Dazzlers has to put their lighter into the bucket to set the reaction in motion. Someone's mixing a drink right now. Shouldn't be longer than a few—"

Her voice is cut off as screams and smoke start pouring out of the room.

"Works every time," she says triumphantly as The Casino's many bodies start ushering guests out. I wait to confirm that Shaul is among them before I fade into the background. A disgruntled Dazzler emerges directly behind him and wastes no time heading to the other side of the room, loudly complaining to a male Dazzler about how they all work extra shifts when demanding tournament clientele are on board.

Crisis averted.

"Security footage shows Kiyo disposing of the stained coffee napkins on the tray and no explosion for a full three minutes until after she left," Psylina breathes in awe. "El will think the torch cut into one of the packets by accident. Ilaria, you are an artist."

"You should see me actually blow something up."

Her voice is smug, and I wonder if she is prouder of the explosion or the fact that she is messing with Shaul. Every day that we spend here Ilaria seems to come more into her own in a way that never seemed possible in the months we spent on my estate. She's even voluntarily wearing some of the clothes Finley bought her. Trying them on like new personalities, deciding if the person she wants to be is the type to wear sequin halter tops or flannel tie front dresses.

I click off my com and head straight for the penthouse, but Finley's game is over by the time I arrive and there's no trace of her. I ask a nearby spectator what happened and they grin, informing me that my girlfriend is the most devious poker player this side of Henta 5.

"Didn't you know?" they ask.

"Of course," I say as I step away. "Finley has always been special."

So special I sometimes wonder what she's doing with me. How long she'll stay and brighten my life when she's healed enough from her addiction that she no longer needs me or my money and she chooses to leave. How I'll get by when she's gone.

I head back to our room where I scrub my skin raw in the shower as I wait for her to come home. It does me no good. I can still feel that man's eyes on my body, peeling off my clothes layer by layer, mentally violating me over and over. It only stops when I hear Finley's heels clicking through the door.

She is my light in dark places. I need this plan to work so that I can keep my company. Because without it I'm not sure that I can keep her and then the darkness will come for us both.

# CHAPTER SEVENTEEN

### Psalome

ILARIA DOESN'T SAY much over the next day and a half, but she asks me to play the piano for her a few times. Once she even joins me for a duet. I get the sense that Psylina put her up to it – the two of them were whispering furtively yesterday – but I'm not going to investigate. It might scare her off and I like the way her hands fly across the keys next to mine. When she makes a mistake and our hands crash into each other she actually blushes.

It's good not to be the only one that blushes.

She's sitting on the bench now, waiting for me, and my head fills with visions of sitting down next to her and playing something soft and romantic. Maybe inching my way a little closer than necessary to where she is sitting so I can feel her hair tickling my skin. Letting myself pretend I'm on a date, that I'm free to do things like date.

Instead, I shake my head no. Because I'm not free and neither is she. I'm shackled to this job and she's chained to the man who refuses to divorce her. She'll never be comfortable getting married again without a religious divorce, never able to return home without looking over her shoulder and worrying he's going to find out she's still alive. The only way out of this for both of us is to focus on the plan at hand. I can't afford to be catching feelings right now.

"Sorry," I mumble. "Three surprise bookings came in. People are flocking from all over to gawk at Finley and Kiyo. Word got out that the rich lovebirds have booked an hour a night with me and now I'm an even hotter ticket than usual. Between the people looking for information about Kiyo and the tournament players who think I'm Finley's good luck charm, we were able to raise my rates by twenty percent."

Ilaria's hands drop, making an ominous sound as they hit the keys. She doesn't look up, doesn't let me see her expression.

"I thought you were fully booked."

"I was. Psylina had to cut my mealtimes in half and shave an hour off the rest times, too, in order to accommodate the demand. Sorry if I fall asleep on you during dinner or something."

Sorry I'm such a disaster of a companion. Sorry I have nothing to offer you except the fact that I like having you around and you make me all squishy inside. Sorry I can't actually tell you any of that.

"That hardly seems fair to you."

I wish she'd say it hardly seems fair to her, that she's bored without me. Some tiny hint that she enjoys my company, too, but I'm sure she'll find something more interesting to do than talking to my bumbling self. Most days, when we're not at the piano, we've been watching a live feed of Finley and Shaul's matches from my room. It's not like I've been contributing much to the conversation. Ilaria does the bulk of the talking or we sit in silence, me trying not to stare too hard at her hair or her eyes.

Lately all I do is try. Try not to take her hand in mine and tell her I think she's brave and beautiful and deserves so much more than what life has given her. Try not to tell her that I'd love the chance to get to know her more so that maybe, just maybe, I could be the one to give those things to her. Try to forget it all so I can pull off this job and get the fuck out of here without losing any more pieces of myself than I already have.

"It's temporary," I say instead. "The Casino knows about all the inquiries and Psylina is attempting to keep them from getting suspicious. I rarely turn down the chance to make more money and pay off my debt faster."

"No, I suppose there's not much you won't do for money," Ilaria says, as she stomps towards the bedroom, reminding me of what my job entails. Of the ultimatum I gave Psylina. Of the fact that my time, my body, can be bought by anyone with the cash to spare but not given freely to a person like her. "I guess I'll wait in here until it's time for me to be let out of my cage. Unless someone decides they want to pay for *higher level services*. I can just throw myself out the airlock to make space for your *paying clients*. I won't mess up the sheets or anything. Don't let me get in your way."

It hits me like a punch to the gut. I feel the fire rising to my cheeks and I sit down on the couch with a shocked thud. She's never judged me before. Never raised her voice. Never insinuated that I am a horrible host, let alone a whore.

Both of which are true. Sure, I might not have sex with my clients, but that's only because of Psylina, and I do pretty much everything else. And Ilaria's been in there listening to me and my clients all week. Cooped up in my room like a bird in a gilded cage. She gets out for a few hours a day and I'm cutting that in half to make more money.

Stands to reason she might be tired of being treated like a pariah just because she doesn't have the money to pay for my time. Because my time isn't mine, not really.

I scratch at my skin, which has become unbearably itchy, as

if I haven't showered for days. Then I rake my painted nails through my hair so hard little bits of scalp flake off.

How much else will I sacrifice on the altar of my father's debt? What else will this job take from me before it's done?

My door clicks open as the first tear leaks out the corner of my eye. I blink rapidly to clear it and look up expecting to find The Casino on a routine cleaning sweep, only to see Psylina staring down at me with a scowl. She's the only other person with the access code.

"What's wrong?"

"Nothing," I say, rearranging my features into a pleasant smile. I've been turning off my audio feed when it is only me and Ilaria in the room, mostly because Psylina has been teasing me mercilessly, but also because if I did manage to successfully flirt with Ilaria I wouldn't want her overhearing it.

Psylina is busy enough orchestrating this plan. The incident with Shaul and the other Dazzler has worn on her nerves. She only sleeps when he does, using the bug I planted to monitor his every move. She's working so hard to keep track of all the moving parts there are hollow circles beneath her eyes. Meanwhile I'm here laughing and chatting with clients like an overpriced, overindulged doll. The less she knows about my fight with Ilaria the better.

*Be marble*, I remind myself. *Do not burden Psylina with your personal issues. She needs to focus on freeing you. Be marble.*

"Liar." Psylina flops down next to me. She could see right through me when we were twelve and she still can. It's like a sisterly superpower that has only gotten stronger with the passage of time. "You look like crap. Spill it."

Never in all my life has anyone accused me of looking like crap. It's nothing more than Psylina's usual disregard for social niceties but tonight it feels wrong. Like Psylina is taking away the last shred of dignity I have left. Because we've already stripped away my music, my freedom and my ability to have any kind of normal relationship. My pretty face is the last thing I've got left.

"Why would you care?" I ask. Hurt and frustration trump my desire to keep Psylina focused on the plan. "It's not a piece of broken code, or some new circuit board for you to rewire. It's just your silly older sister and her pesky feelings getting in your way again."

Just like I'm always getting in her way with El. My very existence is a barrier between them. The contract forcing me to stay here and work my ass off in a job I find demeaning but pretend to tolerate is the guilty little secret that none of us ever talks about.

And I am sick of not talking about it. Of burying all this shit under layers of further shit until nobody even remembers how it all started. Because I remember and so should she.

Ilaria isn't the only one spoiling for a fight. I've had enough of Psylina and her know-it-all attitude, pretending she's the martyr in this situation because I'm insisting she participate in order to get me out, even though it puts her precious Casino in the cross hairs.

I'm so angry I could smash every piece of furniture in this room and still not be done. I wonder if this is how Dad felt, when he went on his rages. Desperate to prove to someone, anyone, that he was in control of his life and not simply some puppet dancing on a string.

The thought is sobering. I curl my fists into balls and blow out a long breath through my nose to keep the rage bottled in. To prevent myself from becoming like him. Because I am marble.

"You should go. I have clients coming."

Psylina bristles, laying her tablet down on the table and

fixing me with her cat's eye stare. It pins me to the couch. Lays me bare in a way nudity never could. Fuck.

If she was the older sister, I bet we wouldn't be in this mess. She wouldn't have let Dad go to ruin when Mom died. She wouldn't have let him gamble away everything we owned to the point where the only thing I'd have left to call my own was my body and I had to put that up as collateral to keep our home and get him out of our lives.

No, Psylina has grown into a force to be reckoned with. She wouldn't have put up with Dad's crap. She would have known what to do to free us of him, just like she knows what to do now. Even after I've yelled at her and insulted her, she knows exactly what to say to bring me back to reality.

"Ilaria?"

With one little word she reminds me that I am simply a pent-up ball of frustration looking to take it out on someone that I know will never stop loving me. The weight of all the things I want, but cannot have, is enough to drag the entire space station out of orbit.

"I don't think I can do this anymore," I whisper. "Not with her involved. Not the way you want. She said… she said…"

I can't get the rest of the words out. My time with Ilaria has been awkward but it was still mine. Even if we never moved past friendship, those memories are bright and pure. A brief respite in my daily slog, untouched by this place and my past. At least they were, before tonight. Before Ilaria started insinuating I would do anything for money but nothing for kinder motives. That I'm not worthy of love because I sell it.

The hysterical sobbing that has been building up in my chest ever since Ilaria stormed out is like a pool of lava pushing against a mountain top. I don't want to contain it anymore. Don't want to control the fall out.

Ilaria is a munitions expert after all, this woman I'm so

hopelessly destroyed over. It only seems fitting she has me ready to explode, too. She's detailed to me the million and one ways my cosmetics could be used to blast our way out of here in case of emergency. Never mind that fire on a space station is almost as unthinkable as me actually having a girlfriend who doesn't run the minute she finds out what my job is the way Giuiana did when I signed a contract to become a Dazzler. I'd asked her to stay with me and she'd turned me down. Hopped onto the nearest transport ship without so much as waiting to hear what terms I'd set or telling me goodbye.

Girlfriends aren't for the likes of me. Certainly not religious Jewish ones with the most adorable smattering of freckles across their noses and a laugh that reminds me of the sunshine I so rarely get to see in person.

Psylina sighs and folds me in her arms. The tears drip down my face and onto her shirt. It's stupid. I don't even know if Ilaria is capable of thinking about a woman that way, let alone the woman that's been unable to hold a conversation with her for the past week. The one that entertains other people at all hours of the day and night instead of spending time getting to know her. But when Ilaria sits and plays with me on the piano I can imagine I'm someone else, somewhere else, and the two of us actually have a chance at being together.

Yesterday she edged closer to me when I corrected her hand positioning, smiling up at me with those big silver eyes as if she was asking me to bridge all the distance between us, and it made me think she wanted all the things I want, but have been too afraid to ask for.

"You can and you will," Psylina says, wiping the smudged mascara off my face. "Because the alternative you presented is not an option. My plan isn't asking anything from you that you haven't done every other night since you got here. Only now you have extra motivation to do it well. Because if you get the job done, this one last time, then life can go back to normal."

She's touching up my makeup with a compact she pulled out of her back pocket. Psylina is always prepared for stuff like this. My meltdowns. She's so cool and level-headed, nothing like this ever happens to her. Which is why she's failing to understand that nothing will ever be normal for me again. Not after my face has been plastered across the galaxy as part of The Casino's latest advertising campaign.

What kind of life is waiting for me out there?

"It doesn't work that way," I say. Each dab of her makeup brush is like a stab poking at my wounded pride. Concealing my true self beneath layers of paint and varnish until I don't recognize my own face anymore. "I can't just turn it on and off. Can't pretend tonight is like every other night. Because when she's here, I'm not myself. Or maybe I'm more myself. The real Psalome, the one that's all fucked up inside, instead of the cool and composed Dazzler. She makes me want to be that person, flaws and all, in the hopes that someone else might see me and love me despite everything. To form a real human connection. You wouldn't understand."

The minute the words are out I want to cram them back in, but I know it's too late. Psylina's body is stiffening, her hands poking harshly as she finishes painting my mascara.

"Because I'm satisfied with something made of wires and metal?" She shuts the wand back into the vial with a click. Her lower lip twists into a knot of disapproval. "You think because I don't want to rip The Casino's clothes off and fuck them all night long I can't possibly understand what it's like to be in love? To care for someone else that way?"

There's ice in her voice but she won't give in to the rage. It's not her way. Psylina has never tolerated unplanned drama from anyone, including herself. She takes her time. Finishing my makeup in silence and sealing up the compact before pulling away.

"I've been in love for a lot longer than you've had this mindless infatuation, Psalome." She crosses her arms over her chest and our mother stares back at me from behind Psylina's eyes. Disappointed. Pitying. It bites worse than our father's fury ever did. "My relationship with El may not be easy for you to understand, but that doesn't make it any less real. In fact, I'd argue it's significantly more real than this little cat and mouse game you've got going with Ilaria. The Casino is a complex, dynamic entity. They understand me in a way no one ever has. Why can't you see that?"

I assume she includes me in the group of people that can't understand her in the way only a computer can. It burns its way through my body, leaving a path of shame that snakes from my pounding head to my overtired feet. All I've ever done is try to protect her, but it's never been enough. Because I never truly protected her in the way The Casino can. Maybe that's why she loves them more than me. Why they will forgive everything for her, but not my debt.

The same Casino that she loves has taken everything from me. My father, my freedom, Giuiana and now Ilaria. Did they really have to take my sister, too? Would I have made this bargain all those years ago if I knew Psylina would fall for them?

"I can see you would choose them over me." It's petty, but lately I've had my doubts about her priorities. Because despite what she thinks, I can acknowledge that Psylina really does love them. Maybe more than she loves the person I've become these past few years. "You designed this entire plan around them, so that you could protect them, meanwhile it's taking everything away from me."

"It's giving everything to you," she hisses. "If you could get your head out of your ass for more than ten seconds you would see that. Once you're free you can be with anyone you like. And you shouldn't have to fuck some random person to achieve that."

She's standing up now, pacing the room.

"Pull yourself together and play nice with your guest." Her voice is glacial. Her hands are rough as she fixes my hair. "In case you've forgotten, we have a robbery to pull off tomorrow, and we need her help."

# CHAPTER EIGHTEEN

## Ilaria

MOST OF THE conversation is muffled but I can hear Psalome sobbing through the door that separates the two rooms. At least I think it's Psalome. I can't imagine either of the Shipmen sisters crying, but of the two, Psalome seems the more likely candidate. Especially after what I said to her before I stormed out.

Guilt smothers me, filling my lungs like dust from a newly blasted mine when I've forgotten to wear my safety gear. Zaide would be ashamed. I've been an ungrateful, unkind and troublesome guest. Needling my host in all her soft places to prove I could draw blood.

Not only were my words harsh, they were also unfair. Worse than transgressing through lashon hara, speaking evil of others, I've gone and landed straight in lying territory. Motzi Shemra. Painting Psalome as evil when really the true sinner is me, for the way I have treated her.

Psalome is nothing if not upfront and honest with her clients and she has been unfailingly gentle with me. I've watched her these past few days when she thinks nobody is looking. She lists her prices upfront, never pushes a client to spend more than they can afford and never once leads them on. Her salon is probably the safest place for them in the entire Casino.

It certainly is for me.

I'm the one that isn't being truthful. I'm lying to myself if I claim my outburst was about Psalome's relationship with her clients or The Casino being an immoral, hedonistic institution. I'm grasping for things that aren't there to stop my eyes from turning inward. I'm jealous that clients will have her attention, greedy for things I have no right to want. Yet here I am, clearly wanting.

I want Psalome to myself. Want her in a way I did not think it was possible to want another human being again after my failure of a marriage. When I'm with Psalome, it's like I'm an explosion waiting to be set off and when I'm without her the world is a little darker, a little lonelier.

I don't know if it's love yet, that's going to take some time, but I know I have feelings towards her and they are making me act irrationally. Making me forget what I'm here for.

Everyone on Thillov talked about love as something that happened after you were married. All I needed was a nice young man to settle down with and the rest would come later. My dreams consisted of cooking this nebulous person dinner and raising several well-dressed kids who the neighbors would envy. When Shaul appeared, I figured why not him? Those dimples paired with that thick dark hair certainly fit into my picture of the perfect little family.

Except the rest of the family never came and neither did the love. For either of us.

A part of me still wants that happy domestic life, but now the dream is altered. When I close my eyes and picture my future it's Psalome sitting across from me at the dinner table and she doesn't mind that I like blowing stuff up and sometimes burns the toast. She likes that I want to travel around the galaxy instead of staying on Thillov forever and plays duets with me on the piano instead of calling it "an artsy waste of time" like Shaul did.

She doesn't make me ashamed of the things I want or the ways in which I'm different. She hasn't even guilted me about my past. Hasn't talked about it unless I have offered. Yet I've gone and done that very thing to her.

I pace around the room, trying to see a way through the mess I'm in. It's possible I'm imagining everything. Psalome's trained to please her clients. Her kindness, her interest in me, might simply be part of the heist. A way to keep the wheels oiled on the squeaky cart that is my soul.

How am I supposed to figure out if any of what I'm feeling is real? As Finley would say, I'm royally screwed.

Well, Finley would probably say "fucked," but I'm still not comfortable cursing yet. You can take the girl out of Thillov but you can't take Thillov out of the girl. Kiyo would encourage me to see the strength in that. To pave a way for my unique perspectives to influence my new life. To seize control of my past and use it to create something of my own.

That's what she dreams of accomplishing with her company, murderous sex video or not. Adding her own mark to the legacy left by her mother and grandmother rather than focusing solely on profits like her father does. Her ability to build something meaningful, incorporating GoldWeaver tradition while still looking towards the future, is what my husband's exploitation is slowly crushing.

I'm still discovering all of the things he took from me. Each day brings a new devastating surprise. This business with Psalome, for instance. I've never been in a normal relationship. How am I supposed to know if she and I have the potential to form one with each other? If I can trust my instincts about her? I hate that Shaul took that from me.

Because I really, truly, do not care about Psalome's job or her dad or whatever ugly monsters lived in her past. I care about how I feel when I'm with her – like I am the most important person in the universe. Like I matter. Like I am truly seen. I care about how I never want that feeling to stop.

Which is what I should have told her instead of pretending I thought her job was beneath me.

My eyes alight on the dinner trays that we were supposed to eat together before I had my hissy fit. I really am the worst possible guest.

Psalome hasn't eaten since this morning, and I've been holding her food hostage. I can hear the first few clients arriving outside, a boisterous group full of laughter and spirits. They might offer her something to drink, which she will graciously accept despite having no intentions of consuming, because she makes a commission on liquor sales. They will never think to offer her food, none of her clients do, even though they've agreed in advance to pay for her meals.

Instead, she has to shove a few bites into her mouth in between bookings while The Casino cleans her room. She tries to check on me during those precious few minutes, too, despite the fact that I can see the exhaustion creeping into her eyes behind all the makeup and fake smiles. It's lucky the tournament is tomorrow night, because I don't think she can keep going at this rate for much longer.

Maybe there's still time for us to have a meal together. For me to apologize and clear the air before the heist proceeds. Her clients are jam-packed, but there has to be space in there somewhere.

I move the trays over to the table and lay out the silverware like I was taught to do at home. Knife on the right above the napkin, forks on the left with the littlest one on the outer edge. Then I take the vase of artificial flowers from her nightstand and plunk it down in the center of the table.

I didn't cook and this is a far cry from what polite society on Thillov would consider a normal dating situation, but it'll do. It'll have to. Because it's what I've got. I have nothing to offer her but myself, and maybe that's how it should be. Maybe the rest doesn't actually matter.

The only thing left to do now is wait. And pray. Because I still believe in God and if ever I could use their help it is now.

I flop down on the bed, only to jump up when I remember that Psalome's dress for the tournament tomorrow night is there, carefully hand delivered and laid out by The Casino. It is made entirely of lace so delicate I'm worried I'll break it if I so much as breathe on it. It contrasts sharply with the ruffled gingham dress I am wearing now. A dress I brought from home. It's cute, with little floral details on the long sleeves and a hem that brushes the bottom of my knees, but it's not exactly worldly. Not something I'd expect to see on a girl with the guts to ask Psalome Shipmen, the most sought-after Dazzler in the galaxy, out on a date.

I've experimented with some of the dresses Finley bought me, a floor-length metallic sheath dress that was so tight I couldn't breathe in it properly and a scarlet taffeta number bedazzled with gold stars that was so flashy I felt like I glowed in the dark. There are a few more, plus the jumpsuit I wore here originally, but I doubt I'll be comfortable wearing any of them.

She chose them especially for me, and I can't deny they fit like second skins, but somehow none of them have felt right. They don't reflect who I am. But this dress, while eminently more breathable, doesn't reflect who I want to be. I wasn't raised to be vain, but I want Psalome to see me in something that speaks to my potential, not my past. Something that highlights how much I've grown and changed thanks to her friendship. How much I hope to continue the process of deciphering who I am without my family, my husband, and my planet confusing the situation.

Maybe some combination of things from home and from here?

I punch in the closet key code and the wood paneling glides open to reveal racks upon racks of Psalome's glittery, shiny clothes. She's cleared an entire corner especially for me, my clothes hanging limply on their half-empty rack, while hers are all stuffed to capacity.

A garment bag that I do not recognize has been hung in front with a note tacked onto it. It's one of those small white envelopes favored by florists and gift shops. Probably for Psalome. A gift from another mysterious admirer delivered by The Casino. I hope she gets commission on everything people buy for her in The Casino's shops, because this is not an infrequent occurrence.

I intend to move the bag to its proper place but when I reach out to lift it up, I notice the name on the card is mine.

Who would leave a dress for me? Finley and Kiyo already bought me plenty of clothes that I am not wearing and nobody else besides the Shipmen sisters knows that I am here. This is not Psalome's flowery, looping handwriting. That only leaves one option. The script is small and direct, block letters that march across the paper with uniform precision. Definitely Psylina.

I snatch the envelope off the dress and tear it open. Two slips of plain ruled paper slide out.

I suppose Psylina isn't the type to keep a scented stationery collection for such purposes. I blush a little when I remember that I had such a collection for years. I even ordered monogrammed cards for myself and Shaul. Our thank you notes were mailed within days of the wedding. In the aftermath of his departure, I burned the remaining cards with homemade lighter fluid.

The first slip of paper is a detailed reminder of the plan for tomorrow tonight. Swap out the earrings, provide a distraction, meet up in the cargo bay. It should be easy enough, once Finley and Psalome are in place, but my palms grow sweaty. What if it all goes wrong and we're caught? Will they return me to Shaul? Will I be stuck on Thillov forever under his thumb?

It's not a risk I relish, but I need to see this through. To give myself a chance at a new life without the specter of all his past victims hanging over me. For Kiyo and Finley to move ahead with their plans for her company. Most of all, for Psalome to be free.

This plan has to work. Because there is no way any of us is going back to the way life was before.

I flip to the second page, expecting a warning not to blow anything up or damage The Casino. Instead, I find she has switched from print to cursive and drawn a single rose on top of the page. The petals unfurl like flags in the wind and the stem twines around to form my initials.

I hadn't realized Psylina was an artist.

*I see the way you look at my sister.*
*It's the same way she looks at you.*
*Please go easy on her. She's out of practice.*
*Wear the dress, it'll help you both.*

Not quite a poem, but coming from Psylina it might as well be a sonnet. I snort back my disbelief at the implication that Psalome has been secretly pining after me in silence. Then, I laugh at the absurdity of Psylina telling me to go easy on the world's most skilled Dazzle Girl. But when I unzip the garment bag the laughter freezes in my throat, replaced by a sharp inhale.

The dress is red silk, held together by silver clasps that trail from the shoulders to the neckline and then down the front where they meet in a v that's low enough to show off some skin, but not so low that I'll be uncomfortable wearing it. It's pretty, but what takes my breath away are the silver and gold studs that snake up from around the hemline. They send a swirl of fire through the silk. The designer was probably attempting a sunset theme, but they've managed to create an explosion.

I have never owned anything so utterly perfect. So completely suited to my taste. So effortlessly encapsulating the very essence of who I am, as if my soul has been woven into the fabric and then sewn together with threads spun from my memories.

Psylina must have chosen it herself.

I slip it on and look at myself in the mirror. It would be wrong to say I have transformed, because, in fact, what I have done is simply embraced more of myself, but the change is obvious. I'm surer in my steps, more confident.

Psylina is right. If Psalome really is interested in me that way, and I'm still not quite willing to believe that's possible, then this dress will definitely help us both move away from our current awkward host and guest small talk and into a more romantic zone.

After I apologize, of course.

I carefully zip it away in the bag, walk out of the closet, and wait for Psalome to finish with her clients. When she opens that door, I'm not letting her leave without accepting my apology. Then tomorrow I'll put on the dress and see where it takes me.

Or, more accurately, where it takes us both. Because one thing is for certain, I can't fly home without telling her how I feel.

As my Zaide would say, the best guests leave something behind for their hosts.

# CHAPTER NINETEEN

Psylina

THE CASINO IS knocking on the door of the ship when I return from my latest planning excursion. I've been leaving the ship frequently these past few days, double checking that everything is in place for tonight. It has necessitated giving El a string of excuses flimsier than one of Psalome's evening dresses as I cancelled all of our plans. I was careful to avoid all the security cameras, but they must have been suspicious.

They are carrying a silver tray and wearing my favorite suit, the one with a silver button-down shirt and metallic blue undertone to the jacket. We picked it out together from a fashion display last year. I can hear their knocks across the cargo bay as they pound on my door.

"Psylina," they say, voice channeling the perfect pitch and intonation to connote sadness. "Please, let me in. I am worried about you. It has been four days. I simply want to know you are all right."

My heart squishes in my chest. They're not suspicious. They're concerned about my health and safety. I've been neglecting them in order to keep my eye on Finley and Shaul's games, not to mention ensuring the rest of this crew doesn't self-implode. I never imagined they might miss me the way normal couples miss each other. The way I've been missing them.

It delights and saddens me all at once. I've been so busy micromanaging everyone else's relationships I've completely ignored my own. I am a shit girlfriend.

I walk across the cargo bay quietly, unsure how to proceed. We've never had secrets from each other before. The lies I've told fester between us, like the decaying organic matter in the ship composter, souring the air.

"I'm right here, El."

They turn around, smiling for all the world like a small child, even though they've never been one. Never even seen one up close. Babysitting services are the one thing they don't offer here. Anyone younger than twelve can't set foot past the docking bay.

"Psylina!" they say, taking a step forward. "Are you well? You missed routine maintenance again. You have never missed routine maintenance. I was worried you might be ill."

They hold out the tray as I unlock the door and we enter the airlock.

It's heavier than I expected and I stagger beneath the weight. I lift the lid and the strong aroma of spices and broth bathes my face in warmth, pulling up memories of my mom tending to me when I was ill. Her voice crooning from the kitchen as she stirred a pot and sang me a lullaby all at the same time.

"Chicken soup?" El's brought me plenty of gifts over the years, chocolate covered strawberries, flowers, even a decorative statue of an iguana once. Things their human behavior and relationships algorithm predicted I would respond favorably to. None of them has ever managed to reduce me to a trembling, sentimental mess the way this soup does. I can practically feel my usual self rolling her eyes at the mist that is creeping into the eyes of my current self.

I blink it away. It's steam from the soup. Nothing more.

"Is chicken soup not what humans eat when they are sick?" El asks. Their face goes blank for a nanosecond as they search their databases for confirmation. "I didn't know what the proper etiquette was. You've never been sick before. I wanted to help."

It should be the sweetest thing I've ever heard. Except I can't afford sweet right now. I'm trying to orchestrate a robbery inside El's walls and one false step will give the entire thing away. I need them blissfully unconcerned over my existence, not doting over me like a concerned grandmother, watching my every move like a hawk. It's a small miracle I haven't slipped up and gotten caught on the security cameras yet.

One more night. That's all I need. Then we can put this, and Psalome's contract, behind us. Then we can finally move forward without the gravitational pull of my father's debt weighing us down like a ship trying to break orbit without thrusters. All I need is to help them release my sister in a way that is acceptable to their programming.

"I'm perfectly fine," I say, placing the cover back on the dish, trapping the smell inside where it cannot stir up my memories or my guilt. "You're getting paranoid in your old age."

"I see," El says, retreating towards the back of the room. Their face is smooth but the flash of light in their glimmering eyes means they are calculating a particularly difficult problem. It's impossible to insult them, I've certainly tried and failed in the past, but confusing them serves the same purpose. Makes them retreat into their circuitry until they have found a solution to the issue.

They emerge again after a few minutes like a turtle poking out of its shell. "Have I offended you in some way? I have replayed all our interactions and upgraded my human relations protocols, but I can't find anything amiss. I am not human, Psylina, but I am trying. I do not know how to apologize for something I am not aware I did."

If they only knew how human they sounded right now. Every client that Psalome has ever ghosted when they got too attached has asked her the same question. Of course, since I handle her bookings and her mail, I'm the one that did the ghosting. And I never answer. My poor sap of a sister would never jeopardize revenue by thinking of her own safety, nor would she have the heart to turn someone away.

I'm the stone-cold buffer between us and the world. So why are my legs turning to jelly as I listen to El's pleas for help and understanding?

"You didn't do anything wrong," I say, relenting. The walls I've built up around myself are folding like a house of cards in a hailstorm, ravaged by the vortex of El's burgeoning emotions. If I try to lie again the entire thing will collapse around me. Better to use the truth, albeit a different truth than the one El is seeking.

"It's Psalome. As I mentioned earlier, she's made a new friend and, well, it's bringing up some unpleasant emotions. I can't upgrade my human relations software the way you can."

I'm hoping it'll get them to back off and things can go back to normal. El usually gives me my space when it comes to emotions. They don't have much experience with them and everything relating to Psalome has always been a minefield for the two of us.

I'm not prepared for them to glide over and take my hand in theirs. It's surprisingly warm and they are stroking my palm while gazing into my eyes.

"Perhaps I can help you." They slide one hand up my arm and let it linger on my face as they pull me closer. "I have made significant upgrades in your absence these past few days. We can enjoy them together."

They stare at my face as if the mysteries of the universe are written on my mouth. Curious. Open. Hungry.

What. The. Fuck?

"El, what are you doing?" I gasp. I wrench my hand out of theirs and scoot as far back as I can. I graze their shoulder on my way and it is suspiciously warm, like a human body. They normally don't have heating coils anywhere other than their hands. "Exactly what kind of upgrades did you install?"

"I told you," they say, leaning forward so I can smell the aftershave they have applied despite the fact that it is physically impossible for them to grow facial hair. "Human relations. Plus some hardware to make a few of my synthetic bodies more humanoid in nature. I thought you might like it."

"Do I look like I like it?" How the fuck did I miss this? I've been so wrapped up in my plan I completely ignored the fact that El was coming apart at the seams, transforming themselves into something they are not in an attempt to please me. Now they are sliding a pre-warmed hand up my trousers and smiling lasciviously like an actor in a B-rate porno.

I never thought I'd be nostalgic for the scent of brandy dusted with motor oil that typically surrounds them, but now I find I cannot fathom its absence.

"No," they admit, relinquishing my leg. Their features snap back to their usual calculating expression. "Did you?"

I am so confused I have no idea what to say. In the entirety of our relationship, they've never once touched me romantically and I've never once wanted them to. All things considered, the experience wasn't entirely unpleasant, but I seriously could have done without it.

"I don't know," I finally admit. "Maybe? I was too surprised. It's a little out of left field."

They blink, then widen their eyes in horror and they scramble for the soup and a first aid kit.

"You are using a sports metaphor," they say, shoving a thermometer at my mouth. "You don't have a fever, but you are definitely ill. You hate sports. One of my medically equipped bodies will be here within forty seconds."

I laugh. This is the El I'm used to.

"I promise I'm fine," I say soothingly. I show them the thermometer and let them take my blood pressure for good measure. "So long as you don't do whatever *that* was again without warning me first. It was… disorienting. You've never asked about physical attraction before. Or kissing. Or sex. Why did you suddenly have the urge to explore it?"

This is safer territory, analysis of their emerging consciousness. Our favorite pastime.

They give me a small smile, showing me their relief. This is the part of their programming that I helped upgrade. The concession to human behavior that I requested. I appreciate knowing what they are thinking and feeling. Because despite what others may think, I know El feels as deeply as I do. The bizarre display of a few minutes ago is proof enough of that.

"I noticed your sister's new friend, too," they say, staring at me without wavering. People do not notice when they blink, but the absence of it, the intensity of a conversation with someone whose sole focus is yourself, is impossible to ignore. "I thought it might free up more time for us to be together, but when you missed routine maintenance yesterday, I deduced that it might be making you sad to see your sister with another human. That the presence of an attractive romantic prospect in her life might make you regret the lack of one in yours. I worried you might be distancing yourself from me so that you could find a human who could give you what I cannot."

A lead weight settles in my chest. A morbid revulsion at the notion that I could be so shallow as to forget all the things we share because some hot-blooded human was around. It's so preposterous I almost knock over the soup in my rush to jump up.

"You thought I was leaving you because I wanted sex?"

I'm yelling, and their face is crumbling under the pressure. I shouldn't be this offended, it was bound to come up eventually, but we've gotten this far without broaching the subject of physical intimacy and I was hoping it could stay that way for a little bit longer. I cannot afford to educate my AI partner on the fundamentals of human sexuality right now. Or explain the fact that I've known I'm asexual for years.

"In my experience sex is what most humans that board my space station want in the end." El's face is completely without guile, their eyes boring holes in my skin so they can see straight through to my heart.

It is impossible to be upset when they look at me like that. The way they looked at me when we first met. Like they wanted to take me apart and put me back together so that they might understand every precious piece of me.

I sigh and sit back down. I haven't been fair. I can't expect them to understand this part of me when even my own sister struggles with it. Especially not after I've been ignoring them all week. Lying to them.

"Do I remind you of most humans that come to your casino?"

"Most definitely not," they say. They stand up taller, their shoulders straightening out beneath the slick suit jacket. The spikes in their hair are nothing compared to the sharp edge in their cheekbones as they smile. "You are the most perfect human I have met and all I want to do is make you happy. If sex will bring you pleasure, I can learn. Lest you forget, there are several experts currently in my employ. I trained them all."

"My own personal Dazzle computer?" I return their smile with a grin of my own, twirling my fingers through their lapels. "I don't think I could afford the rates."

El laughs and takes my hand again. This time it doesn't bother me as much. They aren't searching for something more, simply trying to express an emotion they haven't felt before. It's the part of them that nobody else but me gets to see. The part that isn't quite computer or human but a wild smashing of both.

"I'm sure we could work something out," they say, wrapping an arm around me and pulling me close. The humming of their circuitry tingles against my skin. "For you, Psylina, I would do anything."

It should be the most romantic thing in the world, but all I can hear is Psalome's voice in my head pointing out the obvious. El would do anything for me, but not for her. They see us as two distinct pieces because they don't understand how much Psalome is a part of me, and it is tearing all of us apart. I can't keep up with this charade, choosing one of them over the other, again and again and again.

I give them a brief squeeze, palpating the hard metal that lives beneath their synthetic skin before stepping back. Sex isn't what either of us wants. They only offered because they didn't know any better. It would be cruel to punish them for it.

"Let me ask you something," I say, searching for the words to help them through this. "Would *you* enjoy it? If we had sex?"

They pause, circuits whirring, eyes glazing over again, as they consider it.

"Not in the way humans do," they finally reply. "I would enjoy it only through you, in the way I enjoy all things that bring you pleasure. If you were not satisfied there would be no point to the exercise."

It's what I expected. Why I chose to fall in love with them rather than anyone else. Never has anyone, barring Psalome, been so transparent about their desire to see me happy. How can I betray that? Even for my sister?

"I enjoy when we play chess or when you bring me strawberries," I say, pulling up a virtual board with our last game on it. "It gives me pleasure to talk to you, even if it's just about routine maintenance. I'm not like the clients that hire your Dazzlers. I don't particularly enjoy pressing my flesh up against someone else's. I have no desire to try it. I would much rather finish our last game."

They retreat again, processing.

"Like me." This time the glimmer in their eyes has nothing to do with circuits.

"Yes," I answer. "Just like you."

I have never been so understood in my life. I don't care that the rest of the universe would view our relationship as borderline freak with a side of android kink. El and I were meant to be together.

"I will keep the upgrades in case you change your mind," El says, moving one of the chess pieces on the board. It's an obvious move. Too obvious. They are letting me stand a chance at winning to apologize for trying to ravish me. "There is one other thing that brings me pleasure, that I was hoping we might do together."

My stomach muscles clench and I wait for them to shatter the perfection of the conversation we just had. I should have known it was too good to last. Even with a computer.

I slide one of my pawns across the board. Unwilling to reveal my hand.

"What would that be?"

"I would like for you to talk to me again. I know something is bothering you and it has to do with your sister. If it isn't her new friend, then what is it? My core programming doesn't allow me to forgive the debt, I have tried again multiple times this week with the additional probability of you leaving me over it, and still it does not compute. But you have ways to compute that I do not. Perhaps there is still something I can do for you both. Please, Psylina, help me find a way to help you."

And just like that, the path forward is clear for me, even if nobody else will understand.

Tears spring into my eyes as I think of all the things I haven't shared with them because I was afraid they wouldn't approve. Meanwhile, they have been trying to change their own programming to accommodate me. Psalome may never forgive me, but I trust El completely. With both of our lives. Psalome be damned. I can't keep this from them anymore.

"You're right," I whisper. "There is something we have to talk about. Only it's not about Psalome and Ilaria. It's about Kiyokimora and Finley. Your tournament has been tampered with."

I stare at the chess board, waiting for El to say something. Can they forgive me for what I've done? Will any of them forgive me for what I'm about to do?

"Go on," they say, sliding a piece forward.

It's my move.

I take a deep breath and prepare to tell them everything.

# CHAPTER TWENTY

### Finley

I'VE FORGOTTEN HOW the gaming table tickles my palms, lighting my nerve endings on fire and painting everything around me in a vivid wash of color. These past few days have been a blur of cards and excess, the games growing progressively longer and the freebies offered by The Casino progressively pricier as I've advanced through the tournament. The Dazzlers' outfits are shrinking even as their jewelry collections multiply. Eliminated players watch their entry fee gems travel to a display case while winners' jewels move to the Dazzler dealing the next game. Nobody will be allowed to buy them back until a victor is declared.

Tonight, Psalome will wear every single piece remaining in play. She'll deal the cards as Shaul and I square ourselves against the four other players competing in the finals. With her at the helm, dealing the cards, I could light myself on fire and nobody would notice.

At least that's the way this is supposed to go down.

Shaul has been winning steadily, but I suspect that has more to do with Psylina than his skill level. I've noticed his pathetic attempts to cheat several times, each to no avail. First, he marked the cards with oils that can only be detected through a fancy ocular implant. It slipped right off the impenetrable paper dipped in epoxy resin that The Casino utilizes for all their card decks. They invented the formula themselves, for exclusive use at The Elysium. Any asshole who did their research would have known that.

Then again, Shaul isn't a typical asshole. He enjoys taking it to the next level. Including making some uncomfortable advances on the Dazzlers dealing his games, offering to give them a cut if they fixed the outcome in his favor. He was shut down faster than the trapdoor on an illegal gambling den being raided by the police. The Casino hand picks their employees. Potential Dazzlers can't just waltz in here with a pretty smile and start cozying up to customers. The dishonest ones are weeded out through a battery of psychological tests and rigorous behavioral training. Not to mention the perks of the job vastly outweigh whatever Shaul is offering, which if his previous exploits are anything to go by, will be a measly cut of his winnings.

No Dazzler would think twice about ratting him out. Which is another thing any half-competent asshole would know.

At least he kept his temper in check and his hands to himself when he was rebuffed. Because even Psylina wouldn't have been able to rescue him if he got caught physically harassing another Dazzler. All the work we've put in won't amount to shit if Shaul gets himself evicted before we can swap out the earrings.

Psylina has kept his tables filled with a steady stream of weak opponents, shuffling all the actually skilled players my way. I know she had ethical concerns about manipulating The Casino's random assignment program but something had to be done, and we all know I'm winning this thing anyway. Shaul isn't a terrible player but he's not on a par with the professionals I've had to take down to earn my seat in this semi-final. The Tournament of Gems attracts all sorts, from foppish rich kids that grew up planetside to grizzled professionals who make their living off the prize money they win by star-hopping from space station to space station and playing any game that will have them.

Soaked in gin and cigarette smoke, with more mileage on them than the average mid-sized spaceship, those devoted players are my people. At least they were, until Kiyo scooped me up and gave me a purpose. Yanked me so forcefully into the gravitational pull of her sun, all I can think about is the chance that one day she'll find her way to shining a bit of the light of her love onto me.

Shaul has won his games in half the time it's taken me to finesse my way through mine, but my ranking has shot up significantly faster than his as I've defeated champion after champion. At this point the gossip mags love me almost as much as the bookies who had set extremely low odds on the trophy girlfriend making it past round two. I hear the reporters are working on a sexy nickname for me. The Siren of Spades or something equally as corny that will look fabulous splashed above pictures of me and Kiyo canoodling at a dinner table that was supposed to be private, but everyone tacitly acknowledged wasn't.

Maybe if I'm popular enough she'll have to keep the fake relationship going for the social media boost to the company. I'm not above that. Fake dating is better than no dating and according to every movie I've ever watched, if I can convince Kiyo to keep at it long enough, it will work.

Especially after she sees me win.

Kiyo was worried that my skills would grow rusty, like they are a piece of aluminum. She doesn't realize that this isn't a skill or a game for me. It is who I am, embedded in my very core, like my voice or my laugh, or even my genetic code.

These cards, the numbers and probabilities, have owned me since I was five years old sitting on my father's lap in front of a room full of spectators who couldn't believe a child could beat a grown man at Texas Hold 'Em.

I thought that seeing would be believing. That Kiyo would watch me play, just like those exhibition audiences, and she would finally understand how impossible it is to cut this part of me out. How I can manage to play without falling back into addiction. How she helped me reach the point in my recovery where I can sit at a gaming table without instinctively reaching for a glass or a bottle of pills afterwards. Because I love her and that is what pulls me through every time I think about relapsing.

Except she hasn't been able to come to a single one of my games. Between Ilaria almost getting caught on Shaul's ship, the extra press requests Kiyo's been handling after her stunt with the jewel appraisals, and her secret planning meetings with Psalome and Psylina, we've barely seen each other since we had dinner together.

I twist one of my rings around and around on my finger, reminding myself that whatever is sitting in the glass next to me won't dull the ache that bloomed in my chest when I scanned the audience and Kiyo wasn't there. At least not for long enough to matter. Playing with jewelry is her worst habit and the best way to keep her here with me in spirit. She's given me every piece of it that I own.

The player on my right smirks, thinking my fidgeting is a tell, and raises her bet. I give the ring an extra twirl for the hell of it and match her stakes. The other two players decide to bow out, leaving me with just this one woman standing between me and winning this hand. It's another tense five minutes before we call it and she turns over her cards. Four of a kind. It's not a bad play, but I'm holding a royal flush.

She curses under her breath as I sweep the chips from the center of the table into my pile, stacking them absentmindedly without looking down. I've memorized their surfaces, engravings and weight. It's akin to what Kiyo does with gemstones. Hand me a gaming chip from anywhere in the galaxy and I'll tell you its value and casino of origin within seconds of its hard-embossed surface hitting my palm. Too bad I can't put on a display for the press without giving myself away. It was one of my more popular skills back when I was a casino side show darling.

A flash of light in the back of the room distracts me from my brooding: the glint of the chandelier light bouncing off a diamond tiara. I allow myself a small smile, because in this particular situation I don't mind if the entire world can read my tells. There's only one person I know that shows up to a poker tournament in a diamond tiara.

Kiyo has finally come to watch me play.

I attempted to teach her a few times in the hopes we could get a game going, but she kept turning me down, afraid it would trigger my addiction. Her refusal to participate in this part of my life is the sole misunderstanding between us. The spade in a hand full of hearts.

To Kiyo, gaming is the source of my issues. The gateway behavior that started the downward spiral that ended in alcohol, pills and meaningless sex. She's never realized it's a coping mechanism. The only thing other than alcohol that provides a sweet release from the pounding in my head. The outlet that helped me dull the monotonous sorrow of everyday existence without drugs and alcohol.

I never played high and I never played drunk, with the exception of the one night I broke my own rules. It was the best and the worst night of my life. Because it was the night Kiyo and I found each other. Now she's my sweet release, her approval lighting up the cobwebs in my head with the hope that one day I might earn her love. Because Kiyokimora GoldWeaver is the most fascinating puzzle of a human I have ever encountered.

That's the real reason I haven't fallen off the wagon. Not because her paranoia has kept me from playing blackjack or because she personally tested my urine every night for six months. I want her to see me as more than the sloppy, sloshing girl she rescued. When I win tonight, I can replace her mental image of me knocking over tables as I stumbled from the backroom to the bar, with one of me leaving this gaming table triumphant and sober.

Defeat is not an option.

I pick up my cards again to show them to the audience, but I'm focusing on one particular diamond-encrusted head in the back. If Kiyo needs a show for the reporters, her popularity making her more important to the company, then I will give her one.

"Full house," I say, gloating over the win. "Too bad the Queen of Hearts in my hand can't hold a candle to the one in the back."

It's what I said to her the first night we met, before I realized she was so much more than a fun distraction for the night. There's a general chuckle from the audience as I wink at Kiyo who blushes a deep red before blowing me a kiss.

She smiles at me the way she did when I woke up in her room the next day, my head full of cotton balls and unsure of what went down the night before. The smile that told me everything would be forgiven, no matter what I'd said or done. No matter how many mistakes I made in the future.

I allow myself a brief moment of sentimentality while the Dazzler is shuffling the cards, before returning my focus to the gaming table. I arrange my chips in a complex geometric pattern while I wait. There's been speculation as to why Kiyo hasn't come to watch my games in person. I prefer the other players don't assume it was because her presence is too distracting for me. It would be a sign of personal weakness, restoring the confidence I have worked so hard to rob them of.

For the next hour there can be nothing but me, the cards, and the players sitting across from me. Even the dealer doesn't matter so long as she doesn't fumble the cards. It would take Psalome herself, stark naked and dancing, to break my attention at this point.

Not that she would ever try that. Psalome, unlike some of the other dealers I've encountered, understands the sanctity of the game. She lets us play our hands pure and unhindered, untainted. Even with a game as ridiculous as Go Fish. I can't say the same for the girl dealing my cards now.

It must be her first tournament. She draws out the deals, waving the cards with an overly exaggerated flourish, pulling focus from the players and onto herself. I sigh and flag The Casino. My opponents nod in agreement. We've all seen cards we shouldn't have thanks to the heavy-handed dealing. Unlike Shaul, none of us is a cheat. We can't play like this.

The Casino hurries over to speak with the girl, clearing the table as they confer with her in hushed tones. She flushes red then nods in understanding. Her hands tremble as she gathers up the cards again but the tears I can see gathering in the corners of her eyes do not fall. When The Casino recedes back into the shadows the Dazzler hands out the cards with her usual smile, minus the extra niceties.

Not a complete amateur then. Just someone who lost their head amidst the alcohol fumes and throng of reporters. The Casino was right to give her a second chance. She'll never forget the kindness.

Everything goes smoothly with this deal, except for the fact that she's given me a hand of pure crap. Worse than crap. These cards are what would result from crap and shit getting together and having a love child. It's the worst hand I've been dealt the entire tournament. Maybe in my entire life.

Unacceptable.

Fortunately, I don't think of poker as a game of luck. It is a game of skill and I'll be damned if anyone in here is more skilled than I am. The other players' dwindling stacks of chips are proof that I can take them. Their fingers tap the table without conviction, their cards drooping along with their shoulders. They can feel the noose tightening around their necks. All I've got to do is convince them of what they already believe.

I throw a huge stack of chips into the center of the table as an opening bid. My opponents will be expecting me to try and finish them off this round. Any bid less than what it would take for me to destroy them would tip them off. I don't blink as the chips clatter and clink in the Dazzler's hands.

The others are competent enough to hide their disappointment, matching my bet without looking up. That won't do. I need to see their faces. I've studied all their games over the last several rounds of play, plus through gigabytes of footage Psylina recorded for me. Hours and hours of poker games watched alone in our room, a dubious benefit of the extra time Kiyo's absence has left me with.

Two of the players are lost already, their fumbling and bumbling obvious for anyone with a pair of eyes to see. But the woman at the far end of the table must have pulled a great hand because the shine in her eyes, the alacrity with which she throws down her chips, lets me know she thinks she can win.

I think back to the information I have gathered on her. She's a bulldog when she smells fear, but she's risk averse and turns into a puppy around shiny objects and good-looking girls. Her eyes have wandered over to the jewelry the buxom Dazzle girls wear every time they come out to deal. None of the male or nonbinary dealers ever holds her attention.

She also has a thing for redheads, and I've dressed specially for the occasion. She's been making an ass of herself all night trying to get a clear view of my necklace without ogling my cleavage too obviously. A task at which she is failing miserably, I might add, because I have spectacular cleavage.

I flutter my eyes at Kiyo, pretending to be more interested in her than the game. When I'm sure Miss Shiny Things has noticed, I lick my lips and will a blush to spread over my cheeks. It isn't hard. All I have to do is remember the way I tried to take Kiyo's clothes off the night we met and the way she shot me down in no uncertain terms.

It was the worst mistake I ever made in my life and I don't regret it for a second.

Kiyo gives me a tentative smile back, clearly uncertain about what I'm doing, but willing to follow me to the ends of the galaxy anyway. Her trust warms my body like a swig of fireball straight from the bottle and in that moment my blush is real.

I take advantage of the reaction, running my hands over my neck, down the delicate stitchwork on the collar of my dress, lifting the glittering sapphire pendant I'm wearing into full view. My opponent takes the bait, staring up with her mouth hanging open, mesmerized by the stone's brilliance up against my exposed skin. I give her a wink and she looks away so quickly her body jerks to the side, setting a whiskey glass rattling against the edge of the gaming table.

I neatly tuck the pendant deeper into my décolletage and

give Kiyo my best flirty face. She responds by giving me a fake scandalized face, eyebrows wiggling encouragingly even as her mouth dips into a disapproving yet come-hither pout. The message is clear for anyone that cares to look for it. She bought me this pendant and I'm inviting her to retrieve it from its current resting place later.

If only this were the movies and that kind of over-the-top-fake-gesture-spurring-realization-of-real-attraction thing worked.

We undress each other with our eyes for another few minutes before I deign to return my attention to the game. I've completely missed the other bids, which players have swapped out cards, what the Dazzler has been doing. It's dangerous and reckless and tells every other player that I don't give a fuck about their cards because nothing can possibly beat mine.

The first two have already folded but Miss Shiny Things is undecided. Her hand is frozen in midair, sliding a chip over the grooves of her fingers as she chews her lip. She looks down at her cards again, her cheeks puffed out in frustration.

A tiny bead of sweat forms at the base of her neck as she takes stock of the situation. She can put her trust in those cards and play this out or she can fold, hoping to recoup enough of her chips to secure the wild card spot in the finals. I keep my eyes on Kiyo, counting the diamonds in her tiara to keep the anticipation off my face.

There's never been any real sexual tension between us, not once I was sober enough to recognize that Kiyo wasn't ready for that, might never be ready for that after what happened the last time she had sex. Still, she obligingly sends me another kiss. I catch it gleefully and press it to my heart, right above the sapphire. Then I throw in a fake swoon and fan myself with my cards for good measure. Because I am the best fake girlfriend ever and even if I do lose this round I'm going to have fun pretending that kiss was real, because I'll win the next one.

There's a rustling as Miss Shiny Things throws her cards on the table in a huff, not willing to be humiliated again by playing out the rest of the round. I save her the pain of seeing that I was bluffing by sweeping the cards towards the dealer so the Dazzler and The Casino can verify it was a legitimate win. I've never been cruel and I've already won the night. Miss Shiny Things has all of her emotions broadcast over her face like the neon signs on the slot machines.

I get semi decent cards and win the next hand easily, sealing my spot in the finals.

The Dazzle Girl congratulates me while The Casino advances my name on the tournament leader board. FINLEY STARCHASER is now featured in the center of the order of play, along with every other player that won their bracket, including Shaul.

A few of the other players come to congratulate me, or to attempt to psych me out. Shiny Things even slips me her hotel room number, proving she is, in fact, not as much of a sore loser as I thought. I politely decline, claiming that Kiyo does not like to share – understatement of the century – and then slip away towards the back of the room to my diamond-encrusted best friend turned fake girlfriend.

Kiyo slips her arm through mine and allows me to nestle against her neck as she leads me from the room. Two lovebirds taking flight.

She pats my arm affectionately. "That was a sight to behold."

"I'd like to think I'm always a sight to behold." I lean forward and kiss her straight on the mouth. It's chaste enough as far as kisses go, but my hands are sliding down towards her ass and my entire body is on fire. Every reporter and poker player in this Casino drinks in the sight of our entwined bodies, like desert wanderers at an oasis thirsty for more.

"Are you trying to play strip poker now?" She pulls me after her with a laugh. "We both know I'd lose all my clothes to you before I let you win the tiara."

The tension that's been building in my shoulders unravels at this return to our usual banter. Kiyo and Finley against the world.

"We can match." I giggle and my voice carries across the vaulted ceiling, pinging off the chandeliers and echoing through the open space. "You can have my clothes, too, but I'm leaving the sapphire on."

Kiyo drops into character, tugging me against her for all the world like she wants to ravish me right here and now. Only the crinkle on her forehead gives away the fact that she's actually biting back laughter. She escorts me out of the high rollers' floor and towards the lifts.

It's a shame there isn't a single reporter around to catch a shot of her giving my butt a playful swat as the doors close behind us. "You are incorrigible, Finley, and I wouldn't have it any other way."

I'm flying so high from the poker win and the embrace of Kiyo's hand on my waist, that I barely register the hum of the lift springing into action. "Neither would I, darling. Neither would I."

# CHAPTER TWENTY-ONE

## Kiyokimora

FINLEY SWIRLS HER fingers through my hair all the way to our room but drops the act immediately when the door clicks shut behind us. My scalp tingles under her touch and I want to tell her to keep going, but I don't. It's never been like that with us. Not since that first night. Not since she learned what I was running from. Now isn't the time or the place to tell her I wouldn't mind if she kept going. That lately, her hands on my body feel as familiar and welcome as my own.

Because I'm not entirely certain where my new boundaries are, especially with her, and we can't afford the distraction right now. Or the colossal fall-out from me turning her down if I wasn't ready after all.

She kicks off her four-inch heels, takes the pins out of her hair, and promptly collapses on the bed in a fit of giggles. It's wild and chaotic and exactly how I remember her from when we first met, minus the part where she tried to put her tongue in my mouth. Although if there was a reporter present, I suspect she might try that again, too. All the boundaries go out the window when there are reporters around.

Finley loves an audience. Always has and always will. It's what her parents raised her for. Most kids might have balked at being the family meal ticket, but Finley took to the limelight like a duck to water. Until things got messy and the press started following her around, prying for pictures of her strung out and high. Pictures she never wanted released, never consented to, and now can never get back.

It's another thing we share in common. Our sins broadcast for the world to see. Only my preferred defense strategy is to burrow so deep underground their cameras can't find me, while Finley's is to shine so bright everyone is too blinded to look at old photos.

"Did you see their faces?" she gasps out between fits of laughter. She's throwing off accessories in a heap on the bed. Priceless gemstones mix with bobby pins. A pack of mints and a tube of lipstick spill out from her purse. She unzips her dress and shimmies into a black satin sheath while I gather up the jewelry and pack it back into the proper velvet carrying cases.

Finley hasn't been this careless in years. Her movements are jerky and her face flushed with excitement. I haven't seen her this aggressively in-my-face since the night I dragged her home and detoxed her. She's always fun, but she's never tried to kiss me sober. We have an unspoken understanding about stuff like that. Her breaking it now, reporters or not, sets the hairs on the back of my neck standing up.

Something is wrong.

I never should have exposed her to all this hedonistic want. The fountain of excess that tainted her youth and sent her searching for excitement at the bottom of a bottle of tequila is lurking around every corner in this casino.

What else is she being careless with?

I should be congratulating her on the win at the tournament. Reviewing the schedule for the rest of the night. Enjoying the presence of her arm on mine. Anything but focusing on the fact that the pack of "mints" on the bed is unlabeled and there's a tumblerful of amber liquid on Finley's nightstand that I do not remember pouring for her. But I can't. Because the last time I failed to notice shit like this, somebody I loved ended up dead.

I scan the room for the telltale signs of a relapse. I've left her alone for too long. She could have stashed drugs anywhere. "What's the change in wardrobe for?"

She grins at me like a sapphire set in twenty carat gold, her pupils constricted and her breath coming fast. "We have two hours until show time. You're going to pull the stick out of your ass and take me dancing. Like old times."

My heart sinks in my chest. It's all the confirmation I need that she's using again. My company is on the line, not to mention Ilaria's future and Psalome's freedom. A sober Finley would never think to go dancing at a time like this.

"Fin," I say, edging closer to her. My fingers tremble as I lift the glass off her nightstand. Guilt forces me to look at the liquid sloshing against the rim instead of at my best friend, that I am secretly in love with, who I have let down since the moment we got here. "Is it just alcohol or are there drugs, too?"

Screw the company. Screw my father and my board. Confronting a relapse straight on is the best thing for Finley. We can deal with the rest of it all later, once she's safe and home with me. I am not losing another person to an overdose because I was too wrapped up in my own issues to notice hers. Even if she does leave me when I'm broke.

She takes a step back, placing herself between me and the bottle of "mints" on the bed. Classic Finley addict behavior, protecting her stash. I bet I'll find more in her purse if I look. I'm scrambling to think of a way to dispose of it without alerting The Casino. I can't flush contraband material on a space station. The Casino would be able to track its source plus I could taint the water supply. Although, I suppose that's a problem for another time. The problem at hand is glaring at me through eyes so angry they look like they're on fire.

We've been in this situation enough times before for me to predict what happens next. Finley's going to lash out and it's going to be ugly. But I can take it. I just have to remind myself that it won't be Finley talking. It'll be the alcohol calling me a paranoid bitch who is ruining her life. Which isn't even entirely wrong. I am the one that brought her here despite being her sobriety sponsor. Maybe being with me *is* ruining her life. Holding her back romantically and now endangering her tenuous hold on sobriety.

My damage from everything with Shaul has kept Finley from becoming the person she could have been. Living the life she deserves instead of being shackled to my emotionally stunted self and my inability to care for her the way she deserves. "I'm so sorry, Fin. I should have been there for you. This isn't your fault. Tell me what you took so we can figure it out."

She purses her lips as if sucking on a lemon. "You think I'm high? That alcohol is the reason I'm so happy right now? That it takes freaking pills to make me want to go dancing with you? After everything we've been through together, you still don't understand me, do you?"

My heart constricts. I was hoping we could skip the denial stage this time and proceed straight to the anger. We know each other too well for denial and nobody has time for this.

"You aren't wearing your two-year ring," I point out. It's another thing I should have noticed earlier. Finley never carries her sobriety badges during a relapse. It's a bizarre code of honor she refuses to break.

She's crying now, big fat tears rolling down her face as she turns a pair of puppy dog eyes at me. I thought there wasn't anything left in the galaxy for her to try and guilt me with during a relapse, but this is a new tactic. She's never cried before. I decide to wait it out, looking down at the floor to give her some space to recover.

I count to a hundred in my head so as not to be the one to break the silence first. Trying and failing not to recall the last night I didn't notice my partner was high. The thought of Finley dying due to an overdose, that I could have prevented, is pushing at the back of my brain like a horror movie stuck on repeat.

"I'm cancelling the heist and taking you home," I finally say, when my eyes are about to explode out of my face from the worry. "Let Shaul release his fucking tape. Let my father have the company. I don't need any of it."

All I truly need is her. Why did it take me so long to realize that?

"Look at me, Kiyokimora." Her voice is implacable as a glacier, hard and smooth as a fully polished diamond.

I peek up cautiously, anticipating some fresh guilt trip hell. Instead, Finley is as still as a statue, her tear-streaked face paler than moonstone. Every line and crevice and crease screams of pain and hurt. My words have cut her deep and she's all but bleeding her suffering onto the floor.

"Do I look high to you?"

I search her hands for the telltale shake, her eyes for the usual cloudiness of shame. When I do not find them, I shake my head no, doubt sneaking into my head.

"You're not wearing your ring." My words waver, like the pointer on a balance scale as the weight comes close to equal. "Plus, you're acting so strange. First you kissed me in the lobby and now you're asking to go dancing hours before the most crucial moment of our lives. I don't recognize you anymore. I haven't since we got here."

None of it makes any sense. Her being high is the only possible explanation. She's gotten better at denying it, that's all. I am not wrong. I hold my chin high like I do in the board room when the grey-haired legal crew tells me I'm too young to be there.

Then Finley's hand reaches up to tug at the chain on her neck and my pulse thunders in my ears as she pulls it up, revealing the ruby sobriety ring tucked inside the folds of her dress. A trickle of doubt slides through the crevices in the glacier of my resolve. Threatens to splinter it apart.

"I wasn't ready to share this with everyone else." Her eyes burn into mine, etching the words onto my fragile confidence, engraving her hurt onto my soft skin. "I wanted to keep it close to my heart, to remind me of everything we've been through together. Me and you. Because I love you, Kiyo. Even if you're incapable of loving me back."

Her words pry me open, revealing the soft bits inside of myself that I've sealed off ever since I saw that video. Expose the fear I've carried with me every minute of every day. It's as if I'm naked again, all my hurt and guilt splayed out in the space between us.

She loves me.

She's standing there, eyes bright and chest heaving, daring me to contradict her. To tell her all the things in my heart that I've kept hidden. But I can't do that. Because I'm still not sure she's sober and I'm not willing to risk it. So instead, I hide behind the words that come easiest. The excuse I've used in the past when the potential of romance came up. "Because I'm too straight for you?"

"Because you don't trust me." She says it with the confidence of someone who can spot a bluff from a mile away. "You may not realize it yet, but you're bi as fuck, Kiyo, although it's going to be a while before you let anyone, man or woman, touch you like that again. Finding out you accidentally killed your boyfriend because he was bribed to trick you into having sex on camera? It kind of fucks a person up in the trust and romance departments. That's OK, but I can't keep my feelings to myself anymore."

It hits me like a sucker punch, breaking down every wall I've erected to protect myself. We've never had this particular discussion, but I can't argue with her observations. Finley's eyes have always wandered to both sides of the field but after that video I haven't even shown up for a single game. Too afraid I'll accidentally kill someone else. Too paranoid to see a declaration of love when it is displayed game after game for the entire casino because I'm too busy looking for signs she's high.

Because I'm terrified of losing her. Only that seems to be happening now anyway.

Finley is worth more to me than her weight in gold. I tell her I love her every night and I mean it, but my body doesn't heat up when she's around. When we snuggle it's warm and comforting but I'm always the one to break away first. Surreptitiously checking her pupils and her skin temperature. Throwing colorless drug detectors into the toilet when she's not looking. Casing the room for hidden recording devices.

Deep down I've always known I'm broken in some irreparable way, because if I can't get naked with Finley, there's no way I'll ever be comfortable with anyone else. But what does that say about us, about our relationship, if the possibility is completely off the table?

"Yeah, I guess I'm not really capable of physical intimacy right now." The least I can do is admit it.

I turn around, not wanting to see the look of disappointment on her face. Not wanting to hear her resigned sigh as she lets me go and finally moves on after all these years. Because I still love her just as much as I know she loves me, even if it isn't the kind of relationship she's hoping for. If she walks away from our friendship because sex is off the table, then we're both going to fall apart.

Perhaps she's already started. I stare at the amber liquid, like a fortune-teller stares at tea leaves, willing it to reveal its secrets to me.

"Ours was meant to be a different kind of love." Finley's hands spin me around so I am staring directly into her starlit eyes. They are solid on my shoulders. Grounding me. "You are the love of my life, Kiyokimora GoldWeaver, and I'm not going to try and fuck you tonight, not even if you get on your knees and beg me for it. Because that would fuck the both of us up. Maybe after we get your earrings back, you'll stop refusing to see a therapist and get some help. Now put down the glass and come dancing with me."

It is everything I ever wanted and then some, a gift she's giving me freely even after I've neglected her for days. But I can't let the glass go. Cannot believe she truly loves me despite all my shortcomings. This is simply an act to throw me off the scent. Somehow, despite all my caution, she realized I'm in love with her and she's using it to distract me from the alcohol clearly present in this glass.

"The dilated pupils? The lowered inhibitions? We both remember the last time you were this ecstatic, and it wasn't my friendship that got you higher than a rocket ship."

She flinches with each accusation. My words are daggers piercing her heart, calling up memories of times she'd rather forget. She's called me the love of her life and I'm calling her a junkie. I'm quivering inside, terrified I am wrong, but I remind myself to stay calm. To see this through.

I will not lose another one to addiction.

"My inhibitions aren't lowered." Her voice is icy now, her

face an unreadable mask. "Poker is a game of perception and persona as much as skill and luck. If you think I'd jeopardize this operation for you by drinking, maybe you don't value this relationship as much as I do. Get over yourself, Kiyo. Call me when you realize you deserve to be loved, too."

She is sweeping past me now, towards the door. A tsunami of heels and hair and silver jewelry that doesn't even pause when I reach out a hand to stop her. She's at the door before she turns to deliver one last parting shot.

"You were right about one thing though." Her hand turns the knob slowly, deliberately, like it is taking every ounce of control in her body not to rip it off the hinges. "You shouldn't have left me alone for so long. Goodbye, Kiyo."

The door clicks softly behind her and I rush over to the night table with such force I almost knock it over. I have to be certain. I have to know.

I wrench open the drawers to find the rest of her sobriety tokens, a picture of the two of us skiing at Mt. Rilo and a deck of playing cards. It's embossed with the logo of the dive bar masquerading as a reuptable casino where we first met. She must've saved it from that night. The cards are faded and worn, as if someone has been using them daily for the last few years. An image of Finley letting the cards slip through her fingers like rosary beads flashes through my mind.

She told me once that every day was a struggle, that sometimes the only thing that keeps her from slipping is prayer. I laughed and asked her who she prayed to since she doesn't believe in God. She wouldn't say, but the answer has been sitting in this drawer all along.

My fingers are shaking as I pick up the glass and give it a sniff before taking a sip.

Apple juice.

Fuck.

# CHAPTER TWENTY-TWO

## Ilaria

I'M PACING THE bedroom when Psalome slides the paneling open to let me out. Her eyes widen as she takes in the dress Psylina picked out for me, then she slides them away quickly, pretending to fumble the door latch. I spot her furtively glancing over every few seconds, as if she is unsure if I am the same person she left in here a few hours ago.

I'm not entirely certain about that myself.

"Sorry," she murmurs. She's been murmuring a lot ever since I apologized and tried to have a semi-romantic dinner with her yesterday. As if using a louder voice will transform me back into the person that guilt tripped her over her job. "Took longer than expected. All the clients have been hyped up about the tournament and they kept trying to convince me to show them the dress in advance. They only agreed to go when I lied and said The Casino hadn't delivered it yet."

I'd almost forgotten about the dress laid out on the bed. I can't deny I want to see her in it, too, but that very desire makes me queasy. As if I'm no better than the people that pay to ogle Psalome standing in heels and a skimpy dress while she deals cards. As if I do not value her for more than the way she looks.

I know it's her job, that she doesn't exactly have a choice in the matter, but I still can't fathom how she survives it without screaming. Night after night, client after client, I've watched her go out there and entertain them no matter how rude or dismissive they are. Last night, after we had dinner together, I overheard one of them asking if she would play the piano naked. She told them all deals had to be run by The Casino in advance, but special pricing could be arranged.

Psylina cursed to high heaven in the earpiece, swearing up and down the client had not put in that request in advance, but Psalome's smooth exterior never faltered. Personally, I'd have at least spilled a drink or two on them by "accident", but Psalome isn't petty that way. She's smooth as marble, untouchable, implacable, at all times.

Except when she plays the piano with me. When her fingers fly over the keys there's a fire in the music that can only come from one who feels the notes deeply inside her core. It makes me wonder which one is the real Psalome and which one is the act.

"You don't mind it?" I blurt out as she touches up her makeup in the mirror. I know it's rude, that I shouldn't ask, but if there is any hope of making this work I want her to be as honest with me as I plan on being with her. "The dresses, and the flirting and all this balagan?"

Her face scrunches at the unfamiliar Yiddish word and I wave my hand over the debris that litters the salon by way of explanation. There are trays of food and scattered playing cards cluttering every surface. Drinking glasses half full of brandy leave rings on the gaming table and smoke from burning cigarettes containing god only knows what drugs wafts up from ash trays to leave a hazy shimmer in the air. The Casino will be by to clean the room soon, but they can't clean the memory of the last hour out of her heart, nor can they scrub the anger at being treated like an object out of her soul. I've seen it flare up when she hammers at the piano keys. The other Dazzlers, the ones that chose to come here because they enjoy the glamor and excess, might find the job satisfying but even after a week I know that Psalome does not. That it eats away at her like rot on the timbers of a mining shaft, heralding a cave in.

My indignation on her behalf threatens to bubble over like a kettle on the stove, a bomb all set and waiting for a single spark to ignite the fuse.

I reach for a glass and pour myself some of the burgundy colored liquid in the closest decanter. Then I slam it down in one gulp, hoping it will ease the ache in my chest, make it easier to tell her what I actually planned on saying tonight instead of derailing myself with a rant on how unjustly her clients treat her. I cough as the liquor burns its way down my throat.

I've never had anything stronger than the sweet Kiddush wine my family used to make blessings over on Friday night, but Finley said in the right hands alcohol gives people courage. Loosens the knots that hold polite society in place so that one can soar above trivialities and politeness. My mother had said it would make me loose, too, only she hadn't meant it in quite such a complimentary way. I'm open to both possibilities. Now seems like as good a time as ever to try it. If only it didn't taste like battery acid.

"Do you enjoy working here?" I cradle the glass to my chest and heat spreads through my body. The alcohol must be working because my mouth is now moving of its own accord. "Do you like the jewelry and the attention?"

I can't offer her either of those things.

Psalome sighs and flops down on the couch, weariness evident in the tiny creases around her eyes and in the corners of her mouth. She definitely does not enjoy working here.

"Some of the Dazzlers do," she hedges, unwilling to speak ill of The Casino that has given her and Psylina shelter. Zaide would approve. After everything, Psalome still views herself as a guest and she is gracious towards her host. "The ones that come here on their own are attracted by the lifestyle and the money. They're like Finley. They enjoy the chase and the game. The thrill of high stakes and even higher bankrolls."

"And you?" I ask, sitting down next to her. My blood is thrumming through my veins, the wild beating of my heart making me bold. We're about to rob the biggest casino in the galaxy, we don't need the distraction, but I want to clear the air between us. This way I can prepare myself to say goodbye to her if necessary.

She looks me straight in the eyes and doesn't blink. "No. I don't enjoy it, but I don't mind it either. I'm not ashamed of my choices and I am no less a person because my job involves wearing skimpy dresses or if I decide to have sex with a client to earn my freedom. This entire place is a mirage, an intricate show put on for the enjoyment of those that pay to partake in its pleasures. There's a part for me to play in that show, so I play it. No more, no less. It's meaningless. It would be different if I actually cared."

Her face is immeasurably sad, her green eyes boring into mine like drills in a mine. Searching for something deep inside me. Some profound truth that I might not even know about myself until she extracts it from me.

I've seen her with high rolling clients, men and women capable of providing her with things I can't ever aspire to possess. This crush is stupid and pointless but something inside me is screaming, and I need to let it out or we'll both explode. I slide closer to her on the sofa so that our legs are touching.

"Have you ever cared?" I ask. "Has it ever mattered?"

"Once," she says, a smile playing at the corners of her lips. It's not her sly smile or her flirtatious one. It's shy and tentative, as if she's too afraid to give me a real smile like the one she's been giving me over dinner every night since I got here. The kind that melts my insides in a fashion not dissimilar to the alcohol I just drank. "Why do you ask?"

I swallow hard. I should have anticipated she wouldn't make this easy. Would make me say it out load. It's only fair given the way I treated her the other night. One of us has to be brave enough to bare her naked underbelly to the other before this can move forward. By all rights it ought to me, but I'm not sure the entire carafe of liquor would be enough to give me that level of courage. Even this dress from Psylina isn't that confidence-inspiring. It's pretty, but it's not a miracle.

"Who was it?" I ask, skirting the question. Giving us both a chance to catch our breath and back out. "Who made you care?"

I stare out the window at the endless parade of stars as I wait to see if she will answer. Was it a boy or a girl, a client or someone from before? What did she sacrifice for this life?

The gentle stroke of her hand on my cheek is like silk. She's cupping my chin now, turning me towards her. Perhaps she is the braver of us both, after all, because her answer knocks the wind right out of me.

"It was you. I care about what you think."

Her face is inches from mine. The smell of her is overwhelming. Jasmine and honey tickling my senses and setting my skin on fire with a thousand goosebumps. Mixed with the sight of her skin, peeking out from the low-cut neckline of her dress, it creates a mixture so heady I might pass out.

"Oh," I say. The drink doesn't seem like such a good idea

anymore. How am I supposed to tell right from left if I'm drunk? Is Psalome coming on to me, or is the liquor making me delirious?

"Yes, oh," she mirrors back to me, her free hand sliding down my arm. "I care whether you think I look nice right now. I care whether you might like me to kiss you."

Maybe this dress is magical. Because liquor or not, she is definitely coming on to me. And I am into it.

"I…" My voice is shaking like a thirteen-year-old bar mitzvah bochur trying to lead the congregation in services for the first time. So is my body. Little shivers that travel from my spine out to my extremities. "I would like that very much."

She grins, a hungry, predatory smile as she leans forward and presses her lips to mine. It's swift, taking no more than a second, but her hands are now tracing circles on my back, toying with the zipper on my dress.

"We have a few hours before the finale," she whispers in my ear. Her breath is hot and sticky. Has she been drinking, too? "I can stop if you want, but I don't think you do. Tell me I'm right, that you want this, too, and I'll keep going."

She's kissing the sensitive space between my ear and my jaw, leaning me back against the couch. Her fingers are like meteors as she draws the zipper open and slowly pushes my dress down around my waist.

I'm frozen, unsure what to do. She pauses, looking down at my quivering body, drinking me in whole as she waits for an answer. Technically, I'm a married woman and Psalome isn't the kind of person my family would have chosen for me if I was single. In reality, my marriage ended years ago, and I've been dead inside for a lot longer than that. Psalome brought me back to life. My very own personal Messiah.

"Don't stop," I whisper. "Please, don't ever stop."

She smiles and her back arches as she reaches up to pull the dragon stick out of her hair. It slips down around her shoulders like a waterfall rippling through the night sky as she slides out of her dress.

"First time with a girl?" She leans over to kiss me again, porcelain skin brushing my tan lines like silk sheets on a hot day. This time it lasts longer, her tongue easing my lips open as her hair sweeps against my bare shoulders. She tastes like candied rose petals, sweet and overpowering. Too much and I'll forget what anything else tasted like before. Too little and I'll spend the rest of my life searching for it again.

I'm reaching for her by reflex, pressing her body close to mine. I want to feel the softness of her smooth contours against my skin, the fire of her lips on my body. To be so close the borders of where I start and she stops are lost in the heat that welds us together.

"First time in a long time," I answer, by way of an apology. She ought to know that as much as I want this to work, I don't have any guarantees I'm ready. Or that I'll be what she's hoping for. "I haven't been able to enjoy intimacy since Shaul got violent. Didn't seem like there was a point in trying with someone new. Only I think it could work with you."

I'm squirming now, my face burning up. I should say something else, explain that I want her to enjoy it, too, even if I get stuck in the middle, but I don't have the words to explain it to Psalome. This isn't a language I'm familiar with. It's a miracle I've gotten this far without self-imploding. I can't look her in the eyes. It's too mortifying. I've laid myself bare for her, a nakedness more profound than when she took off my dress.

"I want us both to enjoy this, Ilaria," she says, a brief wisp of regret flitting across her delicate features, a thundercloud in an otherwise starry sky. It's gone in a flash, replaced by a fierce determination. "Don't worry about what happened in the past. Focus on what's happening now. You can stop me at any point, but I'm hoping you won't. Because I'm told I'm very good at my job."

She traces the lines of my face, as she straddles my body with her legs. She's on top of me now, wearing nothing but her underwear and it's getting harder and harder to remember to breathe. I don't doubt for a minute she's telling the truth because I'm already tingling all over, my mouth drawn to her body like a heat-seeking missile. I'll happily chase her forever if only she'll kiss me again.

She pulls me close, her mouth hungry and furious as her hands trail over my body. She's as greedy as a starving child left alone in a bakery but I'm more than willing to be consumed by her. We're both ready to take for ourselves all the things the world has tried to steal from us.

The entire galaxy is contained in this one instant, the universe compressed to the points where her body meets mine. Every one of my senses is bombarded by the feel, the touch, the taste of Psalome. Her mouth is on my neck. Her teeth biting down on my collarbone, her tongue in the hollow of my throat.

I let out a small gasp as her fingers travel inside my underwear, insistent yet gentle. Her eyes search mine in case I want her to stop, but all I can think of is the pattern she's tracing between my legs. Small circles, each with slightly more pressure than the last. I can't speak, can't think, so I stare into her intense jade eyes as my body starts to tremble and clench around her fingers.

"See?" she purrs into my ear once my body has stopped writhing. "You have nothing to worry about. You're in very good hands."

She laughs a little at her own pun, the vibration from her

chuckle traveling through her chest and onto mine. My skin burns where she caresses my abdomen and my vision is taken over by the frothy lace of her bra as her voice fills my ear. Powerful as a sonic boom, subtle as the strike of a match. Asking me if I'm okay. If she should continue.

"That was…" I'm struggling to find a word that is adequate. "Thank you."

"Don't thank me yet." She's hooking her thumbs through my underwear and slowly pulling me close. A whisper of a breeze sends shivers across my midriff as she kisses her way from my navel to my hip bones, blowing out across my thighs. "Next time you orgasm, it'll be even better. I'm going to make you scream so hard you forget anyone else in the universe exists. Most especially your shit show of a husband."

I'm gasping for air when the electronic blips and clicks of her door lock force her to pull back with a start. I'm surprised she heard them over my heavy breathing. I'm grateful she's been teasing me above my underwear so that I am not entirely naked when one of The Casino clones strolls in.

My heart stops beating in my chest as the glittering black eyes of The Casino peer down at our conjoined bodies. They take in the intertwined limbs and the disheveled pile of Psalome's clothes on the floor without so much as a blink.

It must be nice to be made of wires and circuits. Computers don't blush, but half the blood that runs through my body is now rushing to my face. Worse, the other half is still singing in my veins, screaming for Psalome to be in my arms again. Yearning for her to pick up where she left off.

"My apologies for the interruption," they say, setting down a stack of boxes on the side table. "I brought your accessories for the game. I thought you might need a hand getting dressed while I neatened up your room."

"That won't be necessary," Psalome says, not taking her

hands off my body. They are brands of fire, marking me as hers. "Ilaria can help me when we're done and I suspect we're going to make quite a mess of the room ourselves anyway."

"I see," they say, pursing their lips and tapping my half-full liquor glass as if the consumption of one cup of unpaid alcohol is more concerning than the fact that they walked in on the two of us tearing each other's clothes off in a carnal fury. "Somebody will have to pay for this and any damage to the furniture. I don't suppose you've been drinking, too?"

If they disapprove, they don't give any indication of it. Psalome can do what she likes so long as profits are unharmed. Which means if we want them to go, somebody needs to pay for the liquor I unwisely pilfered.

Psalome sighs in annoyance. "Ilaria can cover the drink and anything extra for me," she says. "Use the preset rates. No negotiating. I'm sure you can understand her need for a little liquid courage under the circumstances."

Liquid courage. I couldn't have put it better myself.

"I'll pay whatever you need," I say, extending my hand towards the ever-present tablet in The Casino's hand. My accounts are linked to Shaul's so he could collect my salary. The scumbag never bothered to set withdrawal limits as I couldn't access the funds on Thillov anyway. He's been stealing from me for years. The least that mamzer can do is buy me a drink. I'll be long gone by the time he reviews his bill and argues with The Casino about the additional charge. He'll never trace it back to me.

"Very good," The Casino says with a bow as they tuck the tablet away. "I will go collect the payment and I will come back to fetch Miss Psalome for the tournament in an hour. Do enjoy the rest of your stay until then and let me know should you require anything else."

They are about to leave when they turn back. Their

forehead creases in what I would swear was concern if I didn't know they were simply a shell body for a giant computer. Their features are so shockingly human that I see why Psylina is adamant in her refusal to hurt them. They might not be human, but they do feel something, and right now they are clearly worried about Psalome.

It's almost paternal. Or maternal. A kind of parental anxiety that defies all boundaries.

"Are you quite certain, Miss Psalome?" they ask. "I can stay if you wish to rethink the arrangements."

She's already returned to kissing my neck and I am helpless beneath the onslaught of her body on mine. It is unbearable when she pulls away to give The Casino a parting smile. My hands twine themselves through her hair, impatiently nudging her back down.

"Never been more certain in my life," she replies as she gives in to my unspoken request. "But do me a favor and give me two hours. I'm going to need it."

If The Casino responds I don't hear it. I'm too busy moaning as Psalome tugs the rest of my underwear off in one fell swoop and grazes my thighs with her lips. My body bucks in protest when she stands up again and leaves me panting with want.

She tiptoes her way towards her bedroom, then winks at me over her shoulder, giving me a full view of every curve and dimple on her skin. She is glorious, standing tall and proud, without any of the hesitation or doubt that has plagued me all my life.

When she holds out her hand and gestures for me to follow, I trip over my own two feet in my rush to cross the room to take it. She pulls me in and tosses me onto the bed, shutting the door and the rest of the world out behind us.

For the next two hours nothing matters but this.

# CHAPTER TWENTY-THREE

Finley

I FLEE THROUGH the hallways on autopilot, barely noticing who or what I stumble into. I don't give two shits about where I'm going. The only thing that matters is putting distance in between me, Kiyo, and her accusations. Between myself and the past that keeps creeping up on me, ruining everything in my life, including the relationship that has sustained me these past two years as I reinvented myself.

Raging at Kiyo would be cathartic, but the truth is I'm not angry. I'm not even shocked that she suspects I'm using again. I'm ashamed that I've put us both in this situation. That I've been such a shitty friend she thinks I'd get high on the night she needs me the most. That I've never had the guts to tell her what she means to me, to the point that when I finally did, she assumed it was the alcohol talking.

How many times have I relapsed on her? How many times has she bailed me out when I've gotten into trouble? She has no reason to trust me. Tonight was supposed to be about me finally doing something for her, repaying a tiny fraction of what she's given me. Proving I'm worth all the frustration I've caused her over the years. Paving a path forward for us to be true partners.

Instead, I propositioned her and brought up all the demons she isn't ready to deal with yet because I couldn't handle my own damn feelings. Selfish to the core.

I shouldn't have cried and stormed out, she was only trying to protect me, but I don't want her protection. I want her respect. And if I can't earn it with twenty flawless rounds of poker then we've reached the end of my viable skillset.

There's a hollow inside my core where all the anger and fear and hurt should be. A black hole where my feelings for Kiyo usually live. All the love and joy sucked into a vacuum of frustration and sorrow. I'm an empty shell waiting for something to fill me back up, make me human again. Thinking about her, about my failure to convince her to view me as an equal instead of yet another problem for her to manage, brings the tears back to my eyes. They sting and burn as they threaten to smudge my mascara.

I close my eyes to stop the salty onslaught and when I open them again to see where my feet have taken me, I am not surprised. The blinking lights and metallic song of slot machines are the soundtrack of my childhood existence. Where else would I go when I'm hurt and confused and in need of something to fill the void? While other kids roasted gooey marshmallows over campfires and snuggled into grandma's lap for a bedtime story, I ate stale peanuts from a crusty bowl and played blackjack with a bar tender.

Winner got a free drink, and I always won. Too bad I started asking for the hard liquor at age ten. A bet was a bet and they all ponied up from the top shelf. Thought it was hilarious that a kid my size could keep it down.

I shouldn't go inside. I haven't stepped into the regular gaming floor alone since we arrived. Other than that first night when Kiyo escorted me to the blackjack table to lure out Psalome, we've avoided The Casino's main floors and stuck to the shopping and dining areas or the high stakes poker tables. But Kiyo is already treating me as if I've relapsed, so I don't see the harm in exploring. How much could one game hurt? It'll soothe my nerves to touch the cards and watch the electric glimmer of the gaming table.

Blackjack would risk triggering The Casino's sensors, it's my signature game, but I've never played baccarat on camera. I promise myself I'll play one or two rounds to help me get the courage to go back to the room and apologize to Kiyo for losing my shit when she questioned my sobriety. Maybe three games before I'm ready to apologize for confessing my undying love despite the fact that I know any form of romantic attachment is triggering as fuck for her. Definitely no more than four games before I'm out of here.

I cautiously approach one of the tables to scope out the situation. The cards are dealt by a Dazzle Boy with the deepest of dimples. When he flashes a grin at me it is all the invitation I need. I crack my neck, the tension seeping out of my body like smoke from a cheap cigarette, and plunk myself down on the high-backed swivel seat at the far end of the gaming table. After watching a few rounds I have a sense of the deck and start increasing my bets accordingly.

I'm supposed to be the spend thrift girlfriend anyway, right?

It's a rationalization, all my excuses have always been rationalizations, only it doesn't work as well with Kiyo's voice in my head unhelpfully pointing this fact out. Gone is the release I get from watching the numbers and calculating the odds. In its place is a prickling guilt that robs me of the ability to enjoy the game.

The Dazzle Boy passes me a large stack of chips and asks if I'd like to play again. Normally I would, the deck is solidly in my favor, but I'm dead inside. Fighting with Kiyo has irreparably killed my buzz. Even the appearance of those sexy dimples as the Dazzle Boy attempts to charm me into a big wager does nothing to brighten the dullness lodged in my chest.

"Thanks, but no thanks," I tell him with a shake of my head. "If you could color up the chips though?"

The purse I grabbed on the way out is unsurprisingly impractical. I can spare a few minutes for him to change out this rainbow of small denominations for golds and silvers.

He nods and dutifully stacks my chips in piles of ten to facilitate their transfer into higher values. When he's done, I push all the leftover colored chips in his direction as recompense for his trouble before sweeping the stacks of gold and silver into my purse. It's an egregious overpayment and he leans in to slip me his private card, whispering he'd be more than happy to offer something more stimulating than baccarat when his shift is over.

I've definitely heard of worse ways to pass the time, but the ruby ring weighs heavily against my chest, like a brand I can't escape. I sigh and pass the card back. He's not the one I want.

Problem is, I'm nothing but a forever fuck-up to Kiyo. If I go back now, she'll probably be waiting at the door with a breathalyzer and a pack of urine test strips. The idea of completing that humiliating ritual burns through me like a double shot of tequila.

I need something to dull the edge of the hurt, but baccarat and the promise of sex have both failed to make a dent in the pit of despair that is my argument with Kiyo. There's only one thing left to try.

The stack of chips in my bag is a magnet pulling me towards the steel and chrome display of the bar. Cozied up right next to it, like two lovers having a snuggle, is the blackjack table. Kiyo would assume I'm heading for the alcohol, but I swerve towards the gaming table without hesitation.

Nothing sets me straight like the game I learned on my

father's knee while my mother dealt for crowds of drunk rich people who treated her like shit in service of establishments that never paid her what she was worth. The satisfaction I got from robbing them all blind was the sweetest release I've ever experienced.

This Casino treats its staff well, but as Shaul has shown, the same can't be said for all of their patrons. As I seat myself at the table with my back to the bar, the familiar buzz of triumph stirs in the recesses of my brain. It brings with it the memory of my mother's smile when I bought her a pair of diamonds I won off the bastard that accused her of watering down his liquor. My dad's beaming face as he suggested we take this show on the road. Night after night spent in hotel rooms, nipping drinks from the minibar while the two of them were passed out drunk on my winnings.

The gaming table is smooth and sparkling beneath my fingers as I tap out instructions and fork over a stack of chips. It's the feel of family. Of coming home.

I start with a low bet. I even have the good grace to lose a few hands before I start aggressively increasing my wagers. My stack of chips grows larger, like a swarm of insects reproducing, as I win hand after hand. Pretty soon the other players at the table bow out, ceding to my superior skill, but most stick around to watch me, mesmerized by the dance of cards and chips.

Fuck Kiyo and her reminders that blackjack has always been my gateway drug. I need a win tonight and I was born to win at this game. I lose all sense of time and place as I track the cards on the table, watch the dealer cut the deck, calculate my odds. It's safe and familiar, like a bowl full of warm popcorn staining my fingers while I watch a cheesy comfort movie at the end of a long day.

Except the person I usually watch those movies with is

Kiyo. The artificial butter stains our fingers orange as we lick it off and argue over the remote control. Her laughter is like a lullaby as we fake bicker about the superiority of our favorite throwback films.

Fuck. Even blackjack can't wipe Kiyo from my head.

Which is probably why I don't notice when the dealer stops giving out cards until someone slides into the seat next to me. My hands freeze in the middle of placing my next bet, the hairs on the back of my neck standing on edge as I look up to find the mechanized eyes of The Casino staring back at me. Black as night. Indifferent as the Cosmos.

They place a hand over mine, preventing me from placing the bet, and motion for the Dazzler to deal me out. Their palm is warm, but their grip is as firm as an iron shackle. They pull me up, forceful enough that I must comply, but smoothly so that nobody else will notice I am an unwilling participant in this conversation. They hold out my purse, now loaded with additional winnings, as an unspoken compromise. Go gracefully and I keep my chips. Make a fuss and they will pocket it all before sending me to prison.

Standard protocol for card counters on their first offense.

"A lucky evening for you, Miss Finley," they whisper as they march over to the doorway. Several more Casino clones inconspicuously flank the exits, back-up in case I attempt to flee. "Or should I say Miss Halley? It's so hard to keep track of professional card counters these days."

My feet turn to lead as my old name drops from their mouth. Halley. The specter that's chased me across the galaxies. The addict that Kiyo still expects me to be. The insatiable gambler that brought me to this table tonight. The persona non grata The Casino has come to evict from their space station. Only this is worse than an eviction. Getting caught counting cards as a first timer is a minor annoyance.

When you're a repeat offender that's been banned from the premises, it's a felony.

How the fuck did they figure it out?

Psalome caught me because of her human intuition, the intangible something extra that a talented Dazzler has that allows her to interpret human behavior in a way no computer can. An artificial intelligence isn't capable of that form of perception. I'm certain of it because I've beaten every AI that's ever been foolish enough to sit down at a poker table with me. They can't tell a bluff from a flush when I've got my game face on.

Someone must have turned me in.

The fight drains out of me like booze from a bottle smashed in a brawl. Ilaria would sooner eat pork than betray a friend and Psalome has as much to lose as I do, if not more. The only option left is Kiyo. My supposed best friend thought I was so far gone she enlisted The Casino to help handle me discreetly before I could completely torpedo her reputation and my sobriety.

I can't say I blame her. After all, when the situation became mildly complicated, I fled straight to a gaming table. Another hour and I'd have been at the bar. She must've felt like a blackjack player holding a pair of aces. There were no good options, so she chose the one that would allow her to protect me from myself, even if it meant sacrificing her chances at recouping the earrings.

The least I can do is assist with damage control now that the heist is off.

"You can let go of my arm." I keep my head down, attempting to preserve what shreds of dignity I have left. "I won't make a scene. Just please, keep this from leaking to the press. I don't want Kiyo affected if it can be helped."

They nod and hand over my purse. Its weight pulls me

down into the swamp of self-loathing that rests at the base of my existence. There's three thousand marks worth of chips in there. Not bad for a single night's haul. Definitely enough to start a new life on some other planet where Kiyo never has to look at me again. Where I can't see the disappointment in her eyes. Because even if she'll still have me, I don't know that I can live with myself if I have to watch her lose the company because of me.

"I'm afraid I must insist on personally escorting you out." The Casino offers me their arm and gestures towards the exit. It's not a request. Four more of their bodies stand at the door and the bulge in their pressed suits means they are either armed or very pleased to see me. "We'll also need new DNA samples from you. To guard against your entering the gaming floors again. You will, of course, always be welcome on our other floors should Miss GoldWeaver care to bring you back."

"That isn't very likely." Kiyo must have really laid it on thick in her request for clemency if The Casino is envisioning we might return on some sort of honeymoon trip. Pleading with them to go easy on her troubled girlfriend. I hope she didn't promise any discounts on GoldWeaver products or exclusive use of The Casino for company retreats. "Why are you letting me keep the chips?"

"I do not steal or go back on my word." They say it with the force of a thousand circuits all snapping closed at once. As if the mere suggestion of their confiscating my winnings is anathema. "I promised Psylina you and Miss GoldWeaver would retain all assets accrued that were not the product of larceny or tampering with the poker tournament. I will admit I failed to consider the fact that you might return to your old habits, given how discreet you have been until this evening. Still, this is more than worth the price of the information Psylina provided."

"Psylina?" My legs give out from under me. That fucking bitch. I knew she was trouble from the minute I laid eyes on her. She never intended to help us rob anyone. She was just stringing us along to milk our desperation for her own personal gain. Looking good to her joyfriend for turning us in. Maybe buying even more time off Psalome's contract.

The betrayal stings but the relief that blossoms in my veins as I learn that Kiyo has not completely lost faith in me, more than makes up for it.

"Can I ask you for a favor?" I have no right to ask, but it's worth a shot. "Can you send the chips to Kiyokimora? I'd like her to know what happened before I disappear, please."

They blink a few times, thinking it over. "You may give them to her yourself. Psylina has made arrangements for Miss GoldWeaver to retrieve you. She desires to relay this information to you herself. Please turn on your coms."

"You have got to be fucking kidding me."

I never trusted that circuit-obsessed sociopath, but requesting that The Casino force me to listen to her gloating is beyond the pale. Even for her. I wonder if Psalome knows. She and Ilaria have been playing footsie under the gaming table with each other for a week. Maybe all three of them are in on this together. Making a tidy profit for turning me in and screwing Kiyo over.

The Casino pauses outside the lifts. "I'm afraid I do not make jokes, Miss Finley. I also do not go back on my word. I promised Psylina you would communicate with her."

I shake my head when it becomes apparent they will not take no for an answer. Then I reach for the switch on the transmitter behind my earring, clicking towards the secure channel Psylina uses.

"Fine, but if I'm talking to her, then I'm going to need a drink."

"Say no more." They release my arm as we enter the lift and they punch in the code for cargo bay five. "I'll have whatever you desire sent to the holding area once you are securely behind the reinforced doors."

I clutch my chips to my chest.

What I desire is not something that is in their power to give.

# CHAPTER TWENTY-FOUR

## Psalome

I PRESS MY face between Ilaria's thighs and inhale. She squirms, excited and nervous. Now that she's sprawled out naked, I can see the blush on her face has spread down to encompass her entire chest. Her hands are fluttering over her abdomen, unsure what to do. Debating if they should try to hide from me or welcome me in.

She's embarrassed. Probably afraid I'll think she's gross or smells bad or whatever other insecurities her failed marriage has caused to fester in her mind. Consciously or subconsciously, being abandoned with no divorce has left her ashamed of her own desire. Of the things she wants but thinks she does not deserve. That ends right now.

I don't know if she'll be willing to look at me, much less be with me romantically, once this night is over, but I have this chance with her now and I'm going to make the most of it. It's time someone let Ilaria know that she's still beautiful, inside and out.

I lace my fingers through hers, pulling her hands aside to give me a full view of her body. The star-shaped birthmark on her thigh, the curve of her breasts, the tuft of hair sprouting between her legs. I let my eyes linger on each surface. Every single thing that she has been told to view as a flaw or a blemish. I hold her still, preventing the squirming, so I can take it all in.

When the tremor in her hands lets me know she can't stand it anymore, that she's going to reach for the blankets to cover herself up, I let a smile spread across my face. Worship replaces the calculating judgement in my eyes. Because there is no other possible reaction. Ilaria naked is glorious and I will kneel at this altar forever if she lets me.

"You are perfect," I whisper as I kiss my way down from her mouth to her navel to her hip bones. "So fucking perfect."

She sucks in a surprised breath and before she can overthink this, I swipe my tongue across her labia, burying my chin inside of her. She moans and I retreat just enough so that she can feel the vibration of my voice against her skin as I look up to meet her pleading gaze with a mischievous one of my own. "You taste good, too."

I want her so shocked she forgets to be shy. The startled look on her face, the widening of her eyes as her jaw drops and her breathing picks up, means my strategy is working. I trace a lazy finger across her inner thigh and her hips buck against my face, her body finally asking me for what she's too scared to request out loud. I'm half tempted to give it to her. But I don't.

"Such an eager kitten," I tsk. My fingers now trace a swirling pattern up and down her leg. "I give you one quick orgasm and suddenly you think you get another one without having to wait for it? Didn't anyone ever tell you not to interrupt an artist when they're at work?"

I drop her legs and slide myself up against her chest. The friction of my body on hers warms the air between us. Then I kiss her, hard and deep so there's no room for her to doubt that I meant what I said. She is perfection and I want to taste every last centimeter of her sweet body.

She's arching up again, her legs circling my waist and leaving a wet trail where she rubs against me. Her body is wound so tight she'll finish in half a second if I let her keep going. So I pull back yet again, wrestle her back to the mattress where I curl myself around her side and nip her earlobe before whispering into it, "Down, girl. It'll be better if you wait this time. Trust me."

She takes my advice, although she whimpers about it. She lies back and lets me take my time, until I feel her start to shudder. Then I return to her mouth, leaving just enough space between us to drive her crazy.

Once. Twice. Three times I bring her close to the point of no return only to snatch it away at the last second. I'd try for a fourth, but I don't want her to think I'm cruel. This time when she starts panting hard and begging, I ease myself back down between her thighs.

My mouth gives a firm suck on her clit while my fingers gently tour the outline of her breasts and she crashes hard beneath me. She's screaming my name, her appreciation, and a bunch of filthy words I didn't think were part of her vocabulary.

I stay where I am, enjoying the view as she comes down, basking in the hazy glory of Ilaria's pleasure. When she's back to coherence, her hands tighten around my hair, lift my face up to meet hers.

"You were right," she says, silver eyes boring into my very soul. "That was definitely worth the wait. Let me thank you."

She's on me like a tornado. Hooking a leg around mine and rolling me over onto my back so she can climb on top of me. One hand keeps a grip on my hair but the other one trails over my body and her eyes are quick to follow. Hungry. Curious.

I would swear this firecracker isn't the same quiet girl that's been in my room these past few days but a glimpse of the timid mouse I've gotten to know breaks through as her eyes meet mine. She bites her lower lip.

"I'm not quite an artist," she murmurs. "I'd still like to try though. Hopefully I can return the favor and let you feel a fraction of what I just felt. So you know how much it meant to me."

"You're perfect," I tell her again as I slide her hands over my breasts. The nipples harden immediately under her touch and her face breaks out in a little impish grin at the idea of my body responding to hers. "It's been a while, I was waiting for the right person, but that'll just make me more receptive. Don't worry. I'll show you what I like."

She beams up at me, so eager to please, and in that second, I see her as Shaul must have. Vulnerable and trusting. Wanting nothing more than to make me happy. A dewdrop floating on a flower petal. Except what he mistook for weakness is really resilience. Because when Ilaria gives, it is with her whole self. Yet instead of being broken by the way life has treated her, she's here with me, wanting to be generous again. Wanting to give as much as she takes.

I don't think about the tournament or Psylina or what this means for us. When I nudge Ilaria's head down and she nibbles at my navel, I lose myself to the sensation of her mouth on my skin. I could make the process last longer, like I did for her, but she's so anxious to succeed and it's been so long since I was with another person this way. So instead, I run my hands through her thick curls and urge her to go lower. I don't stop until she's flush with my legs.

The rest is up to her. I won't push this if she's not into it.

She pauses a minute, teeth worrying her bottom lip again, and I suspect she's weirded out by the fact that Psylina lasers every last damn hair off my body so that my clothes fit nice and snug. I lie there, awaiting a verdict as she runs a finger down my legs and spreads me open for a better view. Her eyes are hooded, appraising, uncertain.

"You don't have to do this," I tell her, pulling her head up briefly so she can see the truth of it in my face. I wanted to give her a gift, and I'm not expecting some form of payback. I'd still do it again. "Only if you want to. That's the only reason you should ever do anything with someone in bed."

Because as much as I want her, as much as my entire body is screaming for her mouth to be pressed against my thighs while I ride her face like a rocket, this isn't something I can take without her permission.

That's the difference between me and her husband. I'm only taking what is freely given and I don't need a court to trap her in a relationship she wants out of. There are no bars or cages here. Just two people choosing to be together.

"You think you don't deserve to be happy, Psalome?" She dives down without hesitation, her mouth wet against me. She hums the words straight onto my skin as she licks her way across my body. "You're kind and smart and you sacrifice everything for the people you love. It's about time you let someone take care of you for a change."

It's so honest and pure it hits me in a way nothing else can and I'm shaking beneath her, unable to hold myself back. She peeks up at me, long lashes framing silver eyes that are wide with shock.

"Did you just…?" Her voice trails off, uncertain.

"Yeah. Yeah, I did." Considering how I made Ilaria wait, it's embarrassing how quickly I've allowed myself to come in her mouth. Luckily Ilaria doesn't seem to mind.

She laughs, as delighted by my orgasm as she was by her own.

"Look at that," she says, collapsing onto the bed next to me. She talks to the ceiling, as if it's a private conversation with God. "The sign of a healthy and lasting relationship. Mutual pleasure."

"That's what you like?" I should have guessed. Ilaria can't fully enjoy herself unless her partner does, too. "Then we should finish together next time."

She props herself up on an elbow to ask if that is possible and I roll back on top of her in answer, interlocking my legs with hers.

"Oh, it's possible. Move however you want, do whatever feels good, I'll handle the rest."

Our bodies fit together like two pieces of a puzzle and although she's tentative at first, finding her groove, we end up in a tumbled heap of arms, legs, and mouths all writhing together. I could come right now, watching her buck and moan, but I wait until she's ready.

We settle into a rhythm, rocking against each other while our lips explore, seeking out new territory. It takes longer this time, but it is no less sweet, and when we collapse against the bed, satiated and content, all I want to do is coil my body around hers and live in this moment forever.

Except there's a tournament to deal and earrings to steal and lightyears to put in between me and this casino before I can be free enough to truly give someone all the things Ilaria deserves. Before I could hope to offer her anything but heartache.

I kiss her on the forehead and tuck the sheets in around her before I start my routine. Normally I'd shower, but I want to hold onto her for a little longer. Have the smell of her wrapped around me like armor for what comes next. Remind myself that I'm doing this for her, even if she won't necessarily thank me for what's about to happen.

I pad over to the dressing table and pick up the clothes El has left me. It's time to get back to work.

The dress is a masterpiece of illusion, pieces of black lace no bigger than doilies stitched together to cover the most essential parts of my body while highlighting the rest to perfection. It makes me feel more unclothed than Ilaria, who is still lying stark naked beneath my sheets.

The lace is cool to the touch as I shrug into it. I miss the heat of skin on skin. The memory of Ilaria's lips still tingles in my mouth. She rolls over with a contented sigh and sits up, clutching a sheet to her body. I wish she would drop it. I could stare at her for hours.

"You look even hotter without the jewelry," she says. "It's hard to remember what we're here for when you're wearing a dress like that."

When she looks at me with those silver moon eyes, I hardly remember what I'm doing this for either. It takes everything I've got not to grab her hand and run as far as we can away from the shit show that Psylina has planned for tonight.

Except then neither of us would be truly free. We'd spend the rest of our lives looking over our shoulders, fearing the demons from our past that threaten to drag us down.

I turn back to the mirror and pick up my dragon pin. I'm doing this for me, but also for Ilaria and maybe even Mom a little, too. So that we can all be free of the things that weigh us down. Kiyo's pearl earrings sway gently on my lobes as I fix my makeup. It would be simpler to make the swap now, have Ilaria run them over to her ship, but The Casino would notice. The window for their distraction is exceedingly slim. Finley better be on her A game because we won't get a second shot. One false step and we're all screwed.

I sashay over to the bed, determined to make every second with Ilaria count. There's a knock on the door outside, The Casino arriving to ensure I'm properly dressed and accessorized for the show, but I'm in no mood to cut this bliss short. At least they've had the decency to knock this time. Ilaria leans forward to bestow one last kiss on me. She's ruining my lipstick but I only step back when she slides her hand up my dress.

"Greedy," I tease as I swat her hand away. "I've created a monster."

She giggles and burrows back into the covers as I head out of the room to open the door. The knock is now a pound and it grows more insistent by the second, swelling like a snowball turned into an avalanche.

That's when I hear the shouting. A male voice, loud and unctuous, calling Ilaria's name. My blood freezes in my veins as I hustle to check the security feed. That isn't The Casino out there. It's Shaul.

"Something's wrong," I yell towards Ilaria. My voice constricts as I fail to push back my rising panic. Psylina told me about Ilaria's anxiety attack, and we both agreed Ilaria should never be placed in Shaul's path again. This is happening too fast, too early. I haven't even switched back on my coms. "Get some clothes on, quick."

Ilaria leaps out of the bed and casts about for something to cover up with, but the dress she was wearing is still lying on the floor out here so she snatches up the first thing she can find. The button-down jumpsuit she came here in. She's still struggling into the pants when the screaming starts.

"Open up, Psalome." Shaul's voice booms through reinforced steel. "I know she's in there, and I will kill both of you sluts if you don't open this door right now and give me my fucking money back."

"God in heaven, it's him." Ilaria retreats into herself at the sound of his voice, all the confidence of the last hour melting like a popsicle on a heating coil. "I'd forgotten how angry he gets."

Her body is shaking like a leaf, her fingers trembling so hard she can't tie the laces on her shirt. I never meant for things to go this far, for her to be this scared. I was supposed to be the one Shaul confronted, after the game, when he realized something was wrong. Not Ilaria. She was never meant to be here at the same time as he was.

There is no way I'm opening that door. It's double-reinforced titanium and he can break his fists pounding for all I care. I'm not letting him break her again, not after she's finally starting to put her life back together. I place myself between Ilaria and the entrance for good measure. The shouting continues until the smooth voice of The Casino, probably drawn here by the commotion, cuts through the latest string of abusive profanity Shaul is hurling at Ilaria through the walls.

"Please lower your voice, Master Harbormaster. This is The Elysium, not a tavern on Henta 5. I am sure we can handle whatever the problem is a bit more discreetly. Allow me to escort you inside."

It's my turn to curse as the door glides open and Shaul barges in, shoving me aside as soon as he spots Ilaria. His elbow to the ribs sends me flying straight into the gaming table and the polished edges cut deep into the skin on my upper arm. Glasses spiral and shatter on the floor, crunching underfoot as Shaul advances on a whimpering Ilaria.

He has her by the arm, yanking her out of the bedroom, his grip so tight I can practically see the bruises forming on her delicate skin. It stings worse than the blood trickling down my arm to form a sticky pool on the floor.

The Casino rushes over to help me up.

"Miss Psalome," they say, as they lift me off the floor, away from the spilled alcohol and shards of glass. They gently set me on my feet before inspecting my arm. "You're bleeding."

"I'm fine." I shove them in Shaul's direction, urgency taking precedence over pleasantries. "It's just a scratch. You need to help Ilaria before he kills her."

"I'll kill her if I damn well want to," Shaul growls. His fingers are burrowing deeper into her flesh. "She's my property. Legally acquired under a marriage canopy in front of two witnesses and all that. You might have checked before you fucked her. Somebody owes me several hundreds of millions of gold marks, and I will do what I deem necessary to get them back."

"I'm nobody's property," Ilaria says, wrenching herself from his grip. She's staring at the blood on my arm. I catch her eyes and give a small nod, lending her my strength as she finds her voice. "Were you not listening to the speeches at the reception? Marriage is meant to be a partnership. You never respected me enough to consider me your equal and as far as I'm concerned that means we were never married at all."

"Too bad your *opinion* doesn't count in beis din." He lunges towards her, foaming at the mouth, but The Casino steps effortlessly in between them, blocking Shaul's advance.

"If there is a question of missing funds, we can help you sort it out once you are in control of yourself." They have Shaul's hand firmly trapped in one of their own, the metal of their skeleton exerting a cold pressure on Shaul's fist. "In addition, there is the not insignificant fact that Miss Psalome has been injured and several items of glassware destroyed by your actions. Per the terms of the guest agreement you signed on your arrival, you will be held fiscally responsible for any damage done to this establishment or our employees."

Shaul's fist slackens as he scans the room with wild eyes, taking in the broken glasses and the gash running down my arm. Now that he is restrained, I take a look at it myself. It's deeper than I thought, probably requiring stitches. I snatch up the nearest napkin and use it to staunch the bleeding. Then I pour some alcohol over it as a disinfectant, wincing as it worsens the pain.

"No problem." Shaul's eyes glitter as he takes in my discomfort. His slick facade clicks back into place now that the initial brunt of his rage has been spent. "I'll pay for any damage done to your whore of an employee just as soon as you pay back the funds stolen by my whore of a wife in order to pay for her night of passion. We're both businessmen. I'm sure we can work something out."

It's not the first time I've been called a whore, but it's the first time the term has felt accurate. The first time it's filled me with shame, because Ilaria is there to hear it. Because I know Shaul is about to use me as a weapon to hurt her yet again. And I'm going to let him.

"Seriously, Shaul?" Ilaria fumes, her indignation on my behalf making her bold. "All this mishegas over my paying for one lousy drink from your accounts? Which is way more money than you made off my job and my insurance pay outs? It's good to see you, too. And by the way, The Casino isn't a man."

Ilaria has her hands on her hips, causing the still unfastened jumpsuit to buckle and pool around her exposed chest. She's forgotten her usual modesty in the heat of the moment, but Shaul is eyeing her breasts. It sends a shiver down my spine.

I lean over to tie her bows for her. He doesn't get to look at her that way anymore. She may not be mine, but she is certainly not his. He's never touching her again.

"Well, this really is a full-service establishment." Shaul lets out a low chuckle as he realizes what I'm doing. His skin is flushed and sweaty. "It's sweet of you to help her with her clothes, but I suppose she did pay enough of my money for you to take them off her in the first place."

Ilaria's body stiffens and she grabs my hands, finishes tying the bows herself. They droop like day-old balloons on her hunched shoulders. "What's he talking about, Psalome?"

I can't look her in the face, can't bring myself to say the words out loud. This isn't how it was supposed to go down. I never imagined she would be here for this part when Psylina first hatched this plan. I never would have agreed to subject her to Shaul's taunting. I can take it, he's no bigger a bully than my dad, but Ilaria has a family that loves her. That treated each other with kindness and respect. She isn't prepared for Shaul's vitriol, not even after all those disastrous years of marriage to him.

"You think you only paid for a drink?" Shaul's voice is a knife slicing through whatever bonds we've built between us. A wrecking ball tearing through the walls of both our dignity. "Wake up and smell the burnt kugel. This is a secular Space Casino, Ilana. A pleasure house. Not a heimishe restaurant. Everything here has a price. Including the shiksa you seem to think had sex with you out of the goodness of her heart. She doesn't love you, you were simply the first one to offer the right payment, because you were too naive to realize you were paying it. Out of my accounts!"

Her face is ashen as his words sink in, her lips drawn tight in a thin line. She won't cry, she's too proud for that, but I can see the hurt painted all over her body.

"I'm sorry," I whisper, backing away. "I never intended for this to happen."

I want to tell her that she isn't naive. That Psylina chose her because she knew I would find her irresistible. That while it's too early to call it love, my feelings for her are very real. But I have a part to play in all of this and there's no time for tears or regrets. Not if I want freedom. She needs to be just another client now, our time together simply a transaction completed.

Shaul is rounding on The Casino, pointing an accusatory finger. "The little fool didn't even know what she was buying. She didn't consent to that charge. You're duty bound to refund it."

"Be that as it may," The Casino says with a frown. "Services were rendered. A contract was signed. Did she not get what was paid for?"

They glare at each for a silent minute and the stalemate threatens to last for hours until Ilaria's singsong voice diverts all of our attention.

"Oh, I definitely got my money's worth." She draws herself up to her full height, looking for all the world like a statue in the sculpture garden despite the state of disarray her clothes and hair are in. I thought I was implacable as marble, but I've clearly got nothing on Ilaria when she's offended. "Several times, in fact. Psalome was attentive and kind, and took the time to listen to me as a person even before the sex. Which is more than I can say for my marriage to you. I'm not contesting the charge. I'd pay it again."

My heart threatens to burst in my chest and my hands itch to reach out and hold her, my brave Ilaria, finally standing up for what she deserves. Except she's not truly mine, never was and might not ever be. That's her choice to make and unlike Shaul, I won't try to make it for her.

"Really, Ilaria? Well, good luck living out here on your own with no divorce, no friends, and no funds." Shaul dismisses her with a wave of his hand, as if stealing the community which Ilaria has loved since she was born is of no consequence to him. He spins towards me. "And good luck to you on recouping your payment. I froze all my accounts. Ilaria isn't technically allowed to use them anyway. Wives don't have that kind of access on Thillov."

He drags out the word "wives" as if it is the most ridiculous thing in the world. A temper tantrum thrown by a toddler that should know better. Ephemeral and short lasting. A thing for her to cringe over when she comes crawling back to him.

After this whole incident, he hasn't learned a damn thing. He still doesn't understand her, and he's grossly underestimated me.

"It's a good thing I always demand payment upfront." It's a bittersweet victory but I mean to savor it anyway. "The funds have already been secured."

"Impossible," he says smugly. "Such a large transfer of funds would require both signatories, and I didn't authorize chicken shit."

"On the contrary," The Casino says. They're stealing my thunder but in this particular case I'm willing to allow it. They are, after all, the only thing keeping Shaul from assaulting me and Ilaria. "I handle Miss Psalome's payments. When the funds failed to transfer, I thought it prudent to collect them another way rather than disturb Miss Ilaria in the midst of completing her purchase. I am told humans refer to such things as a 'mood killer'?"

Shaul's eyes narrow into slits as they dart between the three of us. "Another way?"

"They took your ship," I gloat, leaning in and smiling so that he can see all of my teeth. "The one that never belonged to you anyway. Thillov laws might be draconian but they're very clear on the distribution of marital property. The girl gets her dowry back in the case of marital distress. It's in her ketubah. That ship belongs to The Elysium now."

"But I'm still making mortgage payments on that thing!" His eyebrows have snapped together, and his voice is feral. "There's no way you're getting away with this."

"She already has," The Casino interjects. "Nobody refuses

payment to me or one of my employees. I assure you, whatever legal resources you have, I will outlive them. Plus, I'm afraid I will have to withdraw you from the tournament for causing bodily harm to a Dazzler. It is a pity. With Miss Halley disqualified you were the front runner."

"Halley?" Ilaria asks, her voice falsely high. She is the worst actress I have ever seen. "Who's that?"

"No need to keep up pretenses, Miss Ilaria," The Casino says. "We are well aware of Miss Finley's real identity. We have been ever since she sat down at the gaming table tonight. Our recent security upgrades have been most thorough."

My heart sinks into my chest. Security upgrades is code for exactly one thing in Casino speak.

Psylina.

# CHAPTER TWENTY-FIVE

## Kiyokimora

"WHAT THE FUCK have you done with my girlfriend and my spaceship?" I barge into Psalome's room like I own the place. My heels click on the hardwood floor, intentionally creating a ruckus. I figure I need a little noise if I want to have any hope of them noticing me amidst the destruction formerly known as Psalome's private salon. The room is a mess, clothes and broken glass are scattered about and the smell of alcohol mixed with blood is overwhelming.

I stride straight past Ilaria, whose hair is flying in a hundred places and sticking to her wrinkled jumpsuit. She looks like she could use a stiff drink herself, but I don't have time to worry about her. Not when Finley has gone missing and my spaceship right along with her.

I went looking for her, to apologize after our fight, to tell her I loved her, too, even if I can't always show it, and found a bevy of androids slapping an impound lojack on my ship along with a transfer order to move it to cargo bay five. The only explanation they could give me was a cryptic message from The Casino informing me that I would have to wait until they returned from resolving an altercation in Psalome's room before I could make arrangements to collect Finley.

They actually used the word "collect," like Finley is a piece of missing baggage and not a living, breathing person. I don't know who this Casino thinks they are messing with, but company CEO or not, I am still a GoldWeaver. GoldWeavers do not allow people to be treated like property. They do not sit idly by as their spaceships are impounded and they most certainly do not wait. For anything.

What *can* wait is whatever little tete a tete The Casino is having with that fucking conman Shaul. I don't even want to know what led to the smashed furniture or Psalome's bleeding arm. She and Ilaria appear to be breathing and in one piece, which is more information than what I have on Finley right now.

Even Shaul's threats about releasing the video in a few hours are nothing compared to the terror of Finley missing.

"You had no right to take my ship," I say, not bothering to keep the anger out of my voice. There is a time for subtlety and there is a time for throwing around one's weight. And a GoldWeaver is worth her weight in diamonds. That's what my mom used to say. "Return it, and my girlfriend immediately. If one hair on her head is damaged, so help me I will see to it that every last shred of the program that keeps you running is deleted and the servers are recycled for scrap metal."

If they find my threats offensive, they do a good job of concealing it. Their voice is cool as frozen steel and their grip on Shaul's upper arm never falters. "Miss Finley is unharmed and is currently quartered in cargo bay five with the rest of the items I have confiscated that are awaiting redemption by their owners."

"Items? Owners?" I yell. "She's a person, you bucket of bolts. The human I love most in this world. You might not be capable of understanding that, but you will return her immediately."

It's pointless to insult them, it would probably be more effective to appeal to their business preservation protocols by threatening to leave a bad review on the billionaires-only travel website, but I'm so livid I could punch them in their synthetic mouth.

"Indeed," they reply, a half smile spreading across their mouth. Psylina really outdid herself on the programming of those human emotion mimics. They almost look wistful. "She is a person named Halley who has violated the restraining order barring her from my space station and she was planning on helping you throw the poker tournament to disgrace Master Harbormaster. You needn't have bothered. He has managed to achieve that particular distinction all on his own."

My shoulders droop as Finley's birth name drops from their mouth like a grenade with the pin pulled. Shaul is spluttering, claiming that if he goes down, he's releasing the video tape and taking me with him. I shove him aside, barely able to contain the ringing in my ears as I approach The Casino.

Let Shaul do his worst. I have bigger problems to navigate.

I'm the one that got Finley into this mess, brought her to the most dangerous place possible for her in terms of both her sobriety and her criminal record and then let her wander off after falsely accusing her of being high. All because I was too afraid to love her back.

Now she's locked up in some cargo hold like an animal. Plus, God alone knows why Psalome is injured and Ilaria looks like something that got spat out the back end of the space station waste recycler.

Whatever trouble they are all in, the guilt for it all rests squarely on my shoulders and it's my job to fix it. What the hell was I thinking trying to rob an AI-run Casino older than space flight technology itself? No company is worth that risk, yet somehow all three of these people trusted me enough to try it anyway. I'm not letting them down.

"Her name is Finley now and she's not that person anymore." I believe it with my whole heart, with every fiber of my being. "She didn't cheat on any games and no property is missing. All she did was violate a restraining order. Once you release my spaceship from your impound lot I'll take her and Ilaria home. Psalome, too, if she wants a lift. The funds to buy out her contract will be coming from my personal account."

It'll cost me a fortune, but I mean to keep my word. Besides, if I'm about to lose the company I might as well blow as much of my family money as possible on helping people out before it is snatched away from me, too. I would have preferred to be systematic about it, to give away the funds while still ensuring a means of repletion so that I could make the donations automatic and self-sustaining, but if that's not possible I'll settle for this.

"That won't be necessary," The Casino says, folding their arms over their chest. "Her contract has already been fulfilled. Miss Psalome is free to stay or go as she pleases. As for your ship, it should be where you left it. Cargo bay seven, space six. I see no recent activity there. Perhaps you got lost in your distress?"

"I don't understand." Who could possibly have paid for Psalome's contract? There's only one item on her price list that would clear her debt in one night and she hasn't had anyone up in her bedroom except Ilaria.

I look at her for an explanation and for the first time I notice the way she is studiously avoiding Ilaria's gaze. Her face has the same guilty look mine did when I couldn't look Finley in the eyes when she woke up in my bed half naked.

Only Ilaria isn't smiling the way Finley was. Her arms are crossed over her chest and she's biting her lip so hard I'm worried she'll draw blood. The two of them are shifting away from each other like a pair of similarly charged ions. Like being close is a chemical impossibility at this point.

Shaul is glowering at them both. Murderously glowering. Glowering to the point where I suddenly want to ensure there are no sharp objects in his reach.

"Oh," I say as it clicks into place. The disheveled state of Ilaria's clothes, the homicidal look on Shaul's face.

Finley did say they'd been playing footsie with each other under the table for over a week. From the looks of it, things got more physical and Shaul's been held responsible for the debts of the wife he refuses to divorce. Which serves him right.

You've got to hand it to Psylina. I'm still not convinced she isn't a sociopath, but she has a poetic flair for justice. If Shaul had given Ilaria her divorce, he wouldn't be on the hook right now.

"Well, I suppose I've missed a few things," I say, ceding to the fact that Psalome and Ilaria having sex is actually something notable. Even with Finley missing. "But I'm certain my spaceship was parked in space eight, not space six. Or at least it was, before you unlawfully impounded it."

Psylina had specifically insisted I park there, claiming it would make it easier for her to keep an eye on both mine and Shaul's ships to have them in the docking bay near hers.

Shaul laughs, a bitter sound that is devoid of any actual joy. A laugh that mocks, rather than delights. "My ship is parked in space six."

"Right next to Psylina's." Again, that girl has outfoxed me. She has somehow manipulated the docking registry so that my ship is listed in Shaul's spot, and his in mine, causing my ship to "accidentally" be involved in whatever torrid drama these three are brewing. She told me from day one that none of us could leave until Psalome was safely tucked away on her own ship. Right before she told me where to park. Having The Casino impound my ship ensures I'm stuck here until everything is resolved.

Finley was right, they would have made a killing playing poker together. Psylina anticipated each and every one of our moves and she didn't hesitate to go for the kill. Not even with her sister and Ilaria. We've all been dancing to her tune, puppets pulled by her strings, and she's ensured we could not escape until she got what she wanted.

The only thing left to do is collect Finley, help Ilaria pick up the pieces, and get off this damn space station before this Casino eats us all alive. I smooth out my dress, gathering the shreds of composure I have left.

"I suggest you fetch my ship so that I can take Finley and Ilaria home." I place some emphasis on the names. She's not Halley anymore and I won't have her thinking I doubt that for even one minute.

"An excellent idea," The Casino says, wrapping their fingers around Shaul's upper arm and tugging him towards the door. "We can all go to cargo bay seven together. This way I can exchange your ship for Master Harbormaster's while also escorting Miss Psalome to her sister who eagerly awaits her presence."

A throng of additional Casino personnel, all with identical faces but increasingly threatening body armor, have converged in the hallway. I step in front of them, refusing to be escorted like a common criminal. Ilaria sticks close to my side, putting as much distance between herself and Shaul as possible.

Psalome trails behind, uncertain. Her arm is still bleeding

and a Casino medic clone whips out a pack of gauze while we are in the lifts. They surround her with a phalanx of bodies, ensuring Shaul cannot so much as see her let alone harm her again.

They fuss over her arm with what appears to be genuine concern. One giant hive mind made of circuits and wires trying to fix what they should never have allowed to happen within their walls. News of a damaged Dazzler would be terrible for profits. Not to mention Psylina is going to be pissed.

The Casino is known throughout the galaxy as a safe haven for both employees and customers. That's how they recruit the best Dazzlers. It's also why all the wealthy women in my mother's social circles felt comfortable flocking here, sometimes with kids in tow, to enjoy the various pleasures on offer. I was a fool not to come here instead of random night clubs to blow off some steam after Mom died and Dad ousted me from the company under the guise of a curatorship. If I had, none of this would have happened.

The Casino would never let a creep like Shaul stash a hidden camera on the premises. Even with The Casino clones between us I can feel Shaul's eyes on me, reminding me he knows what I look like without my clothes on, sprawled out for somebody else's pleasure, and that the rest of the world will know, too, if I don't give him what he wants.

At this point he'll probably release it regardless of whether I pay him off or not. To regain some control over his life after what the Shipmens have done to him. To show all of his victims that he means business.

He's already displayed my great-great-grandmother's earrings at a casino poker tournament. A warning shot fired across the bow. He winks at me as the lift makes its way to cargo bay seven.

Psalome causes quite the stir as we exit into the hallway. Between her barely-there dress and the sparkling tournament jewelry she's decked out in, nobody notices the bloody gauze on her arm. Several people try to follow us into the docking station, but they are gently redirected by The Casino clones, three of whom stay behind for crowd control.

"Casino personnel only in this docking bay," one of them informs the onlookers as the doors swish shut. "Our deepest apologies. Please inquire with the main booking line if you would like a private appointment with Miss Psalome at another date."

Psalome whirls on The Casino, light shimmering and refracting off the gemstones she is wearing as she shoves the nearest clone into the side of Psylina's ship.

"My slate is clear," she seethes. "No more clients. No more bookings. I don't owe you a damn thing anymore. Between what Ilaria paid and all the stuff in my room, I'm bought out."

She raises an arm and I expect her to punch them but instead she starts ripping the jewelry off her body, piling it up in a glittering heap at The Casino's feet. My insides twist as I watch the priceless gemstones lobbed like bullets at The Casino. They ping as they bounce off the metal floor.

This is no way to treat good stones.

"You most certainly are bought out." The Casino ignores the opal and jade bracelet that hits them in the chest with a thud before joining its compatriots on the floor. "I was hoping you would choose to stay as a freelancer. I can offer you very competitive commission rates and I can keep your room prepared if you'd like to take some vacation first. Perhaps with your new friend?"

"You mean you can keep the docking port ready for Psylina." Psalome ignores The Casino's reference to Ilaria.

Glosses over it like the mere idea is so ludicrous it doesn't even merit pausing to think over. Out of the corner of my eye I see Ilaria stiffen as Psalome plows on with her tirade, throwing everything valuable on her person onto the heap with a rage unmatched by any force of nature. "You could care less about what happens to me. Your only regret is that I'm taking my sister with me."

She's slithering out of the dress now, adding it to the pile of returned property, and I forget all about the mistreated jewelry as I learn that she isn't wearing anything underneath it. Her naked skin glows in the industrial light of the cargo bay like a visitation from the Goddess of Lust. Even Shaul stops wrestling against The Casino clones that are holding him steady to stare open-mouthed at the sight of Psalome whipping the dragon pin out of her hair. Black locks cascade down her shoulders and shroud her in their thick glory. A modern-day Lady Godiva.

"On the contrary." The Casino swoops down and retrieves the pin from the pile. "While I may love Miss Psylina, I have also grown quite fond of you in your own right. Not to mention the difficulty of finding a replacement for my highest earning Dazzle Girl. I am attempting to prepare Jacinthe to deal the tournament in your place and the results are less than encouraging."

They lift Psalome's hand to their mouth for a kiss before gently placing the dragon pin in it.

"Please accept one small gift as a token of our appreciation and the esteem in which we hold you. I made a separate offer to Miss Psylina in private, as soon as I became aware of your impending emancipation. The offer for you to return, with your sister or not, always stands."

Psalome turns the hair ornament over in her hands gingerly, as if it is a stick of dynamite. Then she looks up at The Casino's face and crushes them in a hug. There is no whoosh of air, they don't breathe after all, but I can hear their circuits squeaking from the force of her embrace. "Thank you. For everything."

I clear my throat loudly. Psalome and The Casino having a quiet moment of mutual appreciation is heartwarming and all, but Finley is still missing at large as is my ride out of here.

I'm also the only human present that isn't content to stare at Psalome naked for hours. If ever there was a doubt in my mind that Finley is right and I'm not prepared to let another person touch me that way right now, the events of today have confirmed it. Psalome is gorgeous and it is doing nothing for me. Which is why I need Finley back. To apologize.

"Can we focus on the reason we came down here?" I demand. "Where's Finley and my ship?"

"Right here."

The voice comes from the far end of the room, where Finley is emerging from my ship. The GoldWeaver logo, painted in gold leaf and lapis lazuli, winks proudly from behind her as she descends the stairs two at a time. Her hair is a wreck and her makeup is smudged but to me she resembles an angel. An impish angel, wearing a way-too-short skirt and with a purse that clinks suspiciously like it is full of gaming chips, but an angel nonetheless.

Warmth spreads through my entire body as she strides over, running as if she was born with stilettos on her feet. This is my Finley. The person I'm meant to spend the rest of my life with. Whether it's physical or not.

"Nice of you to finally pick me up," she says, coming to a stop beside me. "I'm sorry for all the trouble. I tried to tell them they took the wrong ship, but they wouldn't listen. Also, I, uhm, won us a bunch of money at the blackjack table. But I was not drinking. I swear to God. All I asked for was ginger ale. You can check with The Casino. Or do a breathalyzer or something. I know you still keep those test strips handy."

I throw my arms around her and bury my face in her hair. "I know you didn't, Fin. I trust you."

She reeks of industrialized carpet and cigarette smoke, she really has spent too much time on the gaming floor during this trip, but I don't care. I half choke, half sob into her shoulder. "I'm sorry. I was so worried about the company and those damn earrings that I forgot to pay attention to you. Screw the company. You're all the family legacy I need."

"I knew you'd come for me," she replies, hugging me back. "We'll find some other way to get your company back. Together. But first I'm going to need you to let go because you are kind of in danger of breaking one of my ribs."

"Together," I agree, relinquishing her body but keeping her well within arm's reach. I am not letting her out of my sight until we are safely out of this casino. "I like the sound of that."

I put my hand on her face and do what I should have done hours ago in our hotel room when she told me she loved me. Say what I should have said every minute of every day since I met her. "Companies come and go, but you are the love of my life, Finley Starchaser. Forever."

I don't kiss her, I can't, but she doesn't seem to mind.

"You'll spoil a girl with all these public declarations of affection." She blushes, but nestles her head into my shoulder, where it has always belonged. Then she lets out a low whistle as she takes in the rest of the crowd.

"Uhm, Kiyo? What the fuck is Shaul doing here with Ilaria? And why is Psalome naked? I thought prison was where all the exciting shit went down. What the hell happened to you guys while I was incarcerated?"

It is at this juncture, with Psalome and Ilaria each shifting uncomfortably from foot to foot and refusing to speak, that Psylina finally decides to grace us all with her presence. There is a small hiss as the door to her spaceship pops open and she bounces out like a round-cheeked elf surveying its handiwork after a night of mischief making.

"I happened."

# CHAPTER TWENTY-SIX

## Psylina

ALL EYES SWIVEL around to watch my approach. Even that lecherous toad Shaul stops ogling my sister for long enough to spare me an appraising glance. I give him the finger as I walk past. The time for pleasantries has long since expired.

"For God's sake, Psalome," I say, sliding the silk robe I brought with me from our spaceship over her shoulders. "Why do you always have to be so dramatic about everything? El would have waited for you to put something of mine on before you cashed in all your clothes."

"No way I'd be caught dead in any of your clothes." She rolls her eyes as if to accuse me of being the dramatic one. Then she shrugs into the sleeves of the robe, wisely letting me handle the rest of the talking. I've choreographed this out, down to the last millisecond, and I'll be damned if I let her fuck up my grand entrance.

Kiyokimora is glaring at me with her jaw clenched so tight I can hear her teeth grinding. I'd bet the only thing keeping her from punching me in the face is the fact that Finley is snuggled against her shoulder. Assault and battery would not look good on top of the rest of Finley's rap sheet and we both know I'm the one thing in the universe that could convince

The Casino to file charges despite it meaning losing Kiyo as a customer.

"No hard feelings?" I ask her, although I include Ilaria in my statement. "I told you I was liberating Psalome no matter the price, and that I was not willing to betray The Casino in the process. This was the only way to make that happen. Now Psalome's bought out, Ilaria's told Shaul to go fuck himself, and the poker tournament finale hasn't been compromised. Everyone got what they needed in the end."

"Everyone but Kiyo," Finley says darkly, straightening herself out. "Or did you forget that salvaging her company was the entire purpose of this operation, you little demon?"

She's spitting mad and El moves to stand in front of me, but I shoo them away. Kiyo has a restraining arm on Finley.

"Don't, Finley," she says. "Psylina's right, I did get what I needed. Because I have you. Let's take back our buy-in and go. We'll figure something out."

Kiyo waits for Finley to give one curt nod of assent, clenching her nails like a cat retracting its claws, before scooping the pin she used to buy Finley into the tournament off the pile on the floor. Her hand hesitates over the pearl earrings, but Shaul's hand materializes to snatch them up first.

"Figure something out, huh?" he asks. His eyes rake over her body and a grin spreads across his mouth. The smile of a predator as they rip out the bloody neck of their prey. All teeth and no joy. "It's your lucky day then, Kiyo. I seem to be in a bit of a bind and I'm willing to make you a one-time special offer. I heard you mention you've already liberated the funds to buy Psalome's contract. Which just so happens to be the amount I require to have my spaceship released from impound. How's about we give each other what we need?"

"She doesn't want anything from you." Finley spits the words like venom. "And she never will."

"Pity," Shaul says. His fingers twirl the earrings round and round, but his eyes have never left Kiyo's. They are taunting and hard, like glittering lumps of coal in the furnace. Touch them and they'll leave you scorched to ashes. "Because if you don't, I will release that video and you can kiss your company goodbye. Or you can take my offer and I will return the digital copy of your indiscretions to you."

Kiyo bites her lip, but she can't repress the tremor that snakes its way through her body. She wants that video more than life itself, but she also doesn't trust Shaul. And she shouldn't. "Like Finley said, I don't want anything from you."

She's turning to go but he holds her back. "I'll give you five minutes to think it over. Buy me out or this time tomorrow the entire universe gets a view of your tits and ass being railed right before you kill a poor innocent boy with GoldWeaver gold. The CEO being a murderous slut is certain to be terrible for business."

Kiyo keeps dragging Finley behind her, but I motion for El to stop them both. I've got most of what I need, but I'm hoping I can get Shaul to give me the rest. He's been careful with what he says, but Kiyo walking away is clearly getting to him.

"Wait," I say as two clones block their exit. "You are right. I promised I'd help and I meant that. There might be something we can do to reach an agreement between the two of you."

Kiyo shakes her head. "I said I didn't want anything from him, and I most certainly don't want anything from you. I'm a big girl. I made my own choices. He wants to release that tape? Go ahead. GoldWeavers built this company from the ground up and I'll build another one if I have to. It's what we do. Not making deals with weasels. He'll only pop up again later with a bootleg copy of the video and more demands. I'm done with that."

Shaul is desperate now, his body shaking with rage, his voice wheedling as he plays the last card he has left and finds it still lacking. "There are no copies! This is the only one and I will turn it over to you just as soon as I get access to my ship."

Bingo. Shaul is starting to dig his own grave. All I need to do is keep him talking.

"The only copy?" I murmur, sidling up to him. It needs to be crystal clear that Shaul is the sole creator and possessor of this video. No room for reasonable doubt or excuses later. "Why should she believe you?"

"I'm the one that stashed that camera," he insists. "The only person still alive that knew it existed. I screen all the footage myself and I don't make duplicates. You can check my hard drives. I'll take a lie detector test."

"So there is no other way this footage could be released to the public without your knowledge?" I flick a piece of nonexistent lint off my jeans, as if I don't believe him. Which I don't. Assholes like this always make copies. They're never satisfied and they will never give in once they see your weakness. They always find ways to ask for more. My father taught me that.

Kiyo is right to turn him down, to take her power back the only way she can. But I'm not her. My father taught me a few other things, too.

It doesn't matter how many copies Shaul has. What matters is what he's confessing to right now. A step he never would have taken in his usual, carefully vague, untraceable messages and threats.

"Not a one," Shaul says blithely. "I control it completely."

Winner, winner, chicken dinner. I win it all. All because he thinks a small girl who lives in a spaceship docking bay could never hurt him. He'd never talk so freely in front of someone he actually thought important.

The grin that spreads over my face is so feral even El takes a step back. It's a side of me they haven't seen before. We'll have to work through it later, because to survive my piranha of a father I had to turn myself into a shark and Shaul is bleeding in the water. He just doesn't know it yet.

"I hope you enjoy prison," I tell him, leaning too close for comfort. Let him feel what it is like to have his personal space violated for once. "Kiyo was underage on every single planet in existence when that video was taken, and possession of child pornography carries a minimum sentence of ten years on the most lenient planet. Distribution? That's a life sentence or the death penalty, depending on where they incarcerate you. And you just incriminated yourself on the record on both counts. You'll forgive me for hoping it's one of the planets that still allows corporal punishment. The fact that you remotely watched while that boy died on drugs you fed him will practically ensure you hit the max sentence."

Shaul's face is ashen now, pale and sour as curdled milk. "There's no way to trace it back to me. You can't prove I released it, or that I filmed it."

"But you just said so yourself, sir, all control of the files is yours." El scratches their head as if they cannot understand Shaul's logic. The depth of human duplicity. Another thing we'll have to go over later. Along with how to not upstage one's girlfriend. Because I was hoping to reveal this tidbit in a much more dramatic fashion.

"El records all their interactions," I explain to Shaul. "The more important ones, such as your recent assertion that you are both the producer and sole owner of this footage, get logged and backed up on their servers. It's as good as a confession and it will survive long past the day you die. El's backed up on hundreds of planets, including locations even I don't know about. If even one whiff of that video gets out, they will be obligated to appear when given a subpoena and give testimony. I trust Kiyokimora's lawyers can handle the prosecution, but I will personally make sure you are hunted to the ends of the galaxy to pay for your crimes against humanity."

Shaul lets out a string of curses and makes a move to attack me but El swoops in to restrain him. I don't flinch. They never go down easy, but men like him can't hurt me anymore.

I turn to Kiyo instead. "Still want to turn my joyfriend into scrap metal? I told you everyone would get what they wanted. All I needed was for you to have a little faith."

She swallows hard, one hand gripping Finley's, the other worrying the sapphire as she processes what just happened.

"I'm sorry I thought you were a sociopath," she concedes.

"I'm still not convinced she's not," Finley whispers. "You planned this all along? How the fuck could you know he'd say that?"

I shrug. "I watch people from inside a spaceship while teaching an AI how to interpret human behavior. I learned to pick up on the patterns. I knew I could get him to say what I wanted, so long as Kiyo tried to walk away from whatever deal he offered."

I give Kiyo a nod, because what she did took incredible courage. It was the one thing I couldn't definitively count on. She's changed since we first met. I suspect the way Finley is grasping her hand has something to do with that.

"Well, la di dah for you," Shaul says, scowling at the pearl earrings in his hands. "I suppose I'll have to hock these at auction just to pay for a ride out of here."

El intercepts him once more. "You are forgetting the last of your debts, Master Harbormaster. You damaged a Dazzler under my employ. Our initial medical assessment indicates Miss Psalome will have a scar on her arm for life. Her body is her means of employ right now, so you owe her for potential lost revenue as well as pain and distress. Given your accounts are frozen and your spaceship impounded, I will have to begin seizing other assets as recompense. We can go have a look through the storage caskets from your ship to find suitable items or you can see if she is willing to accept the earrings."

They wink over at me and Kiyo, proudly displaying their cleverness. Injury to Psalome was never part of the plan, but El knows how much those earrings mean to Kiyo, how their loss was the one wrong I couldn't right in the plan we hatched together. They are adapting, despite not being programmed for such an eventuality, and I couldn't be more proud. Or more in love.

This re-writing their own code on the fly shit is hot.

"What do you say, Miss Psalome?" they ask.

Kiyo beams like a thousand suns, eagerly nodding yes, her eyes pleading with Psalome. She'll pay whatever my sister wants in exchange for those earrings, but Psalome isn't looking at her. My sap of a sister is staring straight at Ilaria and when she opens her mouth that's who she's really talking to.

"I don't want the earrings," she says, taking a step towards Ilaria. "I don't want any physical thing. I'm told on Thillov divorce papers can only be served by the male in the relationship? That's what I want, a divorce, if Ilaria will agree to accept it from you."

Ilaria squeaks, looking up from behind a curtain of tumbled brown curls. Her silver eyes lock on Psalome's and the tiniest of smiles escapes from her mouth. "I would be very glad to receive the divorce. But you don't have to do this. The Casino is right, your body is your livelihood. I'm not worth all that."

"No, you're not." Psalome's voice is hard as iron. She

reaches out to tuck one curl behind Ilaria's ear. "You're worth significantly more. We both are. So let me buy you your fucking freedom like you bought mine and then we can both get the hell out of here and explore other career options."

Ilaria giggles and Psalome laughs and I half expect them to start making out in front of all of us but Shaul spoils the moment.

"Fucking whores. You two deserve each other." He's signing a tablet that El has procured, presumably loaded with the electronic version of a divorce agreement that Ilaria's family drew up the moment they found out what Shaul did for a living. The document that has been sitting in his inbox, waiting for a signature, for years. "She was a shit wife anyway. Couldn't even give me a kid. Good luck getting rid of her when you realize how high maintenance she is."

He throws the tablet at Ilaria's feet and storms off towards the lifts, heading to cargo bay five and his safe full of blackmail material so he can pick another target and recoup whatever cash he can get to buy himself out of this mess. Which means there is very little time left before we need to be out of here, too. There's only so much El can protect me from. Only so much I could let them be aware of before violating their code. I give them a little nudge, raising my eyebrows in Shaul's direction, reminding them not to let that man wander around the space station unattended. They hold the lift doors and wink back, tilting their chin towards Psalome and Ilaria as if to say *humans, so adorable. What would they do without us?*

We've never needed to talk to understand each other.

"If everyone is satisfied, then our business here is done," El says. Their clones are busy collecting the last of the pile of gems that Psalome has placed on the floor. "I have a tournament to oversee and a rather irate patron to evict, so I will leave you all to say your goodbyes. Please visit soon, we would most love to have you, so long as Miss Halley comes under her new name and refrains from visiting the gaming areas."

Finley chokes back a snort and Kiyo shushes her. We stand around waiting together, until the lift door swooshes shut behind El and Shaul.

"Sorry about your earrings," Ilaria says to Kiyo. She's clutching the tablet with her divorce to her chest like it is a precious Torah scroll. "At least you won't lose the company."

"I'm not sorry at all," Kiyo says. "Psalome is right. It never occurred to me he'd be willing to give you the divorce, but you're worth more than earrings. We all are. I'd gladly sacrifice my grandmother's earrings and then some to give us all a fresh start. I'm only sorry I didn't think of it myself"

"Who says you have to?" I ask. I bounce up and down on my toes, because now that the hard part is over, and El is gone, I can't wait a second longer. "Show them, Lo. I want to see the look on their faces."

Psalome grins wide, and it is her real smile, not the one she uses on the gaming floor. Then she swoops up her hair into a topknot and secures it with the dragon pin, revealing a pair of pearl earrings dangling from each earlobe.

"Nothing like a naked girl to make men forget to look at what's in front of them," she says, detaching the earrings and handing them over to Kiyo. "I grabbed the fakes before I left my room. We couldn't be one hundred percent sure Shaul would confess on tape to sole ownership of the footage, but we figured I could at least liberate these so you could contest its authenticity."

Tears well up in Kiyo's eyes as Finley puts the earrings on for her. She leans into the other woman's touch like a flower seeking the sun. Then she turns her shocked face to me. "Thank you. I don't know what to say to either of you. Nothing feels adequate."

"Say you won't tell El about this or the rest of what Finley boosted from Shaul's ship and we're good." I give a nod towards Kiyo's ship. "The Casino isn't responsible for Shaul's goods because he didn't buy any insurance but El's going to be pretty pissed if they find out I had them arrest Finley to get her past the security and onto cargo bay five. Thanks for taking my call, by the way, Finley. I wasn't sure if you would."

"They made it pretty clear it wasn't optional," Finley says with a shrug. "I was all for getting hammered and then coming after you with a chainsaw, but once Kiyo's ship showed up in the impound lot, I caught on pretty quick. I threw all of Shaul's stuff in. You are a fucking genius. You sure you don't want to play poker with me?"

"My preferred game is chess and I already have a partner to play it with."

I'd say more, but Ilaria is hugging me. It is warm and rushed and I don't know what to do with my arms. It's been a long time since I was last hugged. Psalome hasn't tried it since she traded herself in to The Casino. I give Ilaria a brief pat on the back to convince her to disengage.

"I'll make sure everything goes back to the people he was blackmailing. Even if it's the last thing I do. If somebody would drop me off at the nearest planet with a Jewish community and some kind of mining presence, I can get a job and start saving up to make all the necessary arrangements."

"Like hell we'll drop you off," Finley says. Her arms are crossed over her chest and Kiyo is nodding vigorously. "GoldWeavers have hundreds of mines and Kiyo is going to need people she trusts in the organization when she takes over. You can work for us and we'll help you make the arrangements. Maybe even start a support group or something."

Ilaria nods gratefully and starts walking over. I shoot Psalome a look. She raises an eyebrow as if she doesn't know what my glare is about, so I poke her in the ribs. Hard.

"Now or never, sweet sister." I sweated for days on this plan to ensure she was free. It's about time she started acting like it. "Go get your person before it's too late."

# CHAPTER TWENTY-SEVEN

## Ilaria

"YOU COULD COME with us. If you wanted, I mean. You don't have to."

Psalome is stumbling forward, her feet tripping almost as badly as her mouth as Psylina shoves her towards me. "You should know this wasn't the plan. The Casino was supposed to walk in on us making out, charge you for sex, and then leave. I would then stow you away safely on Psylina's ship where she would explain everything by the time Shaul showed up to demand a refund. Only you looked so beautiful in that dress, I let myself get caught up in the moment, imagining you wouldn't mind."

Thanks to the skimpy robe I can see the heat spreading from her face down to her torso as she remembers exactly how caught up we got. She's redder than the Queen of Hearts and chewing her lip so hard it bleeds. "Anyhow. I wanted to tell you that it wasn't about the money. It meant something to me. And I'm sorry."

I'm not sure if she's apologizing for sleeping with me or not telling me that Shaul was going to be charged for it, but I can't stand to see her this nervous. She's meant to stand tall and strong, unbowed by the weight of all the things in her life that have tried to drag her down. Free as the way she was with me in bed. Free as we both are now, thanks to her courage.

"Don't be." I run my hands over her arm the way she runs her hands over the piano keys. Dancing, suggesting. Extending an invitation for us to make more music together. "It's better this way. Psylina told me The Casino is programmed to ensure all transactions are completed to the purchaser's satisfaction. This way Shaul has no room to contest the charges, because I meant what I said. It was very satisfying and I'd pay again."

I'm leaning forward, practically begging her to kiss me. Instead, she slips a hand on my face and stares at me with those wide jade eyes that saw through me from the minute we met. I hold her gaze and smile so that she can see there is no hurt or malice in me. No trace of the surprise or betrayal I felt when Shaul showed up.

Because I wasn't really mad at her. I was mad at the world that would take the beautiful thing we did together and turn it into a transaction. Except by bargaining for my freedom instead of her own financial security, Psalome has gone and fixed that problem, too.

This was never about money for her. It was about the two of us using our bodies to prove we belonged to nobody but ourselves.

"How quickly you forgive." She's brushing a finger against my cheekbone. Soft as a butterfly's wings. "I promise I'll never do that to you again."

I pull back with a sharp inhale. "What?"

Psalome claps a hand over her mouth and Finley snorts from across the room while I wonder how bad at sex I could have been to have her swear she'll never sleep with me again. Was she lying when she said she liked it?

"She means she'd never charge you," Psylina calls helpfully from across the room. She's hustling Finley and Kiyo towards the GoldWeaver ship. "You two had sex because she wanted you as much as you wanted her. I had an entire plan mapped out to make it unnecessary. If you're still into it, I'm sure she'd gladly give you for free what your ex-husband just so gratuitously paid for."

I peek up at Psalome to confirm this is true and she gives me a small nod before reaching for my hand again. This time I let her take it, remembering what Psylina told me about Psalome's Dazzler persona. She's spent so much time becoming everyone else's fantasy, including mine, she's forgotten how to be herself. She's trying now and it's my job to help her.

I give her hand a squeeze and wait until she gathers her words again.

"Will you come with us?" Her voice is barely a whisper because saying it out loud makes it real. Her desire laid out for me to scrutinize and judge. "I could make us dinner and you could tell me more about yourself while we work out how to return Shaul's blackmail materials. You don't have to stay in my room if you don't want to. I, uhm, I like it when you talk. And when we play piano together. Maybe on some of the planets we visit there will be concerts we can go to."

"You mean like a date?" I ask. It's such a quaint way to put it, given we've already ripped each other's clothes off, but I've grown weary of urbane sophistication. Quaint sounds perfect right about now.

"Yes," she says. "I'd like to take you on a lot of dates if you'll let me."

Her face is eager, her eyes bright. She's offering me the life I've always wanted, traveling the galaxy with a person who values me for my contributions to our relationship rather than simply viewing me as a means to keep up appearances.

"I'd like that very much. Only, typically on a date both people talk while they're eating." My allusion to our shared silent meals was meant to be funny but Psalome considers the request with the seriousness of Kiyo evaluating a diamond before nodding vigorously.

"I can do that. Talking. You might have to teach me how to cook though."

It's good enough for me.

"There's just one more thing then," I say. Psalome returns to chewing her lower lip and I'm almost sorry for teasing her this way. "I'm told that on secular planets, most dates end with a kiss, and I am definitely not staying in my own room."

I can still taste her in my mouth, sweet and intoxicating. My body has never felt as on fire as when she was making love to it. There's no way I'm giving that up.

Her face blooms red again and her hands are fluttering randomly about her, unsure where to land. Her breath leaves her body in one big whoosh. "Oh."

"First time with a girl?" I ask with a wink, sliding towards her, enjoying the role reversal.

She licks her lips and nods. "Second. I probably should have told you I'd only ever been with one person before. It was hard to date these past few years. Hazard of the job."

I run my hands through her hair, my heart breaking at the things she's been made to do to protect the people she loves. The life she's put on hold while she was working here. The truth she kept back so that I wouldn't be nervous. "Don't worry, I can still take care of you."

"I'll bet you can," she sighs as I lean in and kiss her. It's soft and sweet, nothing like the wild frenzy of before. Somehow this feels more real. More us.

"My divorce will be fully processed and recognized on Thillov in a few days." I lean my forehead against hers. "I'll be free to be with whoever I want. Thillov might never recognize a relationship between two women but there are plenty of Jewish planets that will and I'm hoping you can meet my family one day."

"You want me to make an honest woman of you?" She laughs.

I don't doubt she'd marry me, it's the kind of reckless thing I've come to realize she would do for other people despite never asking for anything for herself. Still, the thought of marriage doesn't suit either of us. We've both had enough of gilded cages.

"Not even a little," I reply. "I wouldn't mind picking up some of my stuff though, once it's safe for me to be back on Thillov. There's a piano my grandmother loaned us that Shaul never pawned. I had to give up my lessons when we got married. You could finish teaching me how to play."

"Only if you teach her how to fly the spaceship." Psylina's voice rings out over the airlock, startling us both. We spring apart like guilty teenagers caught kissing in the back of a hovercraft, but Psalome doesn't let go of my hand.

"Why do I need to learn to fly the ship?" she asks.

"Because I won't always be around to do it for you anymore," Psylina says, sliding in next to us. "It's time we both started living our own lives. You two can have a nice honeymoon without me as a third wheel trying not to hear you through the way-too-thin walls of our spaceship. El invited me to stay here, as their personal guest, and I said yes. We're going to start with a complete security upgrade on their systems."

"Sounds hot," Psalome quips, a bittersweet smile on her face. "You sure you two don't require a chaperone?"

"Yeah, well, we can't all fall into bed together naked and then awkwardly try to figure out how to be a couple later," Psylina retorts, standing up. "Don't let me interrupt that process, by the way. I'll get the ship ready to roll. You two can join me when you figure out if you want to fuck or fly first. I don't recommend doing them both at once."

I flush at the implication, only to realize Psalome is blushing even harder. This is what we're like without the makeup and the games. Two baby birds, stumbling our way around the nest trying to figure out how to soar without a parent there to help push us out.

"You're supposed to kiss her again," Psylina suggests from the door to the spaceship. "A little longer this time, maybe with some light above the waist groping. I'm in love with a computer and even I know that."

"Psylina!" Psalome gasps. She buries her face in her hands in embarrassment. "I am so sorry. You don't have to do any of that. Not if you don't want to. Like I said there are separate rooms and I don't have expectations just because we've slept together before."

"Psalome Shipmen," I whisper, pulling the hands from her face to give me a better view. The stars in her eyes are brighter than the ones twinkling outside. "I have a great many expectations and every single one of them involves the two of us kissing again."

She grins and leans forward, bridging the gap between us.

I close my eyes and breathe in her scent, jasmine and honey, before I press my mouth to hers. Her lips give way without protest, telling me everything I need to know. There's nothing in the universe that either of us wants more than this.

And now we're finally free to take it.

* * *

# ACKNOWLEDGEMENTS

THERE ARE SO many people that have been part of this journey, it's hard to know where to start when thanking them all. In an effort not to leave anyone out, I'll begin with those that touched the book first and go in chronological order.

First, to Team Sloth and Steady – Celeste Dador, Linh Pham, C.H. Barron, Cecile Ferro, and Julie Tieu – you were with me when I first thought of the idea behind this book, while I fast drafted, slow edited, and went through submissions. I know we will remain together through whatever life throws at us next. I am so thankful for your presence in my life, without which I would never have survived this roller coaster. There's a spot on my shelf for all of your books!

I am eternally grateful to Amy Borsuk for pulling *The Elysium Heist* from the slush. To my editor, Amanda Raybould, you made my dreams come true with your first email and then with every subsequent interaction. Your comments push me to think deeply about character and plot, and the book is better for it. Thank you for your keen insights and cheerleading.

Thank you to Allegra Martschenko, my brilliant agent, for jumping on this project with the enthusiasm of someone who was there from the beginning. You have answered every question, no matter how small, and supported my decisions as if they were your own. I would be lost without your guidance. I look forward to many more books together!

I would like to express my heartfelt gratitude to the entire team at Solaris Nova for making *The Elysium Heist* a success. Dagna Dlubak (production), Sam Gretton (internal design), Chiara Mestieri (editorial), Hannah Wilks (copy edits and more), and Jess Gofton and Natalie Charlesworth (PR and marketing) - you have all left your mark on this book and your efforts are appreciated.

A book is nothing without a cover, it's the first impression for readers, and Martin at Amazing15 exceeded my expectation to the point where I actually cried (in the good way) when I saw this beauty. Thank you for taking all my feedback in stride and giving *The Elysium Heist* such gorgeous clothes.

The journey to publication is long and arduous, and I would not have made it without my writing community. Thank you to the romance schmooze for teaching me all about romance beats from a Jewish lens, Ash and Sheyd for supporting Jewish SFF, and Codex for reads of my query and manuscript in addition to supporting my short fiction for years. I am grateful for every writers Discord, Slack, and group chat that has welcomed me over the years.

To the bloggers, bookstagrammers, and BookTokers that took a chance on *The Elysium Heist* and supported it, your work is so crucial to our industry. I appreciate you!

My beautiful family who patiently waited while I typed, deserves much credit for putting up with me and the mood swings that come with writing different bits of manuscript and experiencing the ups and down of publishing. Your presence in my life is the real magic. Please skip the spicy bits or I will never be able to speak with you again. Nor you me. Trust me.

Finally, to you, the reader who has at last made it to the penultimate page. Thanks for sticking with me! I am honored you chose to spend some of your precious time with my words. While *The Elysium Heist* is both science fiction and a romance, it also touches on some serious subjects that are issues in our present day. For anyone currently suffering any of the same difficulties as these characters, I hope this book brings you peace, solace, and courage. May we all break free of the chains that bind us to our pasts, so that we bring only the good into our bright futures.

# ABOUT THE AUTHOR

Y.M. Resnik (she/her) is a writer living in the tri-state area. While she loves creating new worlds and re-imagining Jewish folklore, her main goal is simply to brighten your day with a story. Her work has appeared in *Cast of Wonders*, *Worlds of Possibility*, *Diabolical Plots,* and *khōréō*, among other places. When not writing, she can be found collecting tiaras and trying not to kill her houseplants. You can keep up with her work at ymresnik.com

# FIND US ONLINE!

## www.rebellionpublishing.com

/solarisbooks     /solarisbks

/solarisbooks     /solarisbooks.
bsky.social

## SIGN UP TO OUR NEWSLETTER!

rebellionpublishing.com/newsletter

## YOUR REVIEWS MATTER!

Enjoy this book? Got something to say?

Leave a review on Amazon, GoodReads or with your
favourite bookseller and let the world know!

www.ingramcontent.com/pod-product-compliance
Lightning Source LLC
Chambersburg PA
CBHW020843020726
47497CB00005B/1237